The Lie of Us

USA TODAY BEST SELLING AUTHOR

CALI MELLE

Playlist

Shattered - Always Never
Waiting for Never - Post Malone
Jesus Christ - Brand New
My Blood - Ellie Golding
Can We Kiss Forever? - Kina
Long Nights - 6LACK
Sleeping in the Benz -
Landon Tewers
U move, I move -
John Legend ft. Jhene Aiko
In My Veins -
Andrew Belle ft. Erin Mccarley
Medicine - James Arthur
Love Me Blind - Joshua Golden
Afterglow - Taylor Swift

To the ones who aren't afraid to reach deep inside the darkest of hearts, only to find the light that they think they're incapable of possessing.

And to the Dramione girlies who have experienced the same pain I felt from reading Manacled. If you want to know who hurt me before writing this—it was that book.

CONTENT WARNING

Please note that there is reference to physical/emotional/mental abuse in flashbacks from the male main character and his father. There is no abuse or violence between the two main characters.

PROLOGUE
WINTER

Past

"I can't do this."

His words were like a blow to my chest as I stared back at him in disbelief. My heart had cracked wide open and I was bleeding out onto the floor as the blood pooled around my feet.

"What do you mean?" I questioned him, my voice small and hesitant. My heart was barely a flutter in my chest anymore.

His jaw clenched and he ran his fingers through his dirty blond hair. I watched him curl his hands into fists, holding on to his hair as he gave the locks a tug. "I mean, I can't fucking do this anymore, Winter. All I'm doing is destroying you."

"You don't get to be the one who makes that decision," I told him as I closed the distance between us. I stepped closer to him as my throat constricted. "Look at me, Kai," I urged with desperation.

He lifted his head with hesitation. His eyes were dark as they stared directly through me and into my soul. "I told you that you should have stayed away from me, Winter. I fucking warned you."

"I didn't want to stay away from you."

"Well, now you don't get the choice anymore," he said with such conviction, it sent a shiver down my spine. His voice was hard and cold. Distant and detached. "I'm leaving tonight."

His words were like a knife twisting deep inside my chest. "Where are you going?"

"As far away from you as possible."

My sternum was being crushed under the weight of his words.

"We had a good time, Winter," he said with such cruelty as the ice hardened in his eyes. The venom dripped from his tongue as his gaze sliced through me. "But that's all it was and all it would ever be."

Tears burned my eyes as I fought to conceal them from him. "Don't do that."

He cocked his head to the side. "Do what?"

"Act like this means nothing to you." I paused as my voice wavered. "Like I mean nothing."

Kai's jaw tightened and his fingers were warm as he slid them under my jaw. His hand was a stark contrast to the coldness he exuded as he cupped the side of my face. "You are everything, which is why I have to leave. Consider it a blessing in disguise. I'm the only one who can save you from me."

"Please stop saying that," I begged him with desperation drowning my words. "You're not damaged like you think you are."

Kai's eyes were wild as he stared back at me, and he dropped his hand from my face. I instantly felt the absence of his warmth. The laughter that spilled from his perfect lips was harsh and hollow. It was rough and raw as it slid across my eardrums like sandpaper.

"I'm fucking broken beyond repair, darling. Please, just stop trying to fix me."

I knew Kai was broken when I met him my freshman year of high school. He was a product of his environment. The lack of nurture had preceded nature and he was left to his own devices. He came from a wealthy family, but money could never buy the love he never received. He was merely a pawn in his father's eyes and he was determined to burn the entire chessboard of his life to a pile of ash.

Whenever he got himself into trouble, his parents were always there to cover things up. They made his problems go away quietly, without leaving a mark on their family name and legacy. It seemed as though Malakai Barclay never suffered from the consequences of his actions to the outside world, but no one knew the truth.

No one else saw the bruises and scars that I did. The way they peppered his olive skin, hidden beneath his clothing. His father was a ruthless man and he wasn't one to be challenged. That only added fuel to Kai's fire and deepened his desire to rain terror down upon his family name.

Everyone thought he was just a troubled kid, but no

one bothered to look at where the root of his problems were buried.

They were buried deep beneath the estate he lived in, entangling and entwining themselves in every empty crevice of his soul. Malakai Barclay was plagued by the demons his father had bred inside his mind.

In Kai's eyes, he would never be enough.

"Please don't leave me," I pleaded as the tears spilled from my eyes. I fought an earnest battle against them, but I couldn't hold them in any longer. The coldness that radiated from Kai had seeped into my bones and I shivered as I viciously swiped at my cheeks. "What about Vermont? We were supposed to go together."

Kai's eyes darkened under the moon that hung above us in the night sky. "I was never going to go with you, Winter."

His words struck me, swiftly draining the air from my lungs in a rush. My lips parted and it felt like my world was turning upside down. "What?"

He shook his head as another frigid laugh escaped him. "What the fuck is there for me in Vermont?"

"Me," I breathed without hesitation as he twisted the knife in my chest while pushing it in deeper. "We were supposed to go together. You and me."

"There is no you and me, Winter. Stop being delusional," he scoffed as the mask of ice slid across his features. "Did you really think college was even an option for me? I only made it through high school because of my father having the board in his back pocket."

4

He was breaking my heart, tearing it to shreds and letting the pieces fall to the ground by our feet. Kai's moments of vulnerability always made him cruel, but he was always different with me. He let me into places no one else would ever come close to touching. He was icing me out and I didn't know how to get through to him.

"But you told me you got into Wyncote University."

His face was blank. "I lied."

Nausea rolled in the pit of my stomach. "You never applied, did you?"

He shook his head and shrugged with indifference as he shifted his weight on his feet. I watched him transform in front of my eyes. The coldness had encapsulated him, but he wasn't here with me anymore. He had withdrawn from me completely.

"This is life, Winter Reign. It's disappointing and fucking pointless. It is never what you expect it to be and I was never meant to be a part of yours."

"You don't mean that." I let out a ragged breath as I reached for him.

Kai abruptly took a step away from me. "You need to leave, Winter."

I shook my head at him. "I'm not leaving you."

A shadow passed over his face. "Go."

"Don't do this." My plea fell from weak lips and my words were barely audible.

Kai ran his hands through his hair in frustration and gripped the strands between his fingers. The ice from his gaze slid through my veins. "GET OUT!"

My chest had finally caved in and his words punctured my lungs. I took a step backward, feeling slightly off-balance. The distance between us was already feeling like it was rapidly growing by miles.

"I hate you, Malakai Barclay."

His face fell momentarily before he recovered and his mask was back in place. "Good."

I faltered and waited two breaths for him to say something else. He didn't. I was met with nothing but silence and his cold gaze that was locked on mine. This was it—this was the inevitable end Kai had promised me from the beginning. He was broken and I could never fix him.

Slowly turning my back to him, I left my heart lying on the ground by his feet and walked away from him forever. Kai made it his mission to push everyone away from him. He had finally succeeded with me, but only after he had let me in and allowed me to see the side of him no one else got to see. He had left a scar on my soul, one that I would never be able to remove.

I should have listened to him when he warned me to stay away.

He never lied when he said he would destroy me.

The only lie was the lie of us.

CHAPTER ONE
WINTER

Present

I stood outside of my childhood home and stared blankly at the massive front door. Never in a million years did I anticipate coming back to Orchid City. To the very place I had tried so hard to stay away from. When I left for college and moved to Vermont, I had every intention of leaving this place and the memories tied to it behind.

Every year when the holidays rolled around, I had an excuse that I couldn't come back home for them. My parents and sister made it a habit to come see me in Vermont instead.

It had been over six years since I had been here.

"Winter, what are you doing?" my sister, Sutton, asked me from where she was standing. She was just beside the door with her dark hair pulled up into a messy bun on the top of her head. "We can't just stand out here all day."

My lips parted slightly, but only a harsh breath escaped me. I inhaled deeply and pushed my shoulders back as I followed her up the steps onto the front porch that wrapped around the entirety of the house. Sutton was sliding her key into the lock and I was burrowing every memory of this place back in my head.

Our parents had both retired last year and they made the decision to spend the next few years traveling. Instead of selling their seven-thousand-square-foot mansion that was nestled on a six-acre property, they wanted to pass it on to my sister and I. Sutton already had her own home and that meant I was the only one left to keep up with the estate.

I had no desire to take on such a task, but given everything our parents had done for us in life, saying no was not an option. I didn't want to leave the life I was building in Vermont. It wasn't much, but it was a life of my own and that was what I wanted. I wanted autonomy and to not be relying on my family's money.

While in Vermont, I was working as a junior editor for a publishing house until I completed my master's degree in English literature. They had a position waiting for me as soon as I finished. My graduation ceremony was two weeks ago. The weight of the piece of paper sitting in the trunk of my car that stated my credentials was crushing.

I had no choice but to turn down their offer.

Sutton snapped her fingers as she stood inside the doorway. "Winter."

She looked like she was growing impatient with every passing second that I was simply standing here.

She had a charity event she needed to attend at the country club tonight and there was no reason for her to even be here. Since she lived in beautiful Orchid City, my parents left the keys for her to give to me.

I supposed she just wanted to get a small taste of nostalgia before resuming her normal life. There was nothing bittersweet about being here and everything devastating about it.

"What's going on with you?" Sutton questioned me as I finally followed her into the foyer. The sound of her heels on the marble floor echoed throughout the vast space. Not a single thing inside had changed and that made it hurt even more.

Everywhere I turned, everywhere I looked, all that greeted me were memories of him.

"Just tired from traveling," I told her as I abandoned my suitcase. "Did Mom or Dad say that there was anything they wanted done with the stuff in the house?"

Sutton looked around and shook her head. "It's all yours to do what you please with it. Since they plan on moving to the house in the Keys after they're finally done with traveling, this is all yours now. Make sure you go see the lawyer on Monday to sign over all the paperwork."

I stared at my sister for a moment as a rock lodged itself in my throat. "I don't want any of this, Sutton."

"You can't sell it," she said matter-of-factly. "It's practically a family heirloom that has been passed down from one generation to the next. Find someone to pay to take care of the place if you don't want to live here," she told me with a shrug.

"I can't afford to pay someone to do that," I admitted, my voice quiet and tentative. My sister had built her own empire and now ran her own architect firm. She was the golden child of the two of us. I was the one who lived with their head in the clouds and went to college for a bullshit degree.

All I had was a piece of paper with my credentials, barely any work experience, and a laptop filled with half-finished manuscripts. It was always my dream to be a published author, yet somehow I ended up on the other side of the publishing industry.

Part of it was because I let my own fear hold me back.

The other part of it was because when I wrote, all I did was sit down and bleed all over the pages. I bled the story of us, the history of him, and it made my heart ache. Ever since that night, I had never fully recovered. I was forced to pick up the pieces and move on in life, but that didn't mean I was ever able to repair the hole he left in my chest.

It was easier to push him away from my mind when I wasn't surrounded by memories of him. Vermont was safe. Vermont was far enough away. He was never there, so I was able to make my own memories without him. I had tucked the thought of him away in the deepest, darkest corner of my mind.

Only now was he pushing his way back to the front.

"Have you thought about what you're going to do

for work? Surely there is some way for you to work remotely with your editing experience."

I stared back at my sister blankly. "I would have worked remotely for the company I had a job with if it would have been possible." I paused for a moment. "I applied for the librarian position at the local library in town."

A small smile touched Sutton's lips. "You and your books."

"Sometimes fiction is better than reality."

She stared at me for a beat as a thoughtful look slid through her green irises. Sutton knew that something had happened to me during that summer six years ago. She questioned me on it one time when we were sitting in my apartment in Vermont sipping a glass of wine. I shut her out completely after she brought up Kai. It was a part of my life that no one would ever have access to.

Her lips parted slightly and it appeared like she wanted to say something. Instead, she closed them and pursed her lips. "Well, I should probably head out so I can get ready for this event. Will you be okay here?"

A laugh escaped me and I shook my head. I didn't know her perception or thoughts as to what happened to me. I dropped my gaze down to my hands as I absentmindedly picked at the cuticle on my thumb. "It's not just here that I'm worried about."

"He doesn't live in Orchid City anymore, Winter."

Her words struck a nerve in me. My head popped up, my gaze slicing to hers. "Good to know."

She nodded as she tested the waters of my patience

in regards to bringing up the one person I refused to speak about. "Have you followed any of his career?"

I stared back at her as it felt like the oxygen was vanishing from the entire house. "Why would I? He was just a friend from high school, Sutton."

She chewed on her bottom lip as she nodded as if she wasn't the one who found him time and time again sneaking into my bedroom in the middle of the night when we were younger. "Right."

"You should probably go," I told her as I motioned back toward the front door. "I would hate for you to be late."

"You can come with me," she offered as she adjusted her Hermès bag on her shoulder and began to turn back to the door. "Maybe that would help you adjust with being back here."

I shrugged as I glanced down at the sweatpants I was wearing. "I don't know that I'm really country-club ready."

"Please?" she said as she pushed out her bottom lip into a pleading pout. "I really don't want to go but I promised Mom and Dad that I would go stand in for them. I would love to have you there to keep me company from all of those stuck-up, stuffy assholes."

I choked out a laugh and shook my head. "I haven't seen them in years." I paused for a moment as a small smile crept onto my lips. "You know what—I'll go. I can't wait to horrify them when I tell them that I'm about to be a librarian."

Sutton laughed with me but shook her head in disapproval. "Are you trying to piss Mom off?"

"Considering the fact that she forced me back here, yes, yes I am."

Sutton half frowned but nodded in understanding. "You have an hour to get ready and no more. I'll be back in forty-five minutes to get you."

My eyebrows pinched together. "You just said I had an hour, though."

"I know you, Winter. You're going to need someone to light a fire under your ass for those last fifteen minutes if we want to get out the door on time."

Sutton left with those as her parting words and as soon as she was out of the house, there was an eerie stillness that settled throughout the space. The house was big—far too big—and I would have been more content in a smaller place where my mind didn't have the opportunity to wander the dark halls.

As I walked up the stairs to the second floor, it felt like he was everywhere. Kai was more than just a friend and my sister knew it. When he didn't have to be at his own house, he was here. Even after my parents prohibited us from seeing one another. That was when he began to sneak in.

My parents were always wary of him and after he got arrested for defacing the side of the clubhouse at the country club, my parents didn't want me tied to his reputation at all.

Kai had lost his safe place to go. I never knew where he was before the sunset in the evenings, but once the moon was hanging heavily in the sky above, he was climbing through my bedroom window. And he was always gone when I woke up in the morning.

Shaking the memories from my mind, I wandered down the hallway to my old bedroom. As I pushed open the door, I inhaled deeply and peered inside. It was just the way it was when I left. My large king-sized bed was on the opposing wall with built-in bookcases in the wall beside me. My heart crawled into my throat as I hovered in the doorway.

It took everything I had to step inside my room. I didn't want to be here.

But even more... I didn't want to be here *without him.*

After setting my things down on my bed, I wandered over to my old desk. My heart crawled into my stomach as I pulled open the middle drawer and reached inside. Tucked away, under an old notebook, was an envelope addressed to him. I slowly took the letter out, giving my eyes a moment to scan over the words I had written to him many years ago. The pain laced in every word scratched at my heart and settled within my bones.

It was a letter that I wrote to him, but I could never bring myself to send it. I bled all over the page, etching my heartbreak, stained with ink. I wanted him to know how badly he broke me, but I knew it would never change anything.

Tucking the letter back inside the center drawer, I abandoned my desk and walked over to my window. The same window he used to crawl through in the dead of night. The pain was palpable. My heart clenched, feeling the weight of the agony as it seeped into my soul.

I was left living with his ghost and it hurt worse knowing that he was out there somewhere living his life. He was living it without me and I would be willing to bet anything that I was never even a thought that crossed his mind. He pushed me as far away as possible and then simply forgot I even existed.

He never looked for me after I walked away from him that night.

After that night, I never heard from him again.

CHAPTER TWO
WINTER

My sister glanced over at me as I fidgeted in the dress she let me borrow for the night. I had brought most of my belongings with me, although there were still some that hadn't been unpacked yet. That included all of my clothing, like what I needed to attend a charity banquet at a country club.

"Are you okay?" she asked me as she looked at me again from the corner of her eye. Her dark hair was pulled back in a French twist and two curled tendrils framed her slim face. "You look about as uncomfortable as a monkey wearing a diaper."

My face contorted and I gave her a questioning look. "What the hell type of analogy is that?"

She simply shrugged as she turned into the drive that led to the main banquet hall at the club. "I don't know. I never said I was any good with words."

I stared at her for a moment. "To answer your question, yes I am okay. It's been a while since I've worn a dress that feels like it's squeezing the literal life out of me."

Sutton smiled. "Well, it's good to know there's still something left inside of you."

My eyes narrowed into a glare but I tore my gaze away from the side of her face and stared out at the golf course as we drove past a few of the holes. It was perfectly manicured with the soft rolling hills across the landscape. My breath caught in my throat as my eyes traveled over the raked bunkers.

Kai would spend hours out here working on perfecting his swing and his drive. Every aspect of golf, he had wanted to master. And according to my sister, since he had made it to the professional level, it seemed as though he was finally living the life he wanted. The one thing he had dreamed of and worked so hard to achieve.

As we passed the third hole, my eyes drifted to the tee box and the gazebo beside it. My heart crawled into my throat, lodging itself like a rock. My chest was collapsing in on itself as I sucked in a deep breath while trying to block out the memories as they came crashing down around me.

———

"No, that's not how you do it," Kai muttered with irritation as he slid his driver into his bag on the back of the cart. "Your form is all wrong."

A frustrated sigh escaped me and my gaze sliced to his. "I don't golf, Kai. How the hell am I supposed to know what my form should look like?"

His lips twitched but he didn't dare smile. "Let me show you."

My breathing grew shallow as the silence encapsulated us and Kai stepped behind me. His chin was just above my ear and his breath was warm against the exposed skin on my neck. Considering it was the middle of summer in Florida, the air was hot and stuffy—borderline suffocating. My hair was pulled back in a high ponytail and my skin was slick with sweat and sticky from the humidity.

Kai's chest was pressed against my back and he slowly slid his hands down the lengths of my arms until his hands were closing over mine. "Like this," he murmured as he positioned the golf club in front of me and moved my hands where they needed to be. "If you have the heel of your right hand resting here, it will make it a more comfortable swing."

"Okay," I breathed as I held my hands in place with him still holding mine. "Now what?"

"Show me your swing now."

He didn't move away from me. He guided me as I pulled the club back and swung it in front of me. The head hit the ground with a thud, kicking up some of the grass with it. Kai chuckled softly and the sound snaked around my eardrums as his breath warmed my skin.

"How did you grow up in this scene and never learn how to golf?"

"I'm a figure skater, Kai, not a golfer," I reminded him. Sadness slid within my bones and my voice dropped lower. "No one ever took the time to show me because the ice was where I was supposed to be."

Kai fell silent and we stayed unmoving, his chest against my back, his hands wrapped around mine.

"My time belongs to you, Winter."

The air around us grew thicker with tension and he slowly loosened his grip around my hands. I instantly felt his absence as he moved them away from mine, but he didn't step away from me. His palms fell to my hips and his fingertips were light against my skin as he held on to me.

"Try again," he urged me, his voice soft and low. There was a tenderness to him that was only ever reserved for me. To everyone else he was cold and indifferent. He was the same to me as well, but every now and then the sunlight peeked around the edges of the clouds and he lowered his guard and removed his mask.

I obeyed his command even though my body felt like I had reached a boiling point. At any given moment, I would surely be melting into a puddle by his feet. Malakai Barclay was working his way under my skin, but I didn't want him to stop. I wanted him in my veins like a drug. He was my addiction, and I would take whatever part of him he would give me.

His hands were firm on my hips and he held me in place as I tried shifting my weight while I swung the club. "There's the problem," he murmured as his lips brushed against my ear. "You're shifting your hips wrong, which is throwing off your weight and messing up your follow-through on your swing."

"What do I do?" I breathed as my lungs struggled against the thick air.

His lips curled upward and his fingers dug into my skin as he gripped me tighter. "You let me show you."

—————

"Earth to Winter." My sister's voice broke through the memory and reality came crashing down around me as I looked over at her. I hadn't even realized that we were already in front of the building. "We need to get out of the car so they can park it."

My eyes widened and I glanced around for a moment as I focused on my actual surroundings. I was no longer in the past, not with the memory of him. Instead I was sitting in my sister's car while she stared at me like I had lost my mind.

"Of course," I told her with a swift nod as I collected my clutch and climbed out of the car. My movements were rushed and the heels felt foreign on my feet. I stumbled on the concrete walkway before Sutton grabbed my elbow. Her eyes flashed to mine, filled with disapproval. "Sorry," I spit out at her. "I'm as far as detached from this lifestyle as possible."

Sutton frowned. "Do you think I particularly enjoy any of this?"

I shrugged at her as I ripped my arm from her grip and righted myself. "You were the one who always fit in."

"Please don't start with some sibling rivalry bull-shit," she muttered as she shook her head. "We're only here to please Mom and Dad. Neither of us want to be here. Don't get mad at me because you could never find your footing in this atmosphere."

I snorted. "Apparently I still haven't."

Sutton let out a sigh as she moved out of the way

and motioned for me to walk through the doors ahead of her. "You're lucky you were able to have your own life away from the one Mom and Dad created."

"What do you mean? No one ever told you that you had to stay here."

There was a moment of sadness that passed through my sister's eyes. "This was where I felt comfortable, like I belonged. The world is a big, scary place. You used this place as your way out. Nothing ever scared you and I was always envious of that."

My footsteps faltered and my brow creased as I assessed my sister for a moment. She looked perfect in her black floor-length gown. She always looked perfect and well put together. There were only two years that separated us, but in that moment it felt as though it were ten. Why would she have ever been envious of me?

I stayed in my quiet corner of the world with my nose in a book or my skates on the ice. I kept to myself for the most part and did my duties as the daughter of a wealthy family that was deeply involved with their country-club community. Other than that, I was practically a wallflower.

When I moved to Vermont, only then did I come out of my shell a bit. It was a new place with new people. There wasn't the intense need or pressure to impress or be the best I could be. Instead, I was able to be who I wanted and do what I wanted to do. It was like a breath of fresh air.

Coming back here was the opposite.

It was suffocating.

"Staying here scared me," I admitted quietly to my sister as we stepped deeper into the room.

She stared at me for a moment with a thoughtful look in her eyes but I watched as her face transformed and the mask was back in place. Sutton Reign had to play the part and as Mrs. Danbury approached, Sutton plastered her best smile to her face and greeted her with the utmost respect.

My smile matched my sister's but I took a step back as they immersed themselves in conversation. It was where I belonged. On the outside; in the background. I had no place in this room with these people. My mask didn't fit as well as it did in the past. There were cracks in it, revealing the true facade.

"It is so good to see you back, Winter." Mrs. Danbury smiled at me as she plucked a glass of wine from one of the server's trays and thrust it into my grasp. "Your mother has told me of your great accomplishments with figure skating and your job at the publishing house."

I took a sip of the bitter liquid and swallowed it back without so much as making a face of distaste. "It's great to be back. I actually had to leave all of that behind when I moved back here."

Mrs. Danbury's face paled slightly but she nodded. "What a great sacrifice on your part."

Sutton narrowed her eyes in warning at me and shook her head.

"Oh, yes. I gave up my dream job, but I'm hoping to secure a position at the local library as their new librarian." I paused and smiled at her, ignoring the look of horror on my sister's face. "I actually forfeited my posi-tion at the club I was competing for with figure skating, but I'm hoping to be able to find a new club locally and skate leisurely."

Two other groups that were standing near us must have been eavesdropping on our conversation as they fell silent and stared momentarily. I glanced at them, smiling sweetly as they all began to duck their heads one by one and fall into hushed conversations.

"You'll have to excuse Winter. She is quite tired from her traveling," my sister interjected as she offered a bullshit excuse. She directed her gaze to mine. "Perhaps you should visit the veranda and get some fresh air."

I nodded while slowly sipping my wine and continued to survey the people near us. "I think I should," I agreed as I smiled back at Mrs. Danbury. "If you'll please excuse me."

The room was already crowded and began to feel stuffy as I began to walk toward the back doors. As my eyes drifted, the air left my lungs in a rush and the oxygen was violently sucked from the room. My gaze landed on the same stormy dark blue eyes that had haunted my mind for the last six years. His gaze held mine, sending a chill straight to my soul.

Malakai Barclay.

CHAPTER THREE

MALAKAI

Winter stared back at me with her eyes wide. I watched her perfect plump lips part slightly. The color abruptly drained from her face, her fingers tightened around the stem of the wine-glass she was holding. She looked just as I remembered her but even more exquisite. It had been six years since I last saw her in person.

She had matured in more ways than one. Her dark hair was pulled back away from her face. Light makeup highlighted the contours of her face and her bright green eyes shined from the chandeliers above us. Her deep red dress hugged the curves of her body before pooling around her feet.

The moment between us was fleeting. I literally blinked and she was gone. I caught sight of her red dress as she pushed through the crowd of people, heading in the direction of the veranda out back. Standing at my full height, I was able to follow the top of her head with my eyes as she moved quickly before I lost sight of her completely.

I knew Winter Reign.

Her fight or flight instincts were stronger than anyone's I had ever witnessed before, you would have thought she spent her childhood getting beat. When things were too much for her, she always ran.

And I always knew exactly where to find her.

I excused myself from the conversation I wasn't even paying attention to and made my way past the groups of people. My feet carried me in the same direction I saw Winter heading. As I push through the French doors that led out onto the veranda, the warm summer breeze greeted me. There were two smaller groups of people standing outside talking.

Two of the older men nodded their heads at me in greeting and I tipped mine back in response but didn't stop to speak to any of them. Winter was nowhere to be seen but I already knew that would be the case.

Stepping off the cobblestone walkway, I walked through the grass toward one of the trees on the top of the small hill that the building sat on. Down below was a pond, but there was a large maple tree that looked down at it with a bench. The bench and tree were in memory of Winter's grandfather.

It was her quiet place, her place of solitude when the people around here got to be too much.

My heart skipped a beat when I saw the outline of her sitting in the dark. Her heels were discarded on the ground beside the bench and she was staring down at the pond. Crickets sang their summer song as I padded through the grass to where she was.

I stopped just behind the bench.

"That was quite the performance with Mrs. Danbury."

Winter's body grew rigid as she straightened her spine. She didn't dare to turn around and look at me. Her delicate hands were folded in her lap. She remained silent, unmoving like a statue, but I saw the way her breathing shifted. Shallow and ragged.

She was sitting on the left side of the bench. I moved around to the front of it and sat down on the opposite side. The night breeze carried the smell of her perfume and I closed my eyes, inhaling deeply as I resisted the urge to reach out to make sure she was real.

Words failed me as the silence settled between us. What could I possibly say to her to fill the void? So much time had passed between us and I was the one to blame for it all. Hell, I didn't even know if she was seeing someone else or not.

The thought alone made my blood boil. My grip tightened around my glass of bourbon and my other fist was in my lap.

I didn't give two fucks if she were seeing someone or not. I was here for her now. Everyone else was entirely obsolete.

"What are you doing here, Malakai?"

Her voice was barely audible but the defeat hung heavily in her words. If I weren't so in tune with her, I may have missed it, but I knew Winter Reign better than I knew myself.

"I came here for you."

An exasperated sigh escaped her and her shoulders sagged a fraction of an inch. "I don't mean why you came out here. I meant Orchid City. Shouldn't you be at some golf tournament or something?"

She still hadn't looked at me and kept her gaze trained on the pond.

"You're why I am here." I took a sip of my bourbon and didn't offer her anything more than that.

Winter slowly turned her head to the side to look at me. And when she looked at me, she looked directly into my soul every goddamn time. "How could you have possibly known I would be here?"

"I didn't necessarily know you would be here tonight," I admitted, my voice quiet as I stared back into the green hues swirling in her irises under the moonlight. "Your parents came up in a conversation with my mother. She mentioned they were leaving their estate to you and you were coming back to beautiful Orchid City."

Her eyes widened. "So you just decided you would come home too?"

"This place has never been my home." I stared at her as my heart pounded against my rib cage. "It was always you. You were my home, Winter."

She abruptly jumped from the bench and onto her feet as she shook her head. "No. No. We're not going to be doing this."

"I'm afraid it looks like we already are."

She bent down beside me as she viciously grabbed her heels. "You don't get to waltz back into my life like you didn't break my heart six years ago." Her eyes were borderline wild and filled with emotion as she stared down at me and crossed her arms over her chest. "You never once tried to talk to me again."

"You don't know what I did, Winter."

She narrowed her eyes and her gaze was colder than the ice she skated on. "Nice try, but I'm not taking the bait. I don't want to know, nor do I care."

I didn't move from where I was still sitting on the bench as I stared up at her. "Yes, you do."

"I really don't," she breathed, the frustration thick in her tone. "You no longer exist in my world and you don't get to just show back up like this."

"Too late, darling," I shrugged with indifference. "I'm already here and I'm nowhere near done with you."

Winter glared at me with such an intensity, it felt like she was driving knives directly into my soul. The venom dripped from her fangs and her nostrils flared. "I hate you, Malakai. I fucking hate what you did to me. That hasn't changed and it never will."

"That's fair." I lifted my glass to my lips and took a slow sip of the amber-colored liquor. "I wouldn't expect anything less."

Her lips parted and her mask crumbled away as there was a chip in her frigid stare. Her mouth abruptly shut and she shook her head. I angled my head to the side as she circled around the bench and left me alone at her spot without another word.

Winter had every right to hate me. I never once blamed her for that, nor did I expect anything different from her. I was the one who did this to her. I did this to us. I ruined everything that was between us, and I ruined her in the process.

It was something I had lived with since that night six years ago. I didn't regret her leaving for college. She thrived while she was away from here and away from me.

There was so much Winter didn't know—so much I had wanted to tell her, but I couldn't. Not now, not with things like this between us. I didn't know how long it would take to win her back or if I would ever be able to.

Forget golf and the prestige. I would have given it all up without a second thought if it meant I would be able to get her back. Unfortunately for me, that wasn't an option. I put my tour on hold the moment I heard Winter was back. She was the only thing that would ever draw me back to this godforsaken place.

Winter was the only person I would revisit this hell for.

After waiting a few minutes as I sat with my thoughts, I finally rose from the bench and dumped out the rest of my Louis XIII onto the pristine grass. I stared out at the pond as the sounds of the crickets grew louder and a toad croaked.

This place was the last place I wanted to be tonight. I was a silent sponsor for the charity event tonight, but there was business I still needed to attend to. Thankfully my parents were out of the country, so I wouldn't have to worry about running into them.

As I walked up to the building, I set my empty glass down on one of the pillars and walked inside. My eyes surveyed the room, looking for any trace of Winter or her sister. When I didn't see either of them, I met with the few men who ran the golf organization at the country club. They wanted me to help with some of their training while I was in the area.

It wasn't a commitment I was willing to make, but I told them I would consider the offer. I didn't need their money and I sure didn't need the job. I had my dream job as a professional golfer waiting for me. I didn't know that I would ever return to it, though.

Winter was something my parents never brought up. My father never approved of our friendship because he didn't think I needed any distractions. What he didn't know was, Winter was my safe place from him. She was my safe haven—the one that I could always run to. She was there for me when no one else ever was. She saved me from myself and my father's wrath.

My mother loved her, but my mother loved everyone. She was a lush and I found out later in life that she was as out of touch with reality as possible so she didn't have to worry about my father fucking his assistant. My family had serious issues that would make the people in this building's heads spin. But then again—maybe it wouldn't.

They all had their own issues and it seemed like once there was money involved and thrown into the mix, the issues were even messier. Winter's parents were the two I never heard anything bad about, except for the fact that they absolutely hated me. It wasn't without reason, though. I was a piece of work as a teenager. I would never blame them for wanting to keep their daughter safe.

And she was never safe with me.

I wrapped up the conversations as quickly as possible before excusing myself from the event. There wasn't a doubt in my mind that Winter didn't go home, but I had to know for myself. I needed to drive past their estate, just to know that she got there safely. I wanted her tucked away inside the three-hundred-year-old house where nothing could touch her.

She didn't know that I kept tabs on her for the past six years. She didn't know that I went to Vermont to see her, even though it was only ever from afar.

There was a lot that she didn't know about what happened after I let her walk out of my life.

And she was about to find out that I would never be making that mistake again.

CHAPTER FOUR
WINTER

Everything was moving around me in slow motion, yet it felt like things were passing by me faster than the speed of light. My senses were heightened. Everything felt too loud, too bright, *too much.* I was in sensory overload and my breathing was growing more ragged with every rushed step I took.

My heart pounded erratically in my chest, so much to the point that it felt as if it were going to burst out of my chest. Faces moved past me in a blur as I pushed through the crowded room. I didn't know where to go. I needed to get out of here. I needed somewhere quiet and private. My walls were crumbling and the facade I had worked so hard to build was falling.

I thought I had caught sight of my sister, but everything was too loud, I couldn't process properly. I was too busy trying to focus on my breathing while trying to plan my escape. My eyes landed on the hall that led to the front door and I knew I needed to go.

Where I was going, I had absolutely no idea, but I just needed to get out of there as quickly as possible. It had been a few years since my last panic attack and I knew that was exactly what was happening.

There was only ever one person who was able to help me through moments like this, but I couldn't go back to him. Not when he was the one who triggered this attack.

I pushed through the front doors in a rush, still holding my heels in my hands. It felt like I was tripping on drugs, like the Earth was spinning faster and faster as it tilted farther on its axis. Nothing felt right and I wanted to crawl out of my skin. My surroundings were completely distorted and I just wanted it to stop.

Stumbling down the walkway, I found a small garden with a bench tucked in the center of it. My feet felt like there were bags of sand tied to my ankles. The grass tickled my skin and the sensation was almost too much for me to handle. The blades were cold, yet it felt like they were burning through my flesh, branding me in the worst way.

I dropped down onto the bench and laid down on my side, pulling my knees up to my chest as I laid in the fetal position. My eyes were squeezed shut and I absentmindedly pulled my dress down to cover my legs. It was borderline embarrassing but thankfully no one was around to witness me falling apart.

"It's okay. It will all be okay," I whispered to myself as I inhaled through my nose and out through my mouth. "It's not real. I just need to breathe."

Counting my breaths, I continued with the method

as I tried to will myself into a state of calm and serenity. It was impossible. My heart felt like it was going to explode and the pressure on my chest was crushing. I abruptly sat up as my sister stepped into the garden.

"Winter," she said softly, her eyes searching mine. She had seen me have panic attacks before and there was a look of understanding that passed through her irises. "Come on, let's get you home."

I swallowed roughly, my tongue sticking to the roof of my mouth. It felt like I had just smoked an ounce of weed with how bad the cotton mouth feeling was. I looked at my sister. It felt like everything was closing in on me. She held out her hand and I nodded as I slid my hand into hers.

Sutton slid her arm around my shoulders and helped guide me over to where the valet parking was. I closed my eyes and leaned into her as I continued to focus on my breathing. I needed to be home in bed, in the dark silence. The exhaustion was beginning to set in and I knew it would be over soon, but the only real solution at this point was forcing myself to sleep.

The car ride was silent back to the house and I closed my eyes as I pressed my face against the cool glass of the window. I hated the sensation, the way it felt like it was burning, but it was a reminder that I was still alive. All of this was real. I just needed to keep breathing and it would eventually pass.

It wasn't long before she was pulling up in front of the house and helping me out of the car. I didn't need her help. I could walk by myself, but I let her help me anyway. "What can I do, Winter? I don't know how to help you."

I shook my head at her as she opened the front door for me and I stepped inside the massive house. "There's nothing anyone can do. I just need to go to sleep."

My sister paused as she stared at me for a moment. Her eyes were soft and gentle, yet she looked worried and helpless. "Let's get you up to bed then."

Sutton walked with me until we reached my bedroom. I hated that my bedroom—my safe place—belonged to memories of him. It didn't even feel like it was my room, but I found myself slipping out of my dress and into an oversized t-shirt before climbing into the bed.

"Do you want me to stay in here with you?" Sutton asked me, her voice quiet, yet overbearing with the way my mind was convoluting and distorting external stimuli.

I shook my head at her and closed my eyes. "I just need to be alone."

She was silent for a moment. "I'll be in the other room if you need me. I'll spend the night here so you're not alone."

Her words pulled at my heart. I wanted to be alone, yet not completely. Panic attacks used to scare the shit out of me and since it was my first one in years, it had left me really shaken up. I didn't feel right at all. The thought of her being in the house so I wasn't alone brought a sense of comfort I had been struggling to find during this attack.

"Thanks, Sutton," I told her, my voice quiet as I peered up at her.

She gave me a small smile and rubbed my arm. "That's what sisters are for."

Sutton left the room without another word and I buried myself deeper beneath the covers. The silence settled around me, but my mind only grew louder. My eyelids were burning, the sheets felt too silky against my skin. None of it felt right. My skin no longer fit the way it did earlier and I wanted to remove it from my body, leaving nothing but bare bones, muscles, and blood.

Seeing Kai was the last thing I had imagined happening tonight. I was completely blindsided, and the panic attack was not something I had planned on either. I had worked through them before on my own, but there was a moment of despair and helplessness.

The one person who could reach me when I was lost in an attack was the very person who had caused it. I couldn't reach out to him, I couldn't ask him to come comfort me. It was conflicting as hell and my soul was splitting in two.

The only place I was safe was in my mind with my memories of him. I kept them buried deep inside, never daring to open Pandora's Box, but desperate times called for desperate measures. I needed him and that was the only way I was going to have him...

———

"Winter," Kai murmured as he shifted across my bed, scooting closer to me. It was late in the evening and Kai wasn't supposed to be at my house, but my parents were away for the weekend and Sutton was at a friend's house.

My panic attacks had become more frequent during our senior year of high school. My mother blamed it on the pressure of preparing for college, but it wasn't from the pressure of that. It was the pressure of life—of the expectations my parents put on me. They were always going on about Sutton and how well she was doing.

Sometimes I couldn't help but feel like I was just drifting, alone and lost in the world. It would happen at the drop of a hat, not necessarily triggered by anything. All it would take was my mind wandering and then I would be hit with the most violent reality check that had everything crashing around me.

Malakai was the only one who could hold it together.

With him, I wasn't lost and alone.

He always knew how to find me.

"Just breathe, darling." He pulled me against his chest and wrapped his arms tightly around my back. "Count to five, in through your nose. Hold for five. Releasing for seven through your mouth."

I listened to the sound of his voice, soft and slow. Quiet and calm. He reached into my soul and soothed me as he continued to count while I breathed along. It didn't eradicate the panic but my heartbeat began to slow down with every rep. My body felt as though I was growing more centered and grounded.

I inhaled Kai's scent. He smelled like sandalwood and spearmint and it was my favorite smell. He continued to *murmur as he stroked my back with his hand. Kai was my safe place. He was the calm in the storm, even though he was a hurricane himself.*

"I got you, Winter," he breathed against the top of my head before pressing his lips to my forehead. "I will never let you go."

Pulling back, I lifted my eyelids to look at him. The waves crashed in his murky ocean eyes as he stared back at me. "Do you promise?"

He nodded but didn't speak the words back to me. Instead, he pulled me back to him. "Just breathe through it. Everything will be okay."

I fell silent and continued to breathe along with the comfort of his voice. Kai was never a person of many words, but the way he whispered the words into my soul, he had me convinced everything really would be okay.

He was able to pull me back from the ledge and talk me down every single time.

I hung on to every word he spoke as I felt the heaviness of sleep beginning to pull me under. I was safe in his arms, he would never let anything bad happen to me. Kai needed me just as badly as I needed him. He was the glue that held me together and I was his safe haven.

"Don't ever leave me, Winter," Kai whispered as his voice cracked around his plea.

I held him tighter. "Never."

———

Lifting my head from the blankets, I slowly opened my eyes as I came back from the memory. There was a sense of peace and comfort, yet it also left a gnawing ache deep inside my chest. Our promises never meant anything. I was just as much of a liar as Kai was.

Letting my eyes fall shut, I began the sequence of breathing. In through my nose, out through my mouth. *Breathe in for five, hold it for five more, and exhale for seven.*

Kai's voice lingered in my brain and I held on to the sound of it as I began to finally drift off to sleep. He didn't come to me in my dreams that night and I was thankful for that. I needed an escape from him, even though the thought of how tender and gentle he once was, was what helped me to feel better.

He shattered my heart and destroyed my mind. The dreamless nights were the only solitude I found anymore.

It was the only place I was safe.

CHAPTER FIVE
MALAKAI

My stomach rolled with nausea as I sat in the sitting room of my parents' house. My mother had called me early in the morning asking if I would stop by. They had flown home early and got in late last night. She didn't offer any information on what was so important, just that she needed to talk to me and see me as soon as possible. Knowing her, it was just a ploy to get me here because she knew how badly I hated being here.

I could have said no, I could have refused, but there was a part of me that would always feel some sort of sympathy for my mother. I mean, being married to Winston Barclay was practically a death sentence in itself. Monetarily, her life was easy with him. Emotionally and mentally, it was hell. But then again, if you drink enough vintage wine, you can erase all of your problems from your mind.

The house was quiet and I picked at the strings on one of the throw pillows beside me. It felt weird being back there, but I also felt like a stranger in the place I grew up in. Our house never fully felt like a home. There weren't any family pictures hanging on the walls. There was never a single thing out of place.

It looked like a staged house rather than a lived-in one.

"Sorry about that," my mother apologized as she stepped back into the room. She sat down on the loveseat across from me. "Doris needed help finding something in the pantry."

I stayed silent and nodded. Doris had been my parents' housekeeper for as long as I could remember. They took good care of her, but I had always felt bad for her. They were never truly grateful for everything she did. I suppose if you paid someone enough to stick around, the money would always talk loud enough.

My mother lifted her champagne flute, that unsurprisingly had a mimosa in it, to her lips before draining half the glass. I stifled a snort and gave her a blank stare. I wouldn't expect anything less from her. She'd be toasty by lunchtime, most likely take an afternoon nap, and then begin round two afterward.

The tiredness had begun to set in around the creases of her eyes. She was probably due for a Botox appointment sometime soon because that was what my mother did. Growing up, I had wished for a different family. For different parents. A different life, even. But this was what I got and what I was stuck with.

"What was so urgent that you needed me to come over for?"

My mother gave me a sheepish grin. "I had this

issue with your grandmother and getting a driver to take her to her doctor's appointment, but I actually got it figured out."

Coldness settled within my gaze and I stared at her with indifference. She was lying. My mother was a wolf in sheep skin. She was a snake in the fucking grass. I knew it was all just bullshit to get me here, but for what? My mother may have loved me more than my father ever did, but she was just as cunning as he was.

"Why did you really want me to come here, Mother?"

She let out an exasperated sigh and shook her head at me. "Would it kill you to come visit your family for once? I know you have a place by the ocean you stay at. You never stop to see your own mother."

"You know exactly why I don't come around."

She frowned, although her face barely moved from how much stuff she had had injected into her skin. "I know your father isn't an easy man to be around, Malakai. Sure, you guys had some rough times when you were growing up, but you need to let that go. He has always provided for us and he cares about you, even if he doesn't show it in the most conventional way."

Her words didn't surprise me in the least. She loved me, but not enough. She would always stand beside my father and love him more than she could ever love me. When my father beat the shit out of me time and time again, she could have protected me, but she didn't. She could have taken me away from here, but she stayed.

My father never laid a finger on her. It was only me.

I was the one who got the brunt of his brutality. His wrath was reserved for just me.

My mother hid from it all behind her charity events and alcohol. She was never blind, nor was she stupid. She just chose to look the other way because at the end of the day, all her needs were still being met. And even though I had zero emotional support, she believed my needs were met as well.

There was only one time that she tried to comfort me after he broke open the skin across my cheekbone. I refused her help. I refused to let her see me crack from what he was doing.

She never tried again.

It was as if she thought I really wanted my space, but in actuality, I just wanted a parent who cared more about me than themselves or their spouse. They both sucked but she was the lesser of two evils and I felt bad. I felt guilty.

Perhaps she was just stupid.

"Sure, Mother," I agreed with her, choosing the easier way out than arguing with her. "When will he be home?"

She glanced at the clock on the wall. "He's not due to be home until later this afternoon, but I was hoping you would maybe come back later for dinner."

I stared blankly at her as I began to dissociate from it all. If I detached, I wouldn't feel. And neither of them could hurt me then.

"Sure. What time do you want me to come back?"

She looked giddy and flashed her perfect white teeth at me as she clapped her hands together. "Try and be here around six-thirty. I'll tell Doris to have the food ready by seven."

I nodded, feeling fucking carved out and hollow inside. I may not have recovered from life in this hell, but I had at least moved on. This was what my family was able to do to me. They were able to strip me down to nothing—leaving me as nothing but a shell.

Over the years, I had learned my own sense of self-preservation in order to protect what little I had left of myself.

Withdrawing and dissociating.

I slowly rose from where I was sitting to bid my mother goodbye. "I'll be back around six-thirty," I assured her without another word as I exited my child-hood house. We weren't like most families and this was how our goodbyes typically went.

My parents hadn't told me they loved me in years.

———

After leaving my parents' house, I drove around mindlessly. My mind was still blocking out the memories this place brought back and I tried to focus on why I was really here. I came back for one reason and she wanted nothing to do with me.

Winter left in such a rush last night and I didn't know when I would run into her again. She had just moved back here herself. It wasn't like she had some type of a routine or structure. I couldn't ask someone where she frequented or where I could find her. Knowing Winter, I could probably find her outside in the gardens of her family's estate with her nose in a book. Or a local ice rink, lost in herself as she spun around on the thin blades beneath her.

Either way, I would find her.

And I was going to do everything humanly possible to win her back.

I wasn't paying attention as I was driving until I realized I was driving down her road. My heart beat erratically in my chest as I neared her driveway. I shouldn't stop. I had no reason to show up at her house unannounced. She probably wouldn't even answer the door if I showed up. Last night was just luck and chance. I had her cornered and she bolted.

Slowing my car down, I weighed my options. The rational, logical part of my brain was telling me to keep driving. I wet my lips as I glanced at her driveway and let out a ragged breath.

Fuck it.

Grabbing the top of the steering wheel, I whipped my car to the left and pulled into her driveway. I never claimed to be one who was logical or rational when it came to Winter Reign. If there was one person who was able to make me do things I had never pictured myself doing, it was her.

She plagued with my head like no other and it was the sweetest torture of all.

There were iron gates that blocked further access onto their property. I put down my window as I pulled up to the small keypad that was by their mailbox. Sucking in a breath, I punched in the code that was imprinted in my mind and hoped the Reigns had never changed it.

The small light on the keypad lit up green and I let out a sigh of relief as I heard the beep and click before the gates started to slide open. I drove my car through and headed down the drive to Winter's house. The logical, rational part of my brain no longer existed.

As I pulled up out front, surprise struck me when I saw Winter sitting on the front porch with a mug in between her hands. She sat up straighter on the chair she was sitting in, but she didn't stand up.

Foolish girl.

For all she knew, I could have been anyone pulling up right now. Their gates could have been destroyed and I would have entered without a single thought. Winter was too trusting, but I could see the panic in her expression. She didn't recognize my car.

I killed the engine and opened my door before climbing out. My sunglasses shielded my eyes from her, but I didn't miss the way her face fell when she realized it was me. She absolutely despised me and it rolled off her in waves.

"What are you doing here, Malakai?" she questioned me as she stood up. Ice slid through my veins. I hated that she kept calling me by my full name.

I stood at the bottom step that led to the porch that wrapped around the front of their house. Winter had a pair of black cotton shorts on, exposing her silky skin. She was wearing an old crew-neck sweatshirt. I squinted my eyes as I attempted to make out the faded words written across the gray material.

Orchid City Country Club.

My breath caught in my throat. It was one of my old sweatershirts.

"I was in the area and wanted to check in on you after last night."

She stared at me with disbelief swirling in her green irises. "Go home, Malakai."

"Not until I know you're okay."

A frigidness settled within her eyes and she barked out a harsh laugh. "You didn't give a shit about me six years ago, why would you care now?"

My jaw clenched. "That's not true," I told her, my voice low.

She fell silent as she crossed her arms over her chest. Her knuckles were turning white with how tightly she was gripping the coffee mug in her one hand. As I stared back at her, I fought the urge to walk up the steps to her. Her iciness slipped into my veins and I pushed back my shoulders.

"You have no fucking clue, Winter," I practically growled at her with my voice still low. "I was an asshole and I shouldn't have pushed you away, but I had no other choice."

She shook her head at me. "I can't do this with you right now. I don't want an explanation—I don't want anything." She shifted her weight on her feet and I recognized the anxious tic. It was a given sign that she was going to flee. "You want to know the truth about last night? I had a panic attack... because of you."

Her words sliced through my soul like a sharpened blade. I would never forget how bad Winter's panic

48

attacks could be and it literally split my heart in two. I was the one who was supposed to help her through them, not cause them.

"Fuck." I swallowed over the knives in my throat as I ran a frustrated hand through my hair. "I had no idea."

She leaned her head to the side. "No, you didn't. How could you have possibly known? You can't see past your own nose."

Winter spun on her heel, the coffee in her mug splashing out onto the porch as she turned around in a rush. She paid no mind to it and didn't mutter another word to me before she disappeared into the house. The door slammed shut behind her, rattling the glass window panes.

I stared back at the door as my heart clenched in my chest. I deserved all of her rage and all of her hate. I'd always been broken, but I never meant to bring Winter down with me. I fucking broke her, and I was the only one who could fix her.

I would fix this.

I would fix us.

CHAPTER SIX
WINTER

Past

My ass slid across the ice as I hit it in a rush. I hung my head in defeat before planting my gloved hands on the ice. My coach stared down at me with a look of disapproval on her face. I climbed back up onto my feet and skated over to her.

"You're not leaving the ice on the correct edge." Her words were clipped and she half glared at me. "Do it again."

My parents had me working with Sasha since I was a young girl and she had not gotten any easier on me over the years. If anything, she had only gotten harder. She expected and demanded greatness and nothing less.

I loved figure skating, but there were times I didn't. This was one of those times. We had been working on the same jump for months and if it wasn't one thing, it was another that I was doing wrong. Even when I landed it, it wasn't perfect.

It needed to be perfect.

I moved my feet, using the muscles in my legs to glide across the ice. Sasha stood over by the boards and nodded as my gaze met hers. I began to move again, practicing the same sequence that was burned into my mind as I attempted the double Axel again. And again. And again...

After landing it a few times, Sasha was a little pleased, but even that was a stretch. I managed to lift off the correct edge but it wasn't perfect. My legs were burning by the time my lesson was over and as I walked out of the ice rink, they felt like they were Jell-O.

Sasha waited for me by the door and we stepped out into the warm evening air as we walked into the parking lot. Her car was parked a few spots from mine and we stopped by my trunk as I put my skate bag inside.

"They are having freestyle ice tomorrow morning at six," she reminded me with her curt tone. "I expect to see you here."

My jaw clenched and I nodded as I forced a smile. "I wouldn't miss it."

Sasha stared at me for a moment as she scrutinized me with her gaze. "Very well. I suggest you go home and get some rest."

I nodded again and Sasha left me without another word. As I climbed into my car, I couldn't help but feel like a deflated balloon. I had a competition coming next month and that was what we were ultimately trying to prepare for, but there was no way I could include a double Axel in my routine. Even if I nailed it, it wouldn't be enough time to incorporate and perfect it.

My parents were a little more lax when it came to demanding excellence. I always had good grades and was a model student, so that was more than enough for me. It was almost as if they had paid Sasha to be the bad guy so they didn't have to be the ones who were pushing me.

My sister Sutton was the one who got the brunt of their demanding nature for her to be the absolute best. Sutton was also more immersed in their life. She golfed and rode horses, just like both of our parents. What she was doing wasn't more important, but there was a shift in the pressure between us.

My parents liked being able to tell their friends that I was a figure skater, but it didn't compare to Sutton. She golfed and competed in her horse shows against other girls whose parents were in the same circle as our parents. There was more of a tie between their worlds and they mixed into one.

I had the pressure of fighting for visibility. I had only turned eighteen two months ago, yet it felt like they were already forgetting I was still their child. I wanted to be the best that I could be in hopes that maybe then I would get some of my parents' attention rather than all of it going to Sutton.

The sun had already dipped below the horizon and the moon was hanging in the sky above. The drive home was quiet and I pushed everything out of my mind as I drove on autopilot. When I got inside my house, my sister was already in her room, as were my parents. No one was around to greet me. I had missed dinner and my mother left a plate for me in the fridge with a note.

I didn't bother reading it before I crumpled it up and threw it into the trash. It used to bother me when I would have late nights like this. Sometimes my sister would wait up for me, but she was just here on a short break before she had to head back to college. She had a lot of work she was doing, so I didn't blame her.

It used to hurt worse when I noticed my parents' absence. My mother used to wait with her or she would be sitting in the sitting room reading as she waited for me to get home so we could talk about all the things. She hadn't waited for me in over a month now and if she did, it was completely random and sporadic.

My feet ached and my thighs were on fire as I slid my food into the microwave and waited for it to warm up. I picked at a stray thread that hung from the bottom of my sweatshirt before grabbing my plate and heading to my room.

My mother frowned upon food in our bedrooms, but how the hell would she know? That meant she would have to actually pay attention to me. Using my free hand, I turned the doorknob and slipped inside my room. As I shut the door behind me, my breath escaped me in a rush when I saw Kai sitting on the edge of my bed.

I paused for a moment by the door. He caught me off guard and by surprise. I wasn't expecting him to be here. He usually didn't come over until much later in the night when everyone was usually asleep.

He was leaning forward with his forearms resting against his knees. His gaze was cast down at the floor beneath his feet. His chin was tucked to his chest and his hood was pulled up over his head. My room was dark with only the soft glow from my night-light. I couldn't make out his face in the darkness, but I could see his hands that were fisted together in front of him.

"Kai?" I whispered as I chanced a step deeper into the room. "What are you doing here? My parents are still awake and they might find you here."

His shoulders sagged and he slowly lifted his head up. His gaze crashed into mine and the soft light illuminated his face. A gasp escaped me as I took in his appearance. My hand shook and I almost dropped the plate I was holding. My heart split in two as I saw the dried blood under his nose and the deep purple bruise developing underneath his eye.

"Kai," I said softly, my voice cracking around his name. His eyes pierced mine and his jaw was tight. I set my plate down on my dresser and dropped onto my knees in front of him.

As I took his hands in mine, I noticed the jagged cuts coated with dried blood across his knuckles. I bit down on my bottom lip as the pain that was radiating from him slipped inside the crevices of my mind. This wasn't the first time he had come to me like this.

And I knew it wouldn't be the last time.

I lifted my gaze back to his and his eyes were trained on mine. I couldn't read them at all and I hated it so much. I scanned his face as I hesitantly lifted a hand to cup his cheek. A sigh escaped him and he leaned the weight of his head against my hand as if it were too much for him to hold up on his own anymore.

There was a cut just across his eyebrow that was still wet with blood. I didn't know how the hell he managed to get that there and a part of me didn't want to know. I knew things could easily get ugly with his father, but I only knew the extent of what he came to me with. I didn't know the full horrors he endured with Winston.

My parents may have been more concerned with my sister and what she was doing, but they would have never laid a finger on me.

"You're bleeding," I whispered as I began to rise to my feet.

Kai's hand darted out and he wrapped it tightly around my wrist as he pulled me back. A storm was brewing in his eyes as his gaze crashed against mine and he shook his head. "No."

I stared back at him as my heart crawled into my throat. "I need to get a first aid kit to clean it up."

"Don't leave me," he choked out, his voice cracking around his words. He pulled me closer to him. "Please, Winter."

He was breaking my heart as he stared up at me with such desperation. I knew I needed to tend to his wounds, but the inside of him needed attention first. Giving in, I stepped closer to him and his legs parted as I stood between his thighs. My hand was hesitant again, careful not to hurt him as I cupped his face in my hand.

Kai's grip around my wrist tightened momentarily

and his eyelids fluttered shut before he released me. I gently brushed the pad of my thumb across his skin. He let out a soft breath as he wrapped his arms around my lower back and pulled me to him. He pressed his face against my stomach and I lightly rubbed his shoulders as I buried my other hand in his tousled hair.

We were silent as we stood in the darkness holding on to one another to stay afloat. His shoulders shook and as the cotton material of my shirt grew damp, I realized there were tears falling from his eyes. My entire soul was splitting apart and his arms tightened around me as I stroked his head.

"It's okay, Kai. I got you," I murmured, not knowing what the hell to do. "I'm here. I'm not going anywhere."

He didn't utter a single word as they weren't needed between us. He continued to hold on to me like I was the only thing that was holding him together. I felt his shoulders sag and he relaxed against me as the tears subsided.

Abruptly, he released me and lifted his head away from me. My hands were still in his hair, but he refused to look up at me. His gaze was trained on the floor beneath our feet. "I'm sorry," he mumbled. "I don't know what the fuck that was."

"Kai, stop," I said quietly as he placed his hands against my thighs and pushed me away from him. He quickly rose to his feet and ran a hand through his hair before gripping the back of his neck. It was as if he were embarrassed by his vulnerability. This was what Kai did. He'd fall apart in my hands and then push me away.

His bloodshot eyes met mine. "I shouldn't have come."

"Don't do this, Kai," I pleaded as I closed the distance between us and reached out for him. "Don't you dare do this."

"Do what, Winter?" he questioned me with a harsh bite in his tone.

"Stop pushing me away."

Torment swirled in his irises and he was fighting an internal battle as he stared directly through me. He lifted his hands to my face. The pads of his fingers were soft as they drifted across my skin. "It's the only thing I'm good at."

"I'm never going anywhere, Malakai. No matter how hard you push, I will never leave you."

His eyes searched mine. "Promise?"

"I promise."

He slid his hand around the back of my neck as he pulled me flush against him. A gasp escaped me as my body crashed into his. His other hand was on my chin, tipping my head back as his face dropped down to mine.

"I can't stand the thought of ever losing you, Winter." His breath fanned across my face, faintly smelling like spearmint. "You're my home. You're the only place I'm safe from this godforsaken world and my fucking demons."

The words were on the tip of my tongue, but I couldn't say them. They would scare him away and that was the last thing I wanted. Malakai Barclay didn't think he was worthy of being loved, but he was. I loved him with every fiber of my being, but the words were too heavy for him.

And he was already tired of carrying the weight of his life.

I stared up at him and I could see it in his eyes. He could feel it, even without me speaking the words. And with the way he looked at me, I knew how he felt about me. His face inched closer and my eyelids fluttered shut as his lips gently brushed against mine. Kai was tender as he stroked the sides of my face and moved his mouth against mine.

His lips were tender, yet his kiss was bruising. Kai was slipping through the cracks in my heart, nestling himself in my soul. I wrapped my arms around his back as he spun me around. He began to walk me backward until the backs of my knees were hitting the edge of my mattress. His tongue slid against mine as he carefully laid me back on the bed and climbed on top of me.

He placed his hands on either side of my head, caging me in while we momentarily broke apart. He stared down at me, his eyes filled with nothing but pain and adoration swirling together in his stormy irises.

"Fuck, Winter…" he whispered, his voice hoarse as it trailed off. His throat bobbed and he swallowed hard. "You're everything to me. I lo—fuck—" He paused as the emotion washed over his face.

I wrapped my arms around the back of his neck and pulled his face back down to mine. "I know, Kai," I breathed against his lips. "I know."

His mouth crushed against mine and there was nothing gentle about the way he kissed me now. A growl rumbled in his chest and his hands were in my hair, his tongue was in my mouth. There was nothing holding him back and I would give him every piece of me he wanted.

Nothing around us mattered. The only thing that mattered to me was Kai and soothing his wounds. Comforting his soul. Silencing his demons. I was his escape from the world that was constantly ripping him to shreds.

Kai rocked back onto his knees, pulling me with him before he pushed my shirt up over my head. We broke apart momentarily, but our movements were rushed and filled with such urgency. I was reaching for his shirt as he was unclasping my bra. It only took a few seconds before our clothes were on the floor. He lifted himself from the bed as he discarded his joggers and boxer briefs on the ground beside the bed.

His fingers slid underneath the waistband of my skating pants and he stripped them away from my body, along with my panties. My breathing was ragged, my chest rising and falling in rapid succession as he stared down at me for a moment. I reached over to my nightstand and grabbed one of the condoms he had buried inside the book I finished reading months ago.

"Goddamn, Winter," he breathed as he took it from my hand and slid it over the length of his cock. "You're like the sunset on the Pacific coast. You're every color from the color wheel, the different hues and shades swirling together. You're a fucking masterpiece and I could stare at you for the rest of eternity."

My breath caught in my throat and my eyes burned

as his words bled into my soul. Kai's eyes were filled with so much emotion, I couldn't dissect them as he climbed back over me.

He settled between my legs and I wrapped them around him as he buried himself deep inside me with one thrust. He stared down at me, brushing the hair from my face as he began to move his hips. I was filled to the brim with his entire length. A soft moan escaped me as he slid his hands across my skin, memorizing the planes of my body with his fingertips.

Kai slid one hand under my ass as he lifted me enough to get a better angle to dive in deeper. His mouth dropped back to mine and he swallowed my sounds as he breathed me in. His hips moved faster and harder as he continued to thrust in and out of me. My head was swimming, my heart was racing, and he was in my veins, running rampant with the pleasure he rained down upon me.

Warmth was building in the pit of my stomach as he stroked my insides with his cock. Malakai Barclay was the first boy I had ever loved and I knew in my heart he would be the only one I would ever love. He had every piece of me that no one else ever had. He had every single one of my firsts and I wanted to give him all of my lasts.

The warmth was spreading, the pressure was building, and Kai kept thrusting his hips, fucking me harder and deeper. His tongue was tangled with mine. He was consuming me, devouring me. *Destroying me.*

He pushed me closer to the edge of the cliff and I was ready to fall. Kai's lips broke away from mine and he stared down at me. His blue eyes were filled with need as he looked into my soul.

"You're everything, Winter," he breathed as he thrust into me once more. "Fucking everything."

His gaze was locked on mine as I split in two, coming apart at the seams. Kai was right behind as he lost himself deep inside me. I shattered around him, my body shaking from the earthquake of my orgasm. We were both caught up in one another. My chest was heaving as his thrusting slowed, yet I couldn't tear my eyes away from his. Not with the way he was looking at me.

He was looking at me like he loved me.

The silence enveloped us as he dropped his forehead to mine and held me close.

I love you. I love you. I love you.

CHAPTER SEVEN
MALAKAI

Present

I sat as still as an ice sculpture at my parents' massive dining room table. It easily sat ten people. There were only the three of us, unless they were hosting people at our house. My mother sat across from me in the seat she had always occupied to the right of my father. I stared at his empty seat for a moment, wishing that it would just stay empty.

It wasn't hard to avoid him the past six years. Even though I had an oceanfront condo about ten minutes away, I made sure that if I were in town, he was away on business. I spent more time in hotels and at resorts while I was on tour. It was easier that way and it gave me every excuse to stay away from the vile man who was my father.

There was only one time that I had run into him since I had moved out of the house. It was the night of my first professional tournament. I was leading in score for the first nine holes. Only as I reached the tenth, did I see my parents standing in the crowd. My mother had her infamous drunken smile as she waved at me.

My father on the other hand—there was nothing but disappointment and hate that came from his cold glare. I shit the bed on the back nine and ended up coming in second after completely fucking up my score.

My mother insisted that we all had dinner that night. My father did nothing but berate me and remind me how much of a failure I was. His disappointment was made crystal clear and it finally took that last moment for me to realize that no matter what I did, I would never be what he wanted me to be.

Countless beatings and having him verbally and emotionally fuck me up couldn't bring me to that conclusion. It took my first professional tournament and his reaction to make me see clearly.

I would always be beneath him.

Doris set a salad in front of my mother and me before she left one at the empty seat at the head of the table. Just as she ducked back into the industrial kitchen, the doors to the dining room were pushed open and my father came striding inside. His entire presence demanded attention and I stared at the lettuce in front of me as my spine straightened.

The hairs on the back of my neck rose and my heart began to pound erratically in my chest. I hated the visceral reaction he caused, but that was trauma for you.

"Hi, Charlotte," he said to my mother as he placed a kiss on her forehead. She stared up at him with the most adoring look and I wanted to throw bleach in her eyes. Couldn't she see what a monster this man truly was? He was the devil in a fucking human suit.

He took his seat at the head of the table and his gaze met mine as he nodded. "Malakai."

"Father," I replied curtly with a nod.

My mother poured him a glass of whiskey, since he always preferred that over the vintage wine my mother sucked down like it was oxygen. "Isn't it so great that Malakai is home?" She smiled at him with her sweet, slurred words.

"Oh, yes. Such a pleasant surprise." My father continued to stare at me with his dead eyes. "Your mother tells me that you're taking a break from your tour and spending some time in Orchid City." He paused for a moment as he took a sip of his liquor. "It wouldn't have anything to do with the Reign girl being back, would it?"

Of course it had everything to do with her.

I gave him a blank stare and shook my head. "Mom mentioned her parents left their estate to her while they were traveling."

"Hmm," my father hummed with indifference as he began to pick at his salad. My father was never fond of the Reign family. To keep up with appearances, he tolerated them and put on a show of being friendly. Deep down, he always viewed them as beneath us because Winter's father didn't agree with some of my father's avenues of income. Because of that, he never liked Winter.

Awkward silence encapsulated us momentarily. I

watched my robotic mother follow his lead as she began to eat her food. The ever proper, picture-perfect wife. God forbid she eat any of her food before he touched his.

Doris brought out the next course as we all continued to sit in silence. I hated it. I hated it all. This wasn't where I belonged. I would have rather been eating a meal alone from a bullshit rest stop in the middle of nowhere on the side of the highway than sitting here with them.

"I just find it peculiar," my father began again as he pierced his chicken breast with his fork. His eyes were back on my face as he slid his knife through the meat. "Are you sure that it's purely coincidence that you are both back in your hometown at the same time?"

"Yes." My voice sounded bored and monotone. Robotic, even—just like my mother. I cocked an eyebrow at him. "What are you implying?"

"Nothing at all," he said with dismissal. "I can't imagine this little break being good for your career."

My jaw tightened and I fought the urge to roll my neck. My hands clenched around the silverware I was holding. I wanted to drive my fork directly through his crystal blue eyes. "It's actually quite common amongst golfers," I retorted as I politely kept my fork and knife to myself and cut through the chicken on my plate. "Research has proven that a mental health break can be beneficial to your overall game."

I couldn't tell him the truth. If I told him the truth about why my mental health was in the trash can, he'd find a way to ruin my career without any of my help. If he knew I was struggling to perform on the golf course because of Winter, he'd find a way to make sure I never thought of her again.

My father may have hated me and he may have wanted me to fail, but he didn't want that strike against the Barclay name. There was a standard I was held to, regardless of his disdain for me.

My father's lip curled upward and his nostrils flared. "I'm assuming that Edgar was the one who suggested that."

Edgar Hastings was my mentor. He was the one who truly took me under his wing and taught me the game. He had taught me everything I knew, including how to not be like my father. He wasn't put off by my ugly attitude or the baggage I came with. Instead, he embraced my flaws and taught me how to hone in my skills.

My father always hated him. He was highly respected in their circles and was still an extremely successful golfer himself. He was everything my father was not.

He disregarded me as he turned his attention back to his meal. His statement didn't warrant a response from me. He knew damn well it was Edgar who suggested it and that I didn't take his advice with a simple grain of salt. It held more weight than any other advice I had ever received in life because it was all in the sake of helping me to succeed, not fail.

I couldn't help but feel like my father was always rooting against me. He was praying for my downfall. He wanted to see me fail.

"How was your day today, Charlotte?" My father turned his attention to her, although his tone was bored and he didn't give two shits about how her day actually was.

"It was good," she smiled at him. She didn't elaborate on what she filled her time with, but everyone knew she was as much of a fraud as the rest of us. She sought her solitude in a bottle, although it was something she would never openly admit.

My father grunted, my mother was oblivious to the growing tension, and they both continued on with their food. I stared down at the chicken on my plate, half wishing it would jump off the table and run away. At least then I would know none of this was real. It was just a hallucination. A bad dream.

"Malakai," my mother half scolded me as she watched me push my food around. I looked up at her, meeting her disapproving gaze. "Is there something wrong with it? I can have Doris make you something else."

My nostrils flared as I shook my head. "That's not necessary. It's fine, there's nothing wrong with it." *There was just something wrong with the company.*

My father's cold stare was now back on mine. "Don't be a fucking prick, Malakai. Eat your goddamn food."

Something took hold of me. The anger that had been welling up inside. He used to push me around and was an asshole while I was growing up. As I got older and met him in height, it turned into more of a fight because I wasn't afraid to hit him back. It never made the situa-

68

tion any better—if anything, it made it worse. He was a more skilled fighter than I was, so usually it was still him that did the damage.

He may have chipped away at me and had broken me down over the years, but I wasn't physically afraid of him anymore.

"I'm not hungry."

His eyes were ice. "I don't give a fuck if you're hungry or not. Stop acting like an entitled brat."

I looked over at my mother. Her eyes were off in the distance and she was dissociating from it all. A volcano of rage was building inside me, the molten lava spilling over the edges as the eruption began.

"Fuck this." I let out a harsh breath as I abruptly pushed my chair back and it clattered onto the floor. The table shifted from my movement, splashing my mother's red wine onto the table. She let out a gasp and my father was already on his feet. "This is exactly why I don't come back here."

"We never asked you to come back, Malakai." My father's tone was low, his voice harsh and frigid. "What a disappointment you've always been."

"And how am I a disappointment now, Father?"

His face lacked any and all emotion. "The amount of money we spent for you to be able to get to the professional level of golf, and you take the advice of some old, washed-up golfer who tells you to take a break. For fucking what? So you can be mentally fit?" He let out a harsh laugh that slid across my eardrums like sandpaper. "I hate to break it to you, son, but you've always been fucked in the head. That's not something any amount of time or medication can fix."

The color drained from my face. The wind had left my sails. Instead of the lava running over, the volcano inside me vanished.

I hated him. *So fucking much.*

Turning my back to my parents, I strode through the dining room, pushing the doors open in a rush as I stepped out into the hall. My mother's footsteps followed behind me as I entered the foyer and walked to the front door.

"Malakai, wait," my mother called out, her voice frantic and her words slurred. She was on my heels as I walked through the front door and her hand darted out to grab my wrist as we stepped onto the driveway. "Your father didn't mean that. He must have just had a bad day. You know how he can be sometimes."

"You always have some kind of an excuse for the way he acts," I shouted at her as I ripped my arm from her grip. "When will you stop defending him?"

She looked back at me like I had just struck her across the face. There was a blankness to her stare, though, and I knew my words were falling on deaf ears.

"Fucking forget it," I breathed, my words barely audible. "I won't be coming back here again, but you know how to get a hold of me if you want to meet at a more neutral location. Without him."

I left her standing there without another word. As I climbed into my car, I chanced one glance back at the front of their house and saw that my mother must have retreated back inside. She was no longer watching me. I knew she went back to see him because if my mother ever had to choose between her husband and child, it would always be him.

As I reached the end of their driveway and pulled through the gates, the weight on my chest was crushing. It was threatening to swallow me whole and I needed to just breathe. I whipped my car onto the road and pressed on the gas pedal as the vehicle surged forward.

I didn't give two fucks about speeding. There were no other cars on the road, so I wasn't putting anyone's life in danger but my own. I was conflicted and torn. It felt like the walls I had built around myself were crumbling. There was only one place I would go in moments like this, but I was no longer welcome there.

I was the last person Winter would want to see, but I couldn't help myself.

I needed to see her.

CHAPTER EIGHT
WINTER

Standing in the center of the ice rink, I closed my eyes and took in a deep breath. My lungs expanded as they filled with the cold air. It burned but I couldn't fight the smile that crept across my lips. It was so familiar and it was exactly what I needed to calm my soul. It was hard to describe the smell, but if you were ever in an ice rink, you would always remember it.

It was similar to the smell of snow. Especially under the moonlight as it fell from the sky above, covering everything around you. There was something about the quiet, calmness. Ice was deadly, yet it was also magical, just like snow.

My parents got it right when they named me. I was definitely a winter child.

I didn't know where else to go after I ran into Kai. I wasn't able to get in with my parents' lawyer until Tuesday morning, so I needed to do something to keep myself busy. My interview was the same day and that had my stomach in knots. I didn't want to have too much going on that day and be stressed out, but it was all going to work out.

If I was going to be back in Orchid City, I needed to do something that was going to keep me busy. I needed to distract my mind, especially since he was back. I wasn't going to let myself sit at home and obsess over the past with him. What was done was done and there was no going back.

I ended up at the ice rink that I grew up skating at. They had changed their freestyle times and it ended up being this evening. I was surprised when I found that the rink was barely occupied. A few other skaters moved around the ice, but it wasn't nearly as busy as it could get. Ice time was always a struggle when you were competing with hockey. Most rinks catered more to hockey than they did to figure skating.

Skating professionally was always my dream. I think it was every little girl's dream who grew up on the ice. My heart clenched at the thought of what I had given up to come back here. I gave it all up, but my head wasn't really in it. As much as I enjoyed competitions, there was a part of me that always hated it. And I had given up trying to compete against my sister and her accomplishments.

Skating professionally and competitively wasn't for me. I belonged on the ice, but on my own time, at my own leisure. I wanted to teach and help mold others who were learning. As I opened my eyes, I began to skate backward, letting the music that played throughout the rink match my movements. Nothing else mattered except for my skates and the way they moved across the ice.

I skated with the best of them and I wanted to use that for more than just myself. I wanted to give back, to help the kids that were starting their own figure skating journeys. I just wasn't sure how to get involved. When I was younger, I used to help with learn-to-skate programs, but that was different from being a coach.

As the freestyle time came to an end, I left the ice and sat on one of the benches as I pulled my skates off. An older woman approached me. Her dark hair was cut short and framed her face. A soft smile touched her lips as she stared down at me for a moment.

"Are you Winter?" she asked me.

My eyebrows pulled together. "Yes," I said with hesitation as I put my skates into my bag and rose to my feet. "And you are?"

"Linda," she told me as she held her hand out for me to shake it. "I run the Orchid City Figure Skating Club. I've heard a lot about you. You're kind of a legend here at the rink with how far you've gone with figure skating."

My throat constricted and I smiled back at her. "Thanks," I nodded. "I don't really compete anymore, though."

Her lips pursed but her face lit up. "That's a shame. You're an extremely talented skater." She paused for a moment. "If you're ever interested in coaching, we can always use someone with your knowledge and skill."

It was something I wanted to do but now that the opportunity was presenting itself, I felt pressure. Pressure that I didn't know I could handle. "It's something I've thought about," I admitted quietly.

"Well, if you're ever interested in exploring that, come find me. I'm here most days in the afternoons."

I nodded at her as I slipped my feet into my sneakers and grabbed my bag. "Thanks. I'll keep that in mind."

"I hope you do come find me, Winter. We have a lot of kids that could benefit from you."

Linda left me with that as her parting remark. It was all too much and too soon. In the short amount of time that I had been back in Orchid City, so much shit had been thrown in my face. I just wanted to get settled in and work in peace at the library. It was conflicting and contradicting.

I mulled over Linda's words as I walked out to my car and slipped inside. It was almost as if the universe heard my thoughts and plucked her out of thin air and placed her in my life for a reason. Maybe it wasn't something I should ignore. I needed time to think about it, but she made it clear that I could help and they needed that.

I knew in the back of my mind that I'd be back to talk to Linda. I didn't know when, but it was something I wasn't going to be able to dismiss. They needed my help and there was no reason why I couldn't do that. It was time for me to give back.

———

The house was eerily quiet even though the TV was playing softly in the background. Perhaps it was because I was in the house alone that made something feel off. It wasn't like I hadn't been home alone before in my life, but being the only one who was occupying the space gave me a weird feeling. It was like there was a void inside the walls and I wasn't big enough to fill it.

As I curled up on the couch with a book, I looked around the room and silently cursed my parents. I wished this place wasn't a family heirloom. I wanted to sell it. I wanted to go back to Vermont and forget about anything that happened over the past few days.

Most importantly, I wanted to go back to my life where *he* didn't exist.

There was a soft knocking sound and I glanced up at the TV from my book. It was a house hunter type show, but there was no one knocking on the screen. I turned the volume down and my heart rate kicked up the pace as my breathing grew ragged. I stared at the TV, waiting for the sound again. As I heard it, I realized it wasn't coming from the show. It was coming from the front door.

Panic welled inside me as I climbed off the couch. I held my phone in one hand and clutched it tightly. I didn't have a weapon to defend myself. There was no reason anyone would be at my front door at this hour. If it were Sutton, she wouldn't knock. She had her own key and was free to let herself in whenever she pleased.

My footsteps were light and quiet on the hardwood floor as I inched closer to the front door. The knocking stopped and I was once again cursing my parents for not getting a door with a window or some kind of a peephole. I flicked on the light switch for the front porch and looked through one of the glass panes alongside the door.

My stomach fell to the floor and my breath caught in my throat as I took in Kai's expression. It was grim and tortured. His hood was pulled up over his head and his hands were tucked in the front pocket of his hoodie. Inhaling deeply, I slowly took a step back and unlocked the door before I pulled it open.

Kai's head was tilted down and he slowly lifted it as his gaze barreled into mine. His jaw was tense and his throat bobbed as he swallowed hard. The air between us was thick with tension and emotion. There was so much brewing in his eyes, I couldn't pull a single emotion out of them without pulling them all out. My breath was caught in my lungs and my eyes desperately searched his.

Words failed me at that moment. The silence between us was deafening. It was suffocating, yet I couldn't move. I was lost in the depths of his eyes, sinking and drowning.

Kai's lips parted and a ragged breath escaped him. "Winter."

There was a heaviness to his tone as his eyelids fluttered shut. His shoulders sagged, almost in relief. There was no reason for him to be here right now. I didn't want to see him, yet I couldn't will my feet to move.

"Is everything okay?"

Kai swallowed again and reopened his eyes. "I

didn't mean to come here. I didn't know where else to go."

The pain and hopelessness was laced in his words. This was the side of Malakai that no one ever saw but me many, many years ago. This was how he used to come to me when we were younger, yet he always let himself in. We were trapped in a weird place where neither of us knew how to act around the other after the damage had been done. It took me a long time to pull myself from the rubble from the wake of his destruction but I did it.

I put myself back together, even though the pieces never fit properly again.

And now he was here, needing me to put him back together as well.

I scanned his face in desperation, but there wasn't a single mark on him. I breathed a sigh of relief as I didn't see that there was any physical harm done to him. There was a part of me that wondered what was really worse. Sure, the physical abuse he endured with his father wasn't healthy but he went through a lot more emotionally and verbally.

"What did he do?"

Kai's lips pursed and he shrugged with indifference as he tried to put his walls back up. "Nothing that he hasn't already done."

I shifted my weight nervously on my feet. Kai cast his gaze down onto the ground. The air between us was growing thicker and it was almost palpable. There was so much pain, so much turmoil that was between us. So much damage. I didn't think my heart would ever fully heal. I never knew the state of his heart because he shut me out before I had the chance to understand what he did to himself that night when he finally had pushed me away.

Taking a step back, I pulled the door open with me. It was possibly the worst thing I could have done, but I couldn't leave him standing on my steps like this. Not when he was so full of despair. Not when he had nowhere else to turn. And certainly not when he needed me the most.

"Come on," I said softly as Kai lifted his head and his eyes crashed into mine. His gaze wavered and there was a look of hope and hesitancy swirling together in his stormy irises.

"Come inside where you're safe."
With me.

CHAPTER NINE
MALAKAI

As I stepped inside Winter's house, it was familiar and just as I remembered. The soft scent of a vanilla candle that was burning met my nose and I closed my eyes as I inhaled deeply. Winter's mother always made sure their house smelled welcoming and it was as if Winter had taken a page from her book. I stood just inside the foyer, listening to the sound of her locking the door.

I knew I shouldn't have come here, but I couldn't help myself. She was who I had always turned to in times like this. I avoided this kind of shit with my father for as long as Winter had been out of my life. It was kind of funny how the two were coinciding now. Life was a fucking mess and it was hard to not wonder what the hell I was really doing here.

I came back home because of her and she wanted nothing to do with me.

"Do you want some water or anything?" Winter

asked me softly as she stopped in front of me. Her bright green eyes stared back at me with a touch of concern.

I shook my head. "Do you have anything stronger?"

Her lips pulled downward and she nodded. "Do you still like bourbon?" Her voice was quiet and hesitant. There was a part of me that was surprised she remembered, but there wasn't much that Winter forgot. That mind of hers was like a goddamn vault.

"I do."

Her tongue darted out to wet her lips and my gaze instinctively dropped down to them. She was nervous, with reason. My eyes shifted back up to hers as she cleared her throat. "I'll be right back."

She spun on her heel and disappeared down the hall in the direction of the kitchen. I watched her until she was no longer in sight before I began to make my way deeper into the house. There wasn't much that had changed. There were never any family photos hanging, except for the massive portrait-style one that Mrs. Reign had hung above the mantle in their family room.

Throughout the rest of the house, it was all expensive art that they had purchased from different shows and events over the years. I was surprised Winter's parents left everything in the house the way it was before they had moved, but then again, there was a lot of shit to move out of a house this size.

Winter hadn't changed anything inside to make it her own. She had just moved back not long ago, but I didn't see a single trace in my venture to the family room that indicated she had even brought any of her own stuff with her. Perhaps she put it in storage. Maybe she still had her apartment back in Vermont and she left it fully furnished the same way her parents did with their mansion.

As I walked into the family room, I noticed there was a house hunter show playing on the TV. I couldn't fight the smile that played on my lips. Winter went through this phase when we were in high school that she wanted to design the interiors of homes. Sutton had jumped on the idea because she was into the actual design of buildings and she had this brilliant idea for the two of them to work together on it.

I didn't know if it had to do with their sibling rivalry or what it was exactly, but after Sutton went down a hole of trying to convince Winter that it was something they needed to do, Winter shut it down. She didn't want to be an interior designer. She just wanted to hide behind her books, in her own little fictional world. There wasn't a single part of her that wanted to be tied to her family. She wanted her own thing and Sutton ruined that.

My eyes traveled across the couch and I could make out where Winter must have been sitting before I arrived. There was a book with a bookmark tucked inside sitting next to a blanket that looked as if it had been pushed aside in a rush. The remote was on the arm rest of the couch and there was a pillow propped up.

"Here." Winter's soft voice snaked around my eardrums as she pressed her wrist against my bicep. I slowly turned around and she held out a glass with amber-colored liquid in it. "Something stronger."

I gave her a nod as I took it from her. "Thanks," I murmured as I lifted the glass to my lips. The pungent smell of the bourbon stung my nostrils and as I swallowed back a mouthful, it burned as it made its way down my esophagus.

"Is this your father's?" I questioned her as I watched her take a sip from her own glass. Winter never had a taste for expensive bourbon, but her father did. And this tasted like it was old and waiting around for a special occasion.

"Yeah," she said with a shrug as she lifted the bottle to look at it. "I suppose if he didn't want anyone to drink it, he should have taken it along with him."

I half snorted and shook my head at her. "I'm surprised they left everything here."

Winter shrugged again as she took a swig straight from the bottle. Her nose scrunched up and the distaste was evident on her face. "They're traveling and couldn't take things along with them. They plan on moving down to their house in the Keys after they're done, but there was no sense in putting their things in storage. I didn't have much to bring along with me and it certainly was not enough to furnish this place."

Silence settled between us and Winter took another nervous sip of the bourbon. She let out a ragged breath and wiped her mouth with the back of her hand. "Come sit," she said softly, her voice practically a whisper as she motioned to the couch.

My feet were cemented in place and I watched her

for a moment as she moved back to where she was sitting before I interrupted her. Her hips swayed and her footsteps were light. She was just as I remembered, yet even better. There was always a grace and beauty to Winter Reign.

I followed after her and took a seat a few cushions away from her. I didn't want to push things between us. Hell, I didn't even know if there was a chance there would ever be anything between us again. In her eyes, I was still the asshole who broke her heart six years ago. And in my eyes, she was still the one who held my heart in the palms of her hands.

"What happened tonight, Kai?"

Of course she would ask. She couldn't just let it be. My mind had drifted away from the shit with my father and now it was crashing down around me. I closed my eyes for a moment as my jaw clenched. I tightened my grip around my glass and opened my eyes as I drained its contents. I held it out to Winter and she filled it again.

"My mother insisted I come over for dinner, so I did to appease her." I paused and let out the breath I didn't realize I was holding. "My father questioned me on why I was taking a break from my tour. I gave him a watered-down explanation, to which he didn't have the nicest things to say."

Her lips parted and her eyes scanned my face. I hoped she wouldn't ask why I was taking a break too. I fought back a sigh of relief when she didn't. "Did he hurt you again?"

I shook my head. "He hasn't laid a finger on me in

many years. The last time was right before I left." I watched the pain wash over Winter's eyes before she blinked it away. She lifted the bottle to her lips once more and took a bigger gulp. "I hit him back that night and got him good. Tonight was the first time I saw him since."

It wasn't completely a lie, but there's no sense in telling her about the time he and my mother came to one of my tournaments. It was insignificant. Winter wanted to know what happened tonight, not what happened over the past six years.

"You haven't been back since then?"

I shook my head. "There was nothing left for me here."

She stared at me for a moment after taking another sip. My glass was magically empty again and I held it out for her to fill once more. "You made sure that I would hate you. You broke my heart and pushed me away."

"I know," I admitted after a beat. "But that didn't mean there was anything here for me if you weren't here. You were the only thing that kept me around."

Winter winced like I slapped her. "You were so cruel."

"I still am."

"So, why are you here? Why come to me?" she questioned me, her voice low. It didn't crack around her words like it once would have. Winter was always strong, but now it was as if she was immune to me. She had built her walls so goddamn high around her heart, the only way I could get through was if I scaled them.

"I don't know," I admitted, my tone clipped. I couldn't help it. There was still a destructive side of me that knew Winter deserved better than I could ever give her. And that destructive side wanted nothing more than to destroy both of us. "I didn't want to come here. I didn't want to come to you."

Winter glowered. "Then why are you here, Malakai?" There was exasperation in her tone and she pushed her shoulders back as she straightened her spine.

We were constantly contradicting ourselves, contradicting one another.

"Because—I don't fucking know." I ran a frustrated hand through my hair before draining my glass once more. The warmth was building in the pit of my stomach and my head was growing fuzzier with the passing seconds. "This is just where I came, Winter. I didn't have time to think. I left their house and drove straight here, even though I knew this was the last place I should go."

She filled up my glass without me having to ask before she took a large gulp. Her eyes were hooded and glossy as she stared back at me. "You haven't changed at all."

Now it was time for my face to contort. "What does that mean?"

"You're hot and cold, up and down, back and forth. You always gave me whiplash, and you still do." She let out a sigh and shook her head. "I could never keep up with your ever-changing thoughts then, and I still can't. You pushed me away, yet you didn't come back here because there was nothing left for you." She pointed the bottle of bourbon at me as her eyes burned holes through mine. "You made me leave without you."

"Because I had to!" I practically yelled at her. I knew this would happen one day, I just didn't expect it to be today. And the alcohol flowing between us was not helping with the emotions at all. We were both getting drunker with each sip and it was like an igniter. It was only adding fuel to the fire.

"You're a liar, Malakai." She glared at me, but her voice was quiet and warm. "Your father is so deep in your head that you believe the vile things he tells you. You think you're worthless and undeserving, but you're wrong. You've always been wrong."

My eyes sliced through hers as anger pushed its way to the forefront of my emotions. As my therapist said, it was a reaction, not an emotion. And Winter had perfected the art of bringing out that reaction in me. "What the fuck do you know, Winter Reign?"

"You," she breathed as she moved closer to me on the couch, closing the distance between us. "I know you."

My jaw clenched. I set my glass down on the table beside me and pulled the bottle from Winter's hand before swallowing more of the liquor. "And what do you think you know, darling?"

"Your father has become that voice of self-doubt in your mind. You've become so critical of yourself because of the way he has plagued your thoughts." She paused for a moment as she took the bottle from me and drank more. "You never loved yourself, Malakai. That's why you could never love me."

Her words were a blow to the chest. They split open my sternum as she reached inside and squeezed my lifeless heart. "You have no idea what the fuck you're talking about," I snarled at her as my hand darted out and wrapped around her wrist. I plucked the bottle from her hand and set it down on the floor while still holding on to her. "You think I didn't love you?"

"I think you did in your own messed-up way," she breathed as I pulled her closer to me. "How could you possibly love someone when you were never taught how to love?"

"You're right," I growled as I pulled her onto my lap. "I never loved you, Winter." I dropped her wrist and slid my hand along the side of her face and around the back of her head. I pushed my fingers through her silky hair. "Love never touched the way I felt about you. You were always so much more than that to me."

She rested her hands on my shoulders and rolled her head to the side. "If that were true, you never would have pushed me away like you did."

I let out an exasperated sigh as I pulled her face down to mine. "When will you understand that I did it because I had to?"

She shook her head at me as she slid her hands around the back of my neck. "I don't understand why you think you had to."

"Because I'm a fucking coward," I whispered against her lips before sucking her bottom lip between my teeth. "Because I never deserved you and I never will, but that doesn't mean a fucking thing right now."

"What are you doing?" she murmured against my mouth as I released her lip and ran my tongue over the half-moon shapes that were indented in her flesh.

The corners of my lips twitched. "Taking what's always been mine."

CHAPTER TEN
WINTER

Kai's mouth crashed into mine as he slowly pulled my soul from my body. He breathed me in, draining the oxygen from my lungs as his tongue slid against the seam of my lips. I wasn't thinking straight. The logical part of my brain was screaming at me to get away from him, but I couldn't listen to it. The sound of my heart beating with his drowned it out.

He always did challenge my heart and mind. He always seemed to be able to override any logical, rational thought that I had. When it came to Kai, I was entirely powerless. Throw some alcohol into the equation and my walls were already lowering. I knew I couldn't let him in, but that didn't mean I couldn't enjoy him in the moment. I could regret it tomorrow morning.

All we were simply doing was repeating history.

It was a common theme between us. Kai was broken and I always did like fixing things. He was a problem I wanted to solve, yet I was never able to. Kai's demons had their claws deep in his skin and he was deep inside my rib cage, making a home out of my heart.

We were toxic. We didn't belong together, but somehow we couldn't fight the pull of the tides between us.

Kai's tongue slid into my mouth, tangling with mine as he deepened the kiss. He was everywhere, surrounding and consuming me. His hands were in my hair, gripping my scalp as he held me against him. His cock was hard, pressing against me through his pants, and I shifted my hips in his lap.

He abruptly broke apart from me, pulling away just far enough that his eyes found mine. "Has there been anyone else?"

I swallowed over the lump in my throat, biting down on my bottom lip as I shook my head. "No one."

There was a part of me that felt pathetic for the omission. In the past six years, I hadn't been with another guy. Not intimately in this way. There was one guy that I dated in college, but I never let it get far. The farthest we ever got was making out and it just wasn't the same. It wasn't what my soul craved, and I couldn't help but feel like I was betraying Kai even though he had cast me aside like I was nothing to him.

I didn't bother asking him because I didn't want to know.

A low growl escaped him before his mouth crashed back into mine with more urgency. His lips moved against mine, soft like silk, yet brutal and bruising. He was cruel with his words and his kisses and I let him take and take until there was nothing left to give.

Kai dropped his hands down to my waist and slid them around to cup my ass. He lifted me up, just enough before spinning us around, and he laid me down on the couch. This was heading into territory neither of us were used to. We were both still damaged and this wasn't going to be good for either of us.

His hands wandered down my body as he settled between my legs. His touch felt like flames licking my skin and I squirmed underneath him as his tongue continued its assault against mine. He was consuming me and I would always let him. It was my own toxic trait. I would let Malakai Barclay strip me bare until there was nothing left.

He was my weakness and he knew it. He used it against me and it was my own fault for letting him.

Kai slid his hands down to the waistband of my shorts. His fingers were soft yet urgent as he pulled them down with my underwear. His mouth broke apart from mine and he rocked back onto his knees as he slid them past my feet before dropping them onto the floor beside the couch.

He moved farther away from me and I stared up at him with curiosity. I wasn't drunk, but I was feeling the alcohol as my head began to swim. It was a deadly combination. You were never supposed to mix drugs and alcohol, yet here I was doing it with him. He was the very drug that had the capabilities to bring me to my knees.

"What are you doing?" I was breathless as I watched

him move down the length of the couch until he was lying on his stomach between my legs.

He fell silent and his eyes searched mine for consent as he slid his arms under my thighs. My knees hooked over his biceps as I wet my lips and nodded. His eyelids fluttered shut as he pressed his mouth to my pussy in the softest kiss. A strangled moan escaped me and my head tipped backward in ecstasy as he slid his tongue against me.

"Fuck, Winter," he growled against my clit as he circled his tongue around it. "You taste just like I remember."

His mouth was against me as he moved his tongue against my flesh, licking, sucking, tasting and teasing every inch. Kai was skilled with his tongue and he knew exactly what he was doing. My hands found his head and I pushed my fingers through his dirty blond hair as he pinned me down and continued to fuck me with his mouth.

Kai had every one of my firsts. He was the only one who had ever tasted me like this. The only one who could ever bring me to pleasure with their mouth the way he did. I never imagined even letting someone else try.

Kai's tongue circled around my clit before he slid it along the center of my pussy and pushed it deep inside me. He growled against me as he moved his tongue in and out of me momentarily before moving back to my clit. His fingers dug into the flesh on my thighs as he held me in place and ate me like a starved man.

It wasn't long before he was pushing me closer and

closer to the edge. My head was swimming, the warmth was building in the pit of my stomach and seeping into my veins. I no longer felt like I was drunk from the alcohol. Instead, I was drunk on him—and I hadn't had my fill yet. I wanted more. My greediness was beginning to take over and I wanted everything he could possibly give me.

It was a vicious cycle. Usually I was the one who was giving and Kai had a habit of taking everything from me. But at the same time, Kai was just the same as me. He gave me every piece of him, even if he didn't know how to love. He did it in the best way he could.

One last flick of his tongue had me coming apart at the seams. The volcano in the pit of my stomach erupted and my orgasm tore through my body like wildfire. It was spreading, consuming me, and I shattered on his tongue as he continued to lick and taste me, drinking from me until the well ran dry.

My body shook with such force as my hips bucked against his face. My hands were tangled in his hair, holding on to him for dear life as I fell from the edge of the cliff. I was falling deep into a state of ecstasy and nothing else mattered.

Kai pulled his face away from between my legs, yet he didn't release my thighs as he stared down at me. "Fuck," he murmured as his lips twitched and a fire burned deep in his eyes. "I love the way you look after you come. The way you look at me with those hazy green eyes and the pink tint on your cheeks. Goddammit, Winter."

My chest rose and fell with every shallow breath

that escaped me. I stared up at him, my eyes bouncing back and forth between his as his eyes continued to burn through mine. I slowly sat halfway up as I reached for him and pulled him back to me.

Regret began to creep in, but I quickly pushed it out of my mind. The past didn't matter. Nothing that had happened before was important in this moment. All that mattered was us replacing the pain with pleasure. Licking one another's wounds while we soothed our souls. It was the simple connection, the binding thread that was always between us, regardless of how frayed it really was.

My hands pushed his shirt up his torso and Kai reached back behind his back before pulling it up over his head. It fell away to the floor and my hands trailed across the planes of his body as I memorized every inch of him. His muscles were more defined than I remembered them. He was always athletic and trim, but there was so much more to him now.

Kai's mouth crashed back into mine after he stripped my shirt and bra away before laying me back down on the couch. I was completely naked and bare for him. A growl rumbled in his chest as he pulled away and began to shove his pants down. His movements were rushed and he wasn't wasting any time as he settled back between my legs.

"Are you on birth control?"

I nodded my response.

"Thank God," he nipped at my bottom lip. A gasp slipped from my lips as he pushed inside me with one thrust. He filled me to the brim with his length, stretching me with his girth. It had been a long time, but my body remembered him, just like his remembered mine.

"Jesus Christ, Winter," he breathed against my lips before tracing them with his tongue. "You're always so fucking ready for me. Soaking and accepting."

His mouth was back on mine and his tongue was in my mouth as he began to pump his hips, thrusting in and out of me. My legs were around his waist, my ankles locked together around the small of his back. Kai grabbed my hair with one hand while the other gripped my ass cheek.

"You were made for this cock, darling," he groaned as his mouth broke away from mine. He lifted his head and his stormy eyes stared directly through me. "It's only ever been you, Winter. It will only ever be you."

"You say that now, but you'll leave me the next chance you get," I bit back at him, feeling the mixture of emotion as he peered inside my soul. I loved feeling him like this. This close, this intimate. It was like the veil had lifted and he removed his mask. This was the side of Kai that was only reserved for me.

But I couldn't help the bitterness that settled within my bones. It always lingered in the background, like a snake lying in wait. I never knew when it would resurface and finally strike.

"You're wrong," he growled as he thrust into me harder. "I'm here to stay. You're my home. This is exactly where I belong."

My legs tightened around him and my nails dug into the skin on his back as he fucked me harder. His movements were vicious like his tone, but his words were a contradiction. They were soft, they didn't match.

"I can't let you back in, Malakai," I promised him, my breathing ragged and shallow as the warmth began to build in the pit of my stomach again. "I won't let you back in. I'm done letting you hurt me."

"That makes one of us," he breathed as his grip tightened around my hair. "All I've ever known with you was pain, but yours was the sweetest kind. I want it all. Don't ever stop hurting me." He let out a breath and clenched his jaw. "And stop saying my name like that."

He released my ass and slid his hand between our bodies as he continued to thrust his hips faster, harder, deeper.

"I hate you," I cried out as his fingertips brushed across my clit. "God, don't stop—yes, right there," I moaned as he began to circle his thumb.

Kai pulled my bottom lip between his teeth and bit down as he dove in deeper. "Hate me all you want, darling. I want your anger. I want your rage. Give it all to me."

"Please just stop," I begged him as I raked my nails down his back.

He abruptly stopped moving and his eyes slid back and forth between mine with confusion. His gaze was troubled and he looked panicked.

I narrowed my eyes at him as I bucked my hips. "What are you doing?"

"You told me to stop."

A sigh of annoyance left my lungs. "I meant for you

to stop talking, not for you to stop what you were doing."

Kai didn't move. Something dark and mischievous passed through his eyes. "And what is it that I was doing?"

Heat instantly spread up my neck and across my cheeks. "You know what you were doing." He was going to make me say the damn words and I could die from embarrassment thinking about it.

"I do," he said matter-of-factly. "But if you want me to start again, I need to hear it from you."

My eyebrows were drawn together as I shook my head. "Absolutely not."

Kai lifted an eyebrow and slanted his head as he continued to stare at me for a moment. "Okay," he said slowly as he nodded. "Well, I can just see myself out then."

A groan slipped from my lips and I locked my legs around his waist as I turned my head to the side. "I want you to keep fucking me."

His hand gripped my chin and he turned my head to face him. "Say it again. Like you actually mean it."

"Fuck me, Kai. Fuck me until there's nothing left of me."

His mouth twitched, but he didn't dare smile. "That's better."

He released my chin and laid his palm against the side of my face. His touch was soft and tender as he began to move his hips once again. It was different. There was a shift between us as his eyes burned through mine. The way he moved, it was slow and torturous. His brutality was a completely different kind of torture.

He wasn't fucking me anymore.

He was breaking me apart from the inside out.

Kai's other hand brushed against my clit, making my eyes roll back in my head from the ecstasy. His hips shifted and he kept a steady pace, stroking my insides with the length of his cock while he played with my clit. I was seeing stars, my back arching and my hips involuntarily bucking, wanting more from him.

His hand that was on the side of my face was now back under my chin. "Open your eyes, Winter," his bourbon-tinged breath fanned across my face. "I want to see you while you shatter into a million pieces."

My eyes were on his and I was slowly losing myself. I fought against the urge to close them as he pushed me over the edge. His thumb brushed my clit once more and my orgasm tore through my body like a whirlwind. He stared down at me, thrusting into me harder as he lost himself deep inside me.

We were both riding the high of one another. His thrusts slowed, until he fell still. A ragged breath escaped him as he slowly pulled out of me and slid between me and the back of the couch. His arms were around me and he pulled me in, holding me close.

"I still hate you," I breathed against his chest as I pressed my face against his warm skin.

"Shh," he murmured as he smoothed my hair along my back. "You can hate me tomorrow."

My arms tightened around him. "I will."

"Good."

The silence wrapped itself around us, but Kai was still consuming me. There was a coldness—a bitterness—to his tone, but his body was warm. He was just as I remembered him to be. Just as contradicting, and a complete whirlwind.

We always were a fucking mess.

And we were never destined for anything but utter devastation.

CHAPTER ELEVEN
MALAKAI

"Shit," Winter mumbled as she wriggled in my arms. "Shit, shit, shit."

"Be quiet."

She stilled in my arms. I wasn't ready to wake up. I wasn't ready for reality and for this moment to be over between us.

"You need to go, Malakai."

Well, there went the moment.

I opened my eyes and met Winter's green ones staring back at me. They were wide, yet there was something lingering in her expression that I couldn't quite put my finger on. If I really tried to read it, I would guess it was regret mixed with panic.

"You're regretting last night now, aren't you?"

Her nostrils flared and her chest expanded as she inhaled deeply. "Yes—no—" she paused and shook her head while her shoulders sagged in defeat. "I don't know, Kai."

My heart crawled into my throat. Winter appeared

distressed, yet I knew I wasn't the one who could comfort her at this moment. She was distressed because of *me*. Because of what happened between *us*.

"Very well," I replied with a coolness in my tone. She was already dressed and turned around as I stood up from the couch. I stared at the back of her head for a moment as irritation pricked my skin. She had seen me naked countless times. Hell, she just did last night and this morning, but whatever. She was dealing with a myriad of conflicting feelings right now, so I'd let her have that.

I put my clothing back on and found my car keys lying on the floor. As I bent over to pick them up, I caught Winter looking at me over her shoulder. She slowly turned back around and I stood upright as we faced each other. The tension was thick and heavy, permeating the air. I wanted to sweep my arm through it and chase it away.

I wanted to pull her into my arms and tell her that I was such a fucking idiot in the past. That I would never hurt her again like I did then. I just wanted her to let me make it all better, but I knew I couldn't. Fuck. I couldn't bring myself to do it.

There was a part of me that couldn't help but feel the sting from her rejection and regret.

We stared at one another for a moment longer and I knew I had to go. My legs felt like they were being weighed down by bags of sand. My heart fought against me as I forced myself to turn around and head in the direction of the front door. I didn't hear her behind me as I stepped into the foyer. My hand touched the cool metal of the lock and I slid it to the side.

"Kai," Winter's voice sounded from behind me. Soft and tentative. "I'm sorry for last night."

Her words sliced through my heart like a sharpened blade. My chest constricted and my throat closed in on itself while the ice settled in my veins. I hated her, but only because of the goddamn pain.

I pulled the front door open and stepped through the doorway before I turned back to look at her. Her bright eyes shined from the sunlight that slipped in.

"I'm not."

Winter's lips parted and a breath escaped her as I closed the door behind me. I left her standing there as I walked out to my car and climbed inside. As the engine came to life, I didn't bother looking back in her direction again. My foot pressed down on the gas and the distance between us was growing as I drove down her driveway and out onto the road.

There was a part of me that understood it all completely. After the history between us, there was no reason for her not to regret last night. But that didn't take away from the visceral pain. Knowing she regretted it dismissed everything that had happened in the moment last night.

Pushing the thoughts from my mind, I felt the coldness settling inside.

Winter could have her regret.

And I would feel nothing instead.

———

I paced around my condo. It had been four days since I last saw or spoke to Winter. Four whole fucking days of forcing myself to feel nothing. And there was nothing that was helping to close this gaping wound in my chest.

The driving range did nothing for me. Standing there under the hot sun hitting golf balls as hard as I could did nothing. Laying on the couch in my own misery was just depressing. I didn't want to go sit at the bar alone and get drunk, although I was running out of options.

My mother reached out and wanted to get lunch next week, but I told her I would get back to her. I didn't know what the hell I was doing, but I was losing my mind. There was a part of me that wanted to go see Winter, to force her to hear me out and understand, but I knew I couldn't do that.

She wanted space from me and I owed her that much.

I didn't even know her phone number. Trust me, I had tried to call the one she had when we were in high school and that one was long since disconnected. I tried years ago and discovered she changed her number, most likely to avoid hearing from me.

I could have called my old friend Nico to see if he wanted to get together, but I never was one who really hung out like that. We were closer when we were in high school, but we had grown apart over the years. He was busy with hockey and I was busy sitting here rotting into a useless corpse.

My pacing eventually stopped and I busied myself

with getting a shower. It was getting late in the day and I had yet to eat anything. I had been living off of takeout for the past few days because, fuck me for never learning how to properly cook. The best I could do was a grilled cheese. And if I was lucky, I wouldn't burn it to a crisp.

The shower did nothing to help me. The hot water provided no resolve from the turmoil in my mind. When I was alone, the mask could come off. I didn't have to appear unaffected and cold, although I still felt the anger shielding me from the other emotions. I tried to tell myself that Winter didn't matter, but all that did was cause an internal argument.

I needed to blow off some steam, but there were no healthy outlets for that since hitting golf balls as hard as I could did nothing for me. I was sleep-deprived and hungry, agitated and haunted.

What I needed was to get shit-faced so I could pass out and finally get some goddamn sleep.

My condo overlooked the ocean and there was a small strip of oceanfront restaurants and bars within walking distance. It was perfect. I could get as drunk as I needed and not have to worry about driving home. It didn't matter if I made it home or not. I'd sleep on the side of the street if it meant that I finally got some sleep that didn't have her bright green eyes haunting my dreams.

I ended up at Saltwater Tavern right along the beach. It was busy when I got there, but I was able to find a seat at the bar that overlooked the water. After ordering my drink, I absentmindedly stared out at the ocean, watching as the waves crashed against the shore. It was a clear night and the moon cast its light across the water.

My mind kept drifting back to Winter fucking Reign and the regret on her beautiful face. It was conflicting. I barely noticed as the bartender slid the glass in front of me. Lifting it to my mouth, I took a sip and felt the coldness of the ice cubes as they brushed against my lips. I knew why she felt regret and her reasons for hating me.

I wanted to hate her equally, but I never could.

She may have pissed me off beyond belief, but I could never hate her.

Music in the bar played loudly and the crowd was only growing thicker and louder. It was beginning to be too much. It wasn't enough to drown out the thoughts in my mind anymore. My emotions were trickling into the cracks of my heart and I needed some kind of peace. I only stayed at the bar long enough to finish my drink and pay my tab before I wandered out to the beach.

I kicked off my shoes and held them in my hand as I felt the grains of sand slipping beneath my toes as my feet sank in deep. I preferred the beaches on the Gulf Coast or at the Keys, but there was something about the ocean regardless of where it was that had a way of grounding me.

There was a figure in the distance walking along the shore under the moonlight, but I disregarded them as I got close to the water and sat down after dropping my shoes. I was just far enough away that I was still on dry land. My knees were bent in front of me and I hung my arms over the tops of them, lacing my fingers together as I stared out at the ocean.

I needed to find a way to get through to Winter and I had no clue what to do.

The figure that was yards away was now only feet away. I hadn't noticed them as they moved closer. I glanced over as they walked through the water in front of me. It was a girl who looked oddly familiar, but I couldn't figure it out until she turned to look over at me.

It was Nico's younger sister, Giana. She paused in front of me as a smile pulled on her lips. She raised her hand to wave at me, but didn't speak a single word. Giana suffered from permanent hearing loss when she was a kid.

I lifted my hand up to her, but gave no indication that I wanted to speak with her. Giana's feet left the water and she walked over to sit down next to me as she pulled out a small notepad. It was too dark that it would have been difficult to read any signs. Giana always carried around a notepad and pen or used her phone to type to communicate with people who didn't understand ASL.

I watched as she scribbled something down and handed it over to me.

Nico said you were back in town. How have you been?

A sigh of irritation escaped me and I handed her the

notepad back without writing back to her. She let out a frustrated sigh and pulled out her phone. Giana was only a couple years younger, but we weren't exactly close friends. I only knew her as Nico's little sister. She and Winter were friends because they were both book-worms, but that was the extent of what I really knew about her.

I never truly paid attention to anyone except for Winter. She was the only one who ever mattered to me.

Still an abrasive asshole, I see.

I stared down at Giana's phone with a typed out message to me. My face did not display a single ounce of amusement as I lifted my eyes to hers. She lifted an eyebrow at me and pushed her phone into my hand.

An exaggerated breath left my lips and I took the phone from her and typed my own response.

Not in the mood for any company.

Giana took the phone and responded back imme-diately.

There's no surprise there. Half the time it only seemed like you tolerated my brother.

She showed me her phone and I narrowed my eyes at her as I pushed it away.

"What's your point, Giana? What do you want?" I questioned her with a bite in my tone. She couldn't hear it, but with the way her lips pursed, she got everything she needed from my expression. I knew it was hard for her to read my lips in the dark, but I wasn't in the mood for conversation. She typed something else out on her phone before showing it to me again.

> I just wanted to see how you were doing. Nico was worried about you after he saw you and said you were here on a ghost hunt.

I stared at her for a moment. "It's not a ghost hunt. She's here."

Her head tilted to the side as her eyebrows drew together.

> Winter moved back home?

I nodded as I rose to my feet. "Go see her. I'm sure she could use a friend."

Giana climbed to her feet with a look of confusion on her face. Her phone screen lit up her face as she furiously typed something on it and shoved it back in my direction.

> Why could she use a friend? What did you do to her now?

"Excuse me?" The venom dripped from my tongue as I lifted my head to glare at Giana and her assumptions. "What exactly are you implying?"

She shook her head at me after reading my lips. She typed something else out for me to read.

> She was never the same after you
> broke her heart.

"How would you know?"

> We were friends, Malakai. She told me
> things... I tried to keep in touch with
> her over the years, but she kind of iced
> me out.

My hands curled into fists by my sides. Just another reminder of what I had done to Winter. I knew I broke her heart. I knew I fucked her up, and I thought I knew the extent of it. Perhaps I didn't.

"That's between the two of you," I told her with indifference. I couldn't take the past back. I couldn't undo what had been done, including how Winter handled her relationships with her friends. "She's back at her parents' house and supposedly working at the library. I'd start with either one of those places if you want to find her."

Giana stared at me for a moment with a look of suspicion and distrust.

> Why could she use a friend, Malakai?

A muscle in my jaw twitched. "Because she knows I'm back for her."

I left Giana standing by the ocean as I walked back through the sand to the small boardwalk. There was nothing left to be said and if she knew the way I broke

Winter's heart in the past, it was enough of an explanation as to why she could use a friend right now.

There was literally nothing that would stop me from getting what I wanted now.

And that had always been Winter Reign.

CHAPTER TWELVE
WINTER

As I walked through the aisles in the library, I paused by the nonfiction section to slide one of the returned books back into its respected spot. A few days ago, I handled the business with my parents' lawyer and their entire property was now legally mine. There was a heaviness to it that I didn't particularly care for, but at the same time, I planned on taking my own life back.

It wasn't ideal.

I wanted to be back in Vermont, but this was where I was now. My autonomy from my old city needed to carry over to being back in my hometown. I could build my own life that wasn't attached to my family. I may have never reached Sutton's superiority, but I could make something for myself that I could be proud of.

The library hired me on the spot. I didn't know if it was because they were that desperate to fill the position or because they actually liked me that much. Either way, I managed to secure a full-time position as the new librarian at the Orchid City Library. There wasn't a single thing about the job I didn't like.

I was completely in my element, spending my hours being surrounded by books. I loved the feel of them under my fingertips. I loved the smell of the pages beneath the covers. Most of all, I love the quiet. The library was like my own personal sanctuary, it was somewhere safe where I could just be. I could merely exist without fully owing anyone anything.

Yeah, I still had a job to do, but it was easy. Everything about it was exactly what I needed.

As I sat back down at my seat behind the desk, I lifted my eyes and surveyed the areas I could see. There were only a few people inside and they were all in their own little worlds, scanning the rows of different fictional places they could get lost in. I pulled out a brand-new notebook I had purchased a few days ago and flipped to the first page.

On my laptop, I had at least half a dozen books I had started and never finished. Every romance I attempted to write always ended up taking a darker turn. It had a way of following down the same path that Kai and my story went. I was left with something always pulling the characters apart and I had no idea how the hell to bring them back together.

I decided I was going to try something new. Something old that worked for people years and years before my own time. I was going to write with a pen and a paper. It didn't mean I would do anything with the words, but I needed a new approach. Something fresh.

Perhaps I could craft a story better by bleeding onto

the page instead of through my fingertips on a keyboard. Maybe it would never work out. Only time would tell, and I was ready to make a conscious effort.

As I put pen to paper, my mind began to wander as different story ideas floated in my head. Instead of grabbing one and diving straight in, I began to jot them down. My hand moved furiously across the page as I tried to pluck the details from thin air and secure them in the notebook in front of me.

"I knew I would find you here."

My stomach sank. My heart pounded in my chest. My breath was stuck in my throat. And the sound of his voice—fuck—it was like a melody that instantly had my body responding.

I lifted my eyes up to the man standing in front of me. I never heard him enter the library, let alone noticed him walk directly up to where I was seated.

"Malakai," I said softly, my eyebrows pulling together as I cocked my head. "Hi."

His hands were tucked in the front pockets of his pleated shorts. My eyes scanned him as I took in his appearance while my mouth instantly went dry. His baseball hat was on backward and his polo shirt hugged the curves of the muscles beneath. *The muscles I had just touched the other night.* He was dressed like he had just finished a round of golf.

"Hi."

I grabbed my water and took a sip in an attempt to wet my mouth. "What are you doing here?" I asked him with a hesitant tone.

"I came here to see you, obviously," he deadpanned

with a hint of boredom in his voice. It was almost as if he was saying, *Duh, why else would he be here?*

I stared at him for a moment. "You can't just show up at my job like this."

"Says who?" Kai slowly looked around the room before his stormy eyes met mine. "I don't see your boss anywhere."

"Please don't mess this up for me," I said to him with a bite in my tone. My voice was hushed yet I saw the way his jaw ticked. "I like this job. I *need* this job. I can't have you here distracting me."

Kai fell silent as he reached into his back pocket and pulled out his wallet. I watched him for a moment with confusion laced in my expression as he plucked out his ID and set it on the desk in front of me.

"Give me a library card then."

My eyebrows were pinched together. "For what?"

"So I have an excuse to be at the fucking library."

Panic instantly filled me. This was my safe place. I shook my head. "Absolutely not."

He lifted an eyebrow at me as the corners of his lips twitched. "Are you going to deny someone who is requesting a free library card?"

"Your parents have a massive library. Go read the books there."

"Already have," he said with a smirk as he planted his palms on the desk and leaned forward slightly. "Plus, there is far more interesting material here than there is in their library."

I cut my eyes at him. Kai was back to his games, and a part of me was excited by it. While he showed me his softer side behind closed doors, something about this side of him always had a way of irritating me and making me clench my thighs together simultaneously.

"Are you going to give me a card?" he questioned me as the smirk vanished from his lips. A fire was burning in his eyes as he stared down at me. "Or shall I call your boss and tell her that you're refusing to give me one?"

Instinctively, my tongue slid out to wet my lips. "You wouldn't dare."

"Is that a challenge, Winter Reign?" There was nothing playful about his voice as his eyes continued to burn holes through mine. Kai wanted me to challenge him, he wanted me to test him. I watched him grow up this way—constantly testing the limits around him.

"Do it," I growled as I leaned forward into his face. His minty breath skated across my face as he let out a breath. "I dare you."

I didn't mean it. I didn't want him to actually call my boss, but I wasn't going to be the one who cowered and backed down from Malakai Barclay. He already had too much power over my emotions and my life and I was done with it. If he wanted to play these stupid games, he had better be prepared to lose.

"You do know all I have to do is make a call and they will terminate your position here?"

I nodded. "I know the power you have, Malakai. I know the pull your family has." I paused for a moment as I straightened my spine. "I'm not afraid of you."

His jaw tightened. "You never were."

"Because this is just the side you show to the rest of

the world. I know this Malakai and I never cared much for him."

A cruelness settled in his irises as he didn't break eye contact. "That didn't stop you from following me around everywhere I went."

Kai always acted like an asshole in moments of vulnerability. The times he actually let me in when his guard was down were few and far between, but I had been inside his soul before. Kai's walls were up so high in this moment, there was no way to see past them or through them.

"Because I know the real you. I can see past you being an asshole because I know there is good inside of you, even if you refuse to believe it."

What a turn this conversation had taken.

Kai's expression gave nothing away, but he couldn't quite hide the wave of emotion that passed through his stormy irises. He was good at hiding the way he felt, but his eyes always betrayed him. Even in the coldness and the ice that settled around them, I could always see the warmth lingering inside.

He may have acted like he was made of ice, but there was really a fire burning inside him.

"So, are you going to call my boss or not?"

He remained silent and his gaze faltered as he pushed away from the desk. He stood at least a foot higher than me and his form loomed above me as his gaze collided into mine again. "No," he said softly as he shook his head. He took a step back. "Keep your safe little job, Winter."

I crossed my arms over my chest defensively as I

refused to be the one to look away from him. If he wanted to be like this and have these little stare-downs, I was not going to be the one to lose. He called my job safe like it was a bad thing. *Like he was never safe for me when in reality, he was the one who had always protected me...*

I waited for him to speak another word, but he didn't. He simply spun on his heel and stalked toward the front door of the library. He left me feeling confused and a little thrown off from it all. As I looked down at the desk, I saw his ID still sitting there. Turning to the computer, I pulled open a new entry and began to enter his information.

Kai always worked in self-preservation. He appeared selfish, but he was really just living to protect himself and survive. I knew it had to do with his past and Kai stopping here was a moment of vulnerability for him. He had no idea if I would be here or not, yet he still put himself out there; he took a chance and his ego was bruised from it.

I glanced out the front window and saw Kai as he climbed into his car. My eyes kept traveling from the computer screen and back to him. I watched the lights on his taillights as he put the car in reverse but then they went off when he didn't move.

I didn't feel bad for him. His ego definitely needed a reality check. I couldn't help but feel like I was just adding more height to the wall around him. I was simply helping to build it higher by fighting against him. I would never willingly give in to Kai and his bull-shit, but I also didn't have to be part of the problem.

Like how things used to be—maybe there was some way I could help him now.

The plastic card printed out and I slid it into an envelope with his ID. I looked back to the window and saw Kai getting out of his car. A smile pulled on my lips and I knew this was my chance. I moved out from behind the desk and walked through the library until I was pushing on the same door he was pulling open.

I was asking for nothing but trouble, but I couldn't ignore the way I involuntarily gravitated toward him.

I held out the envelope to him and Kai's eyebrows were drawn together as he took it from me.

"What's this?" he questioned me, his voice quiet as he opened the envelope and looked inside. He pulled out his ID, along with the library card I made for him. His gaze lifted to mine and there was a storm brewing deep inside him.

"You're free to come here whenever you want, just don't distract me from my job."

The corners of his lips twitched as mischief danced in his eyes.

"I will."

CHAPTER THIRTEEN
MALAKAI

Past

I looked out the window of her bedroom, watching the sun as it had begun to rise. A sigh escaped Winter and I glanced back at the bed and watched as she stirred a bit. Her eyes were still closed and her face was relaxed as she slept. Her dark hair was a contrast to her white bedding and it was splayed across her pillow.

I wanted to climb back into bed with her and run my fingers through her silky hair. I wanted to bury myself deep inside of her and never resurface again. Winter was the only thing I needed in this world and I knew I was going to have to let her go eventually.

Today was the day my parents were having a meeting with the school board. I had missed too many days and had reached the maximum days of suspension for stupid shit I had gotten myself into. It wasn't that I had a problem with figures of authority, I just had a problem with listening to people when they tried to tell me what I could or couldn't do.

I lived with it at home, I didn't want it in every single aspect of my life.

"Malakai," Winter murmured softly as I watched her hands reach across the bed. My heart constricted at the sound of my name rolling from her sleepy tongue. She was still naked and I resisted the urge to touch her soft skin.

I wasn't supposed to be here. *I wasn't allowed to be here*.

I was always careful and I always made sure I was gone before Winter woke up. Last night was a fuckup on my part. I slept later than I planned and lingered by the window, watching the sunrise like it actually mattered. I did it every day. There was nothing particularly special about this one, except it was almost like it was my judgment day.

My parents had no idea about it until last night when they received an email as a reminder. That was what set my father off. That was what earned me a fist to my face. I knew it wasn't going to be good, so I threw out any piece of mail that came to the house from the school. It went undetected and unnoticed. My parents had no idea that I was constantly skipping school or leaving early.

The only way they would have known is if they would have actually paid attention to something other than themselves.

I didn't want my father's attention but I earned myself a hefty dose of it last night. The pain was heavy in my bones and my face was swollen. No one would suspect a thing with the amount of trouble I already got myself into. Fighting with others wasn't something I shied away from, so no one would have ever suspected that it was actually my father who rained his fists upon my face.

Lifting the window open, I quickly slid through the opening and out onto the roof above the Reigns' porch. I watched Winter slowly sit up in bed and wipe the sleep from her eyes as I closed the window behind me. Her gaze met mine, one laced with confusion and longing as she stared back at me.

I hated leaving her, but I knew I had to go.

I was homesick every moment I was away from her.

Winter was climbing out of her bed in a rush, undoubtedly heading directly to my escape route. I moved along the roof and found the spot where I was able to climb down the stone wall of their house. There were a few that jutted out just far enough I could hook my feet and hands in them. It wasn't a far climb and if I fell, it would probably do less damage than my father did.

As the damp grass met my sneakers, I glanced back up to Winter's house. She was standing by the window, watching me as I made my way through the yard. She lifted her hand and placed it against the glass as her gaze glued to mine. My throat constricted and I gave her a curt nod before I ducked into a small patch of trees on their property. I just needed to make it to the end of the driveway without being seen.

There was a small spot in the woods about half a

mile from their front gates. That was where I left my car unless I had Nico come pick me up. After last night and with what was happening today, I didn't want to see him. I was tired of lying and didn't feel like explaining myself to anyone.

My body felt weighed down by the heaviness of life as I walked down the street in the direction of my car. My phone vibrated in my pocket and I let out a sigh as my footsteps paused and I pulled it out to read the message. I already knew it was her before I looked at it.

WINTER

Come back.

My breath caught in my throat and my shoulders sagged. She had more power over me than she would ever know. The hold she had on me was one I never wanted to be rid of.

MALAKAI

I can't. Your parents will be up soon and you have to go to school.

I watched as the three bubbles appeared while she typed her response. My actions didn't match my words. I was no longer moving in the direction of my car. Instead, I had involuntarily turned around and was already walking in the same direction I had just come from.

WINTER

If you hurry, they won't see you. Please come back and we will figure it out.

My mind and soul were at war. My feet went to move, to carry me back in the direction of her, but I knew I couldn't. I had already disrupted her life enough. For once I wished Winter could just see past her feelings for me.

MALAKAI

I can't.

I powered off my phone and tucked it back into my pocket before turning back around in the direction of my car. I forced myself to make the walk there, and it was even more of a struggle getting inside and starting the engine. I needed space from her to think because when I was with her, I couldn't think about anything but her.

As I drove down the road, I contemplated on where to go. My parents undoubtedly would have noticed that I wasn't home. Their meeting wasn't until later this afternoon, but my father still had to go into his office for the morning. I could sneak in after he left and make sure I was gone before dinnertime.

The plan wasn't the best, but it was my only option unless I wanted to drive around mindlessly. If I went to the country club, they would probably know since they now knew I wasn't at school when I was supposed to be. It was my senior year and there was no way I was graduating with honors now. Shit, I would be lucky if I even graduated at all at this point.

College was not something I ever saw myself wanting to do. Winter insisted I go to Vermont with her, so to appease her, I filled out a damn application for

Wyncote University. My only plans for the future were golf. It was a foolproof way for me to make money. My father wouldn't be thrilled when he learned of my real plans.

I was supposed to follow in his footsteps and become some big shot realtor like he was. If there was one person's footsteps I would avoid, it was that man's.

I waited outside of my parents' house until my father left and then I made my way onto the property. My mother wasn't cruel like my father, so even if she caught me, she wouldn't punish me for it. If I caught her at a good time, there was a chance she wouldn't even rat me out to him. When I walked into the massive house, though, there was no one there.

There was an envelope sitting on the counter and my stomach sank as I saw it was from the admissions office from Wyncote University. I slowly opened it and the bile rose in my throat as I read the rejection letter. I knew it would come from any college I tried to apply to, but reading it just solidified the fact that I royally fucked up my chances of anything for my future other than golf.

Anger soared through me and I shoved the paper back into the envelope before I began to rip it to shreds. There was no sense in keeping it. Reality set in and I swallowed back the bile in my throat. I already knew that Winter had gotten in and she was planning to move to Vermont in the fall. She would be leaving me after the summer was over.

That realization and hurt was a visceral pain I had never experienced before.

"Are you already drunk?" Nico asked me later that night as I got into his car.

I spent the afternoon, well into the evening, sitting in the parking lot at the country club, drinking a bottle of vodka I took from my parents' liquor cabinet. I was definitely feeling the effects of it, but I wasn't drunk yet. I had barely even gotten through a quarter of the bottle by the time Nico picked me up.

When I finally turned on my phone, there were multiple messages from him and Winter. I ignored the ones from Winter. After receiving my rejection letter earlier, she was the last person I wanted to see. The thought of her leaving without me was one I couldn't bear right now. There was one missed call from my mother along with a voice message that I didn't bother listening to.

"No."

Nico wrinkled his nose as I shut the door behind me. "It smells like it."

"Well, I'm not."

Nico drove out of the parking lot and pulled his car onto the road. There was supposedly a huge party going on tonight at Lucas Davenport's house. I needed any reason to stay out and it was a good enough reason to not return home. Plus, I would be able to forget about the shit day I had. Scratch that—it wasn't just a bad day, it was a bad fucking decade.

"I heard about your parents meeting with the board today," Nico said with a hesitant voice.

I looked over at him as he continued to stare at the road ahead. "Oh yeah? What did you hear?"

He glanced over at me with his eyes wide. "You haven't talked to your parents about it yet?" He paused for a moment. "I just overheard them talking when I was in the office today. They weren't going to expel you."

"Of course they didn't," I scowled and half sneered. I twisted open the top of the vodka and took a long gulp. It burned my throat as it slid down and warmed my stomach. "My father's pockets are deep. I'm sure he paid someone off to get his way."

A part of me wanted to get expelled just as another fuck-you to my father but I already expected this. I knew I would be fine because he had made it so I was practically untouchable by anything and everyone but himself. My father was the one who held all the power and he frequently exercised his control.

Nico was silent for a few moments as we were nearing closer to Lucas's house. "Is Winter coming tonight?"

I gave him a blank look, giving nothing away. "No."

I didn't invite her and she usually didn't come out unless it was something I invited her to. I was hoping she wouldn't come here, that she wouldn't come looking for me, but I knew Winter Reign. I could only keep her at arm's length for so long. She would always come looking for me.

When we pulled up to Lucas's house, the party was already well underway. As Nico and I walked up to the front door, the bass was already pounding from the speakers his parents had installed throughout the house. His parents traveled a lot for business, so his house was frequented for parties like this. We stepped inside and found ourselves having to push through bodies as we made our way to the kitchen where all the alcohol was.

Nico filled a plastic cup with beer and I clutched onto the neck of the bottle of vodka I walked in with. I had no intention of sharing it with anyone, not when they all had access to the various bottles Lucas arranged in his kitchen. As I left Nico in the kitchen, I walked through the house, brushing past people as I made my way toward the back door.

I honestly wasn't sure why I even came. I didn't want to be around any of these people. All of the friendships and camaraderie, they were all superficial. I just knew I didn't want to be home tonight. And I was tired of feeling like a burden to Winter.

As I sat down on one of the chairs by Lucas's pool, a sigh escaped me and I hung my head heavily.

I was just fucking tired.

CHAPTER FOURTEEN
WINTER

Past

Kai was going to be mad if he knew I was here, but I didn't know where else to go or what else to do. I hadn't seen him since this morning and even that felt like it was a dream. I was awake enough for my brain to register that it was him slipping through my window. I watched him as he headed into the wooded area of our property in the direction of the road. When I asked him to come back, I knew he wouldn't, yet there was a part of me that hoped he would.

Today was the day he had been dreading. He didn't tell me much about it, but I knew he was in trouble. I knew he was in jeopardy of being expelled. I also knew that if his family could get him out of it, they would. And low and behold, that was exactly what happened.

Kai got a slap on the wrist and I wasn't even sure if he knew it or not. He had been ignoring my calls and texts all day long. When I overheard there would be a party at Lucas's house tonight, I wondered if this was where Kai would come.

I knew him better than anyone. I knew the last place he would want to be was home, and I was right. He wasn't there and he wasn't at my house. He wasn't exactly someone who enjoyed the party scene, but he enjoyed the escape from reality. And if there was a party with substances that could provide that escape for him, he would most likely be there.

As I pushed through the different rooms in the house, I couldn't seem to find him anywhere. Familiar faces tried to strike up conversations, but I wasn't here for any of that. I was here for one purpose and one purpose only... and I couldn't seem to find him anywhere.

I caught sight of Nico in the kitchen and made my way over to where he was. There was some girl attached to his side who had captured his attention, but his head lifted as he saw me approach. He stepped away from her.

"Winter," he said softly with a hint of confusion on his face. "What are you doing here? Kai said you weren't coming."

I shifted my weight nervously on my feet. I wasn't a big drinker, but I felt the need to drink something at this moment. "Can I get a drink?"

"Of course," Nico nodded as he grabbed a cup and filled it with some vodka and cranberry juice. "This is what you drink, right?" he asked me as he handed it over. "I remember Kai saying you don't like beer."

I forced a smile. "This is good, thanks." I quickly took a huge gulp, needing all the liquid courage I could get. "Is he here?"

"He's around here somewhere," Nico said as he glanced around with a touch of concern in his eyes. "I haven't seen him in a while, though, so I don't know where he ran off to. Does he know you're here?"

I shook my head. "I haven't heard from him all day."

"You know how Kai is," he shrugged with indifference, "sometimes he just needs to be alone. I'll let him know you're here if you don't see him before I do."

The girl Nico was talking to had captured his attention again and I stepped away with a simple nod. Nico and I weren't exactly friends, but Kai was the common denominator between us. He was the only real connection between us and that was just because we both cared about him. I knew Nico because we both skated at the same rink, but the hockey players and the figure skaters didn't exactly mingle.

The plastic cup was sweating in my hand and I hated the damp feeling. I lifted it to my lips again and took another sip as I headed out of the kitchen. There were people crowding every room and it was almost too much. None of that mattered, though. I just wanted to find Kai and make sure he was all right. After the state he was in last night, I knew he was in a bad place mentally.

All the air left my lungs in a rush as I watched the back door open and Kai came walking inside. I should have been relieved to see him, but I wasn't. He wasn't alone. Dana Walters was hanging onto his arm, laughing as he said something to her. My stomach sank and bile rose in my throat. Oxygen promptly left the room and I was frozen in place.

They stopped together just inside the room and I watched her entering his space. Kai wasn't smiling at her, but his face was dipping down to her ear to say something again. I watched her hands as they went to his waist. His hands were wrapping around her biceps and I couldn't watch it anymore.

Spinning on my heel, I rushed out of the room, blindly pushing my way through the groups of people. I reach the bottom of the stairs that led to the second floor of Lucas's parents' massive house. My chest rose and fell with every shallow breath from my anxiety. I didn't know where I was going, but I ended up making my way upstairs instead.

There were a few couples making out in the hall and I found myself ducking into the first room that wasn't occupied. As I shut the door behind me and leaned against it, the smell of old books instantly flooded my senses. It was all I needed to feel a sense of relief. I was inside their family library.

A smile didn't touch my lips, but it helped to soothe the anxiety and the pain. I lifted the plastic cup to my mouth and swallowed down the rest of the alcohol. I stepped deeper into the room as I admired the floor-to-ceiling bookshelves. It was nowhere near as exquisite as the one in Kai's home, but it was a close second. It was closer to the one in my own house. I walked around the room, my fingertips dragging along the spines of the books as I perused Lucas's family's collection.

The door to the library suddenly opened, drawing me away from the books. I spun on my heel, my breath trapped in my throat as I whipped around to see who it was. I sighed in annoyance when I saw it was Elias. I had known him for most of my life, as his father worked for mine. Elias had developed a crush on me some years ago and he was convinced we were supposed to end up together.

"Hey, Winter," he slurred his words as he stepped farther into the room. A crooked grin formed on his lips and his eyes were bloodshot as he stumbled slightly. "I didn't know you were here."

"I was actually getting ready to leave."

Elias frowned. "So soon?" He stepped closer, closing in on me. I attempted to duck away from him, but his hand caught my wrist and he spun me around to face him. "Stay and hang out with me, Win."

"Let go of me, Elias," I demanded, my voice harsh as I tried to pull my wrist from him. "You're drunk."

"Come on, Winter." I could smell the alcohol on his breath as he pulled me flush against him. "Stop fighting this between us. You know we were always supposed to be together."

I tried to plant my hands against his chest, but he pushed them out of the way. "We're just friends, Elias. I told you I don't have feelings for you."

"But you could," he insisted, his warm breath on my face as he closed the space between us. "I could make you love me."

"Stop, Elias," I told him, shaking my head as he held my wrist by my side. His other hand was around the nape of my neck and mine was back against his chest. "Let go of me."

I was shaking my head at him, my eyes clamped shut. Suddenly, he was stumbling backward and his hands were ripped away from me. My eyes opened in a flash and they widened as I saw he wasn't moving of his own accord. Kai's hands were wrapped around Elias's throat and he was dragging him backward.

Elias's hands clawed at Kai's and I watched in horror as the muscles in Kai's arms flexed as he tightened his grip around Elias's neck.

"Kai, stop." My voice came out as a whisper as I watched a shadow sliding across his expression. His eyes lifted to mine and they were filled with rage. "You have to let go of him," I urged him louder.

Kai released his hands and Elias fell to the floor in a rush. He turned his back to me as he stepped in front of Elias.

"What the fuck, man?" Elias slurred at him as he rubbed at his neck.

Kai grabbed the front of his shirt and hauled him back to his feet. He didn't utter a single word as he drove his fist into the side of Elias's face. It was as if everything was moving in slow motion, yet it was all happening so fast. I knew I had to do something. Kai kept hitting him and if he didn't stop, I didn't know what the hell was going to happen.

I reached for him, wrapping my small hands around

his biceps as I tried to pull him back. "Malakai, stop. Please, just stop hitting him."

His body stiffened and I watched his jaw clench as he stopped his fist from hitting Elias's face again. Instead, Kai grabbed Elias's shirt with both hands and was pushing him back toward the door. "If you look at her again, I will gouge your eyes out with my bare hands. If you breathe in her direction, I will collapse both of your lungs. And if you touch her again, I *will* kill you."

He dropped one hand to the door and opened it before he shoved Elias through the opening. Elias stumbled backward across the hall and crashed into the wall. Kai slammed the door shut and let out a ragged breath as he turned to face me.

The rage had vanished from his eyes. The darkness still lingered, but there was concern and terror mixing in his stormy irises. He closed the distance between us, instantly lifting his hands to cup my face.

"Are you okay?" His eyes scanned my face with desperation. "Did he hurt you?"

I shook my head. "I'm fine. He just caught me by surprise."

"Surprise?" There was a harshness to his tone. "He was seconds away from assaulting you." He paused for a moment as his eyes narrowed on mine. "What are you doing here?"

"I came here looking for you."

He raised an eyebrow. "In the library?"

The memory of what I saw downstairs bombarded me and I took a step away from him. "I came here because I needed to collect myself after I saw you downstairs with Dana."

"What are you talking about?"

I cut my eyes at him. "Don't play stupid, Malakai. I saw you both walk inside. I saw her hands on your waist and you whispering something into her ear." I paused for a moment and I took a deep breath as I felt my anxiety heightening. "You ignored me all day and then you were here with her."

Kai stared back at me. "You just believe everything you see, don't you?"

"I know exactly what I saw."

"You don't know a damned thing, Winter," he snapped at me as he took a step closer to me again. "Looks can be deceiving."

"Then tell me I'm wrong."

He was in my space, sliding his hands around the back of my neck as he pulled my body flush against his. His hands slid down my torso as his face dipped to the side of mine. His breath was warm against my skin and his lips were soft along the shell of my ear. "You're wrong, darling."

"Why were you with her?"

His mouth dropped down to my neck and his hands were on my waist, pushing under my shirt. "Does it really matter?"

My breath caught in my throat. His hands were distracting me. His lips and tongue were touching the sensitive skin on my neck. We had never really had this conversation before, even though we had been together numerous times. "It does," I breathed as he pushed me back against the bookcase. "I don't want you with other girls."

"We're not together, darling." There was a hint of sadness and pain in his voice and it confused me.

"That doesn't mean I want to share you with anyone else," I admitted as he lifted me into his arms and I hooked my legs around his waist. "If we're going to keep doing this, I don't want you to be messing around with other girls."

Kai let out a breathless laugh as he carried me over to the desk on the far side of the room. He pushed some books out of the way with one arm before lowering me onto the surface. "There hasn't been anyone but you since that first time, Winter." He stared down at me, his eyes unreadable. "Dana was trying to make Lucas jealous. I saw you from the corner of my eye when you left the room in a rush."

"That's how you knew I was up here."

He nodded. "I'll always find you, Winter."

"Promise?"

His mouth dropped down to mine. "Always," he breathed against my lips before claiming them with his own. He sealed his promise with a kiss, our tongues tangling together before he began to strip my clothes away from my body.

It was just the two of us, locked away in the library. His hands were in my hair as he discarded both of our clothing on the floor beside the desk. He kissed me with desperation, like he was clinging to me like I was his lifeline. As he pulled away, he hooked his arms behind my knees and pulled me to him. My ass moved along the edge of the desk and he slid a condom over his erection before pressing against me.

"You're mine, Winter Reign."

He pushed into me with one thrust and a moan slipped from my lips. My legs wrapped around his waist and he leaned forward as he pressed his hand over my mouth. His head dipped down to mine again and his lips brushed against my ear.

"As much as I want to hear you scream, I need you to be quiet, darling," he whispered to me as he slowly thrust his hips. "No one sees you like this, but me. If someone walks through that door, I won't hesitate to make sure they never see again."

I let out a breathless moan as warmth spread through me. Kai was scary, but he never scared me. Although I liked the possessive side of him. It did things to me that I couldn't even put into words.

He moved his hand away from my mouth and captured my lips once more in a quick kiss. As he pulled away and straightened his spine, his hands slid down my thighs until he was cupping my ass in his hands. His fingers dug into my skin as he began to thrust into me harder and deeper with every movement of his hips.

My hands clawed at the desk and my nails felt like they were chipping away at the wood as I tried to grab onto anything I could get ahold of. He moved faster and the piece of furniture was groaning under the force of his thrusts. My legs tightened around his waist as my orgasm began to build.

"You want to come, don't you?" His voice was quiet

and breathless as he stared down at me with a fire burning in his eyes.

He released one of my ass cheeks and slid his hand between us as he brushed his thumb across my clit. I bit down on my bottom lip in an effort to silence myself. My hips bucked involuntarily as it felt like a bolt of lightning struck me.

"That's my girl," he murmured as he continued to pound into me, whilst circling my clit with the pad of his thumb. "You be quiet while I fuck you senseless."

Kai increased the pressure and I was so damn close. He stared down at me, his cock deep inside me as he rolled his thumb once more. "Come for me, darling."

An earthquake rolled through my body and my vision blurred as Kai buried himself deep inside me while he came undone. My orgasm flooded my body and I could taste the blood on my tongue from biting my lip so hard. The fire was rapidly spreading between us and there was no way to extinguish it.

And for Malakai Barclay, I would willingly burn until I was reduced to nothing but ash.

CHAPTER FIFTEEN
MALAKAI

Present

The head of my golf club hit the ball with a loud smack and I watched as it soared through the air. It sailed straight down the fairway and a frown pulled on my lips. Golf was absolutely maddening in the most frustrating way. Unless you played, you didn't realize how much of a mental game it truly was.

"I'm confused," Nico said with his eyebrows scrunched together as I climbed onto the golf cart with him. "I thought you were struggling to play. Your ball landed at least seventy-five yards past mine and is dead center in the fairway."

"Putt," I corrected him. "Nothing else is wrong with my game except putting."

He had been after me, wanting to play a round of golf since he found out I was back in town. I put it off for long enough and I knew I couldn't keep stalling. It was the first time I was playing a real round since I completely fucked up the last tournament.

"Have you been working on it at all?"

I stared at the side of his face as he drove down the cart path, closer to where his golf ball had landed. "No."

"If that's the part you're struggling with, though, shouldn't that be your sole focus right now?"

My jaw ticked. I didn't owe him an explanation, but I did owe him some pleasantries. He meant no harm and wasn't saying any of it to be an asshole. Nico was simply trying to help and it was the last thing I had wanted from anyone.

"Probably," I admitted with a shrug. "I don't know if I even want to play anymore."

Nico parked the golf cart and whipped his head to look at me like I had lost my mind. "Why the hell not?"

"It's not important right now."

He climbed out of the golf cart and grabbed one of his clubs before he turned back to face me. "The reason or golf in itself?"

"I'd rather not talk about it right now."

Nico stared at me for a moment as if he were assessing me with growing concern. He frowned slightly but offered a curt nod before he walked to his ball to hit his next shot. I was a professional golfer. How the hell was I supposed to explain to people that I didn't want to do it anymore because it no longer brought me joy?

How pompous of me to tell them that I hated the traveling it required. That I just wanted to relax and not worry about the enormous amount of pressure that was constantly placed upon me. That I couldn't putt to save my life because every time I did, I thought about Winter and the way she was smiling at that asshole at the bar when I saw her six months ago.

The only one who knew was my therapist, and even that was far-fetched. He only knew the extent of what I shared with him—and it was the bare minimum. He didn't know the reason I saw Winter was because I showed up to Wyncote without her knowing I was coming. She never saw me that night, but I saw her. And I hadn't played the same since I saw her with someone else.

She lied to me that night when she told me there was no one else and she had no idea I knew it was a lie. That solidified how damaged things were between us.

Nico strolled back over to the cart and climbed on. "My sister said she ran into you at the beach by Salt-water Tavern." He paused for a moment with his lips pursed. "She said you were as friendly as a grizzly bear."

Guilt hit me. "I wasn't in the best mood."

"When are you ever?" Nico rolled his eyes with a huff as he drove me to my ball. "She said you told her Winter would need a friend. What's going on between you and her?"

I stared at him for a moment as I contemplated an explanation. Nico watched me carefully as I grabbed my club and walked through the grass. Pushing the thoughts from my head, I lined up my shot and focused on what I needed to do. My club hit the ball and sent it directly onto the green.

I stood unmoving and glared up at the flag that shifted from the warm summer breeze. This was the part I hated. I could already feel the anxiety coursing through my veins. It was riddled in my bone marrow and I didn't know how to work through this.

When was life ever going to feel easy?

Nico was waiting for me with an expectant look on his face. "Well?"

My chest expanded as I sucked in a deep breath. I slid my club back into my bag and climbed back onto the golf cart. "I honestly don't even know. It's all a mess."

"A mess that you could have avoided if you had been honest with her before."

I leaned my head to the side. "Would that really have changed anything? You know Winter well enough to know that if I had been honest with her, she would have thrown everything away to follow me wherever I went." I paused for a moment as I ran a frustrated hand through my hair. "I had to let her have a chance at her own life that wasn't plagued by my existence."

"And how did that really work out, Kai?" Nico questioned me with a hint of disapproval in his tone as he stepped on the gas. "Sure, she went off to Vermont and built her own life, but you know damn well she never recovered from whatever happened between the two of you."

Propping my elbows on my knees, I dropped my face into my hands. I didn't know what I was doing.

The only thing I had planned on was winning her back, but I never fully thought my plan through. All I had known was, I was willing to do whatever it would take.

I lifted my head and stared out at the green as Nico stopped the cart again. "She gave me a library card."

"What?" Nico angled his head as confusion passed through his expression.

"She works at the Orchid City Library," I told him as we both grabbed our putters and walked together. "I went in and saw her and she gave me a card."

Nico's eyes filled with curiosity. "She works at the library?"

I nodded. "I overheard her talking about it at the charity event at the country club. I stopped by there the other day and she was there."

He stifled a laugh and shook his head as he walked over to the hole and pulled the pin out for me to make my putt. "You showed up there without knowing she would be there?"

"How was I supposed to know she would be there?" I questioned him with a blank stare.

"Um… I don't know? Maybe asking her like a normal person would?"

I stared at him as I toyed with the putter in my hand. "I don't have her number and she wasn't really happy to see me the last time I showed up at her house uninvited."

"Dude, what is wrong with you?" Nico looked at me like I had lost my mind. "No wonder things are a mess between you both. You can't just keep showing up wherever she is like that if you want her back."

"Why not? She never minded it before."

He gave me a dumbfounded look. "Well, that was before you broke her heart, man. Shit's changed since then."

I was stalling from putting and I was genuinely needing his help. I wasn't inept when it came to interacting with people. My parents taught me how to behave appropriately, not that I ever did anyway. Nico was right. I was going about this all wrong, but I didn't know where to start with her.

"So, what am I supposed to do?"

"For starters, I would suggest getting her number." He paused for a second as he motioned with his head for me to take my shot. "Start there and maybe try taking her out or something. I don't know. Just stop being a fucking creeper and showing up everywhere unannounced."

I mulled over his words and nodded. He was right. Crouching down, I studied the greens for a moment before positioning my shot. I pulled back just enough and slowly brought the putter to the golf ball. All of my doubts hit me like a ton of bricks, causing me to hit the ball at a shifted angle. My breath was held in my lungs as I watched it hook to the right. I let out a sigh of frustration as it came to a stop just beside the hole.

"Do you have her number?"

Nico's eyes followed me as I walked over and simply grabbed my ball. It was right beside the hole so there was no sense in hitting it in. If I missed a shot like that, there would be no sense in me ever golfing again. I grabbed the pin from him and he went to hit his in.

"No," he said slowly as he shook his head. "I haven't personally talked to Winter in years. I just know what I know of her from Giana." He paused for a moment. "She probably has her number, but I suppose it would be better if you got it from Winter directly. You know, to make yourself seem less like a stalker."

I watched him as he lined up his putt and made it without any issues. This hole was one I shouldn't have had any issues with, yet I scored worse than Nico. His words continued to float around in my mind as we packed it in and headed back to the clubhouse. My brain was making me question everything. The logical and emotional parts were definitely waging a war on one another.

He beat me on that last hole, but I still ended up winning the round. As he pulled the golf cart up to our cars, we both hopped off and started to load our bags into our trunks. I turned to look at Nico once more before we parted ways.

"How do I get her number without seeming like a stalker, since that's how you seem to view me now?"

Nico chuckled softly. "Jesus, Kai. You really have no idea what you're doing, do you?" He let out an exasperated sigh. "You have that library card, right?" His lips slowly lifted into a smirk. "I think it's time to put it to good use."

He wasn't wrong. I had no idea what I was doing. This felt like unfamiliar territory, yet Winter was the most familiar thing in my life.

"You're right," I agreed with a nod. "Thanks, Nico."

"Of course," he said with a smile and a wink. "I'm always right."

I shook my head at him and bid him farewell before climbing into my car. I glanced at the clock and saw that the library would still be open for another two hours. It felt like an irrational decision to go there now, but there was so much lost time between us that I would never get back.

I had already wasted six years without her.

And I wasn't going to waste any more time.

CHAPTER SIXTEEN
WINTER

The library was particularly quiet during the week. Occasionally there were a few mothers who would come in with their younger kids. Mrs. Parker, who was now the retired librarian, would come in around eleven each day and have story time for any of the children who were here. There were a few who made it a point to show up just to listen to her read them a book.

Some days if she wasn't too tired, she would include a little craft that she would do with them. It depended on how she was feeling. She wasn't her young, spry self anymore. Old age had settled into her bones and you could see the tiredness hidden in the lines on her face. Her eyes weren't as bright as they once were.

It had been quite some time since I last saw her. Mrs. Parker remembered me from when I was a kid because this was where I spent a lot of my time. It was always quiet and safe. Peaceful and content. I didn't have to deal with the outside world when I could be in my own little world.

Mrs. Parker retired after her husband passed away six months ago. That was why there was a permanent position open here. They had just been filling it with temps or she would help out when she could during that time period. But you could see it on her face—the toll his death had taken upon her.

They were married for over fifty years. It was an anniversary that was almost unheard of anymore. My heart ached for her. I couldn't imagine loving someone that long, let alone having to live life without them afterward. It almost made you question what the purpose of it was anymore. It sounded like it would be extremely lonely. And lost—so lost.

As I stood in front of the romance section, I slid a few books back into their designated spots. I ran my fingers along the spines of the entire shelf. I loved the way that they felt beneath my fingertips. There was something about it that had a way of grounding me. Books were always my solitude.

"Any books that you would recommend?"

The sound of his voice snaked around my eardrums. My spine straightened and my breath hitched as I was momentarily frozen in place. There was a part of me that had been anticipating this moment since I gave him that damn library card.

I slowly turned around to face him. Kai was dressed in a pair of golf shorts again with his polo tucked in beneath his waistband. I dipped my head to the side, a touch of confusion mixing in my expression. It was a common outfit for Kai to be wearing, considering the fact that he did play golf. But he was dressed in similar fashion the other day when he was here, and I was beginning to wonder what his daily agenda looked like.

Focus, Winter. It didn't matter what Kai did with his time.

"That depends," I said softly as I straightened my head and focused on his warm gaze. It was a stark contrast to what I was used to from him and it had me questioning everything. "What are you looking for?"

My heart beat once, twice, three times, as his gaze was glued to mine, never wavering. "I've found exactly what I'm looking for."

I struggled to swallow over the lump in my throat and Kai stepped closer to me. I took a step back, but he didn't stop moving until my back was pressed against the bookshelf. He lifted his arms, placing his hands on the shelves beside my head as he caged me in.

"As much as I enjoy reading, I'm not here for the books, Winter."

"I know," I whispered, not fully trusting my voice as my eyes slowly searched his. "You never were."

He shook his head. "You're correct."

"Why, Malakai?" I questioned him with the desperation in my voice. "You let me go once before."

"And I did what I had to do for you, darling," he said softly as his minty breath fanned across my face. "But if I had the choice to do it again, I wouldn't. I would be selfish and keep you for myself. Letting you go was the gravest mistake I've ever made and I don't intend on repeating that mistake."

It broke my heart, hearing him finally speak the words I had waited years to hear. All I ever wanted was for him to come back and tell me he messed up. I wanted him to take it all back and soothe my soul. I questioned the timing now. So much time had passed between us. He had plenty of opportunities and now it just felt like it was convenient because we were back in our hometown at the same time.

"You don't know how long I waited for you to say that to me," I admitted, my voice still barely above a whisper. "We can't undo what has already been done. There's so much hurt, so much pain. I'm just afraid that it's too late."

A muscle in his jaw tightened and I watched a wave of pain wash through his blue irises. "Have you moved on?" There was a coldness to his tone and his body fell rigid.

My shoulders sagged in defeat. I couldn't lie to him, even though I wanted to. "I tried."

I wasn't going to tell him I had gone on dates with other men in an effort to get over him. That I had even been in a relationship with another guy, but I couldn't bring myself to actually sleep with him because I felt like I was betraying Kai. I didn't lie when I told him there was no one else, because there never was. Regardless of how hard I tried to move on, I never could.

"And you still feel as though it's too late?"

I stared at him for a moment. "I don't know if it is or not. What if the damage between us is irreparable, Kai? You absolutely broke me."

His lips parted and a soft sigh escaped him. "Let me

put you back together, darling. Let me make you whole again."

"I don't need you to make me whole. I put myself back together without you."

Kai's expressions were unreadable as his eyes continued to penetrate mine with such intensity. I couldn't quite read a single one and my mind was reeling as I tried to dissect them. Kai simply blinked and I watched them vanish as his mask went back into place. This was him protecting himself from the emotions that were hitting him in rapid succession.

"Let me fix what I've broken."

His words settled in the thick air between us. I was trapped, facing an impossible decision. I knew he was bad for me, especially considering our history, yet that was a long time ago. Perhaps he had grown, even though he still operated from a place of self-preservation. That was his childhood trauma and I wanted to reach out and wrap my arms around his broken soul.

I knew I would never survive the same heartbreak from him again.

Kai would obliterate me this time.

"I won't stop you from trying," I told him gently as a sad smile pulled on my lips. "But I'm not going to make this easy for you."

He fell silent for a moment. "I wouldn't expect you to. I know I have a lot to make up for."

"I can't promise you it will work," I admitted with a soberness in my tone. I was lying and we both knew it but Kai simply nodded in response. He was the only one who could break through my walls.

He wanted to rectify the damage he had caused. I couldn't deny him that. Even if it didn't work, he deserved a chance. Everyone always deserved a chance.

"I just have one question," I said carefully as I stared up at him. Neither of us had made an attempt to move and his face was still close to mine. "And I need you to be honest with me."

His throat bobbed and his jaw tightened as he swallowed hard and gave me a curt nod. Kai had lied to me in the past, but he always claimed it was for my own good. He omitted a lot of truths from me, but I knew it was because admitting the truth out loud made some things too real for him.

"Are you choosing now because it's convenient?"

A storm was brewing in Kai's irises. "Nothing about this is convenient, Winter. Nothing about this is a coincidence."

His words suspended me back to the night at the country club. When he had followed me outside and told me he was there for me. I didn't think he was serious at the time, I thought he'd just meant it in that moment, but now he had me questioning everything.

"When you said you were here for me... what did you mean by that, exactly?"

"I told you, darling." His hand dropped to my face and he brushed a piece of hair behind my ear. "I heard you were back and it was time for me to come for you."

His expression was giving nothing away. I believed him—I truly did—but I knew there was more to the story than he was giving me. He was taking a break from playing golf and I knew that was part of the reason why he was back as well.

I stared back at him, not sure whether or not I should push the issue. He gave me the honesty I had asked for, even though he was still holding back from me.

"It just seems strange to me that you would come back now. You knew where I was in Vermont, so why wait? Why not come to me there?"

His jaw clenched and his nostrils flared. Something was boiling inside of him, yet his touch was still gentle as he stroked the side of my face. "It's complicated. One day, I'll explain, okay?"

I wanted to know, but I knew better than to push him in this moment. This was his way of asking me to let it go. He wasn't ready to talk about whatever it was that he was holding inside and I at least owed him that much. I didn't owe him much of anything, but it was human decency. Respect. The one thing I expected in return from him.

"I've really fucking missed you," he breathed as his eyes searched mine. "Please give me a chance to make this right."

My lips parted as a ragged breath escaped me. My arms had been pinned to my sides, but I couldn't help myself as I reached out to touch him. Kai inhaled sharply as my hands touched his waist.

"I told you I won't stop you from trying."

His fingers were splayed along the side of my face as he pressed his palm against my cheek. The warmth of his hand seeped into my soul as he pushed his fingers through my hair. He held the back of my head and tipped it back. I could see the torment and the doubt in his eyes, but as I pulled him closer, that was the reassurance he needed.

Kai's lips collided into mine. They melted against mine as he drained the oxygen from my lungs. Our surroundings faded and my mind no longer registered where we were or what was going on around us. The only thing that mattered was his warm body pressed against mine and the way he was distracting me with his mouth.

The air was electric between us. His touch was burning with such an intensity, I thought for sure my body would go up in flames. He deepened the kiss as his tongue danced with mine. He tasted like spearmint and he smelled like leather and sandalwood. Expensive and exquisite. He breathed me in as he consumed every one of my senses.

The bookcase behind us groaned as he pressed me harder against it. One of the books tumbled from the shelf and fell onto the ground. The sound echoed through the library, abruptly pulling me back to reality.

My hands found his chest and I pushed him back. He didn't move, but his lips left mine in a rush. My chest rose and fell with every shallow, ragged breath that escaped me. This was the power Malakai Barclay had on me. He could walk right into my life and shake everything up without a second thought. And by the time my mind had finally caught up, he was already tearing my walls down one by one.

"You're doing exactly what I told you not to do," I said breathlessly as I stared up at him.

Mischief danced in his eyes and he couldn't fight the smirk as it lifted the corner of his lips. The soft dimples in his cheeks were on display and my chest constricted. I could probably count on one hand the amount of times I had seen them.

"I never said I was good at following directions."

"I can't have you here distracting me," I told him softly as I glanced around to see if anyone had seen us.

Kai slid his hand back to my face and grabbed my chin before guiding my gaze back to his. The mischief had vanished from his eyes and instead there was a touch of curiosity deep in the brewing storm. "Why did you change your number, darling?"

There was no sense in lying.

"Because as much as I wanted you to come back for me, I also didn't."

He didn't frown; there was no falter in his expression. He nodded like he accepted my answer without any question or hesitation. "That's fair, I suppose. Although, not having your number is forcing my hand. I have no choice but to show up at your work and use means of distraction."

I laughed softly as I moved away from the bookshelf and ducked under Kai's arm. Without a second thought, I slipped my hand into his and pulled him to the front desk with me. His hand fit perfectly in mine, with our fingers laced together.

My heart pounded erratically in my chest as we stopped in front of the desk. I glanced at him and noticed he was staring at both of our hands woven together. I quickly released him and grabbed a piece of paper, ignoring the tightening feeling in my chest.

"Here." I slipped the paper with my number scribbled on it into his hand. "Now you can get a hold of me like a normal person."

The corners of his lips twitched. "As you wish."

My heart had crawled into my throat and I watched with conflicting feelings as he left the library without another word. I wanted to hate him for what he did to me—to us—yet I was finding my resolve becoming obsolete. I was no match for the effect Malakai Barclay had on me.

I had given my heart to that beautifully broken boy many years ago.

And much to my dismay, he still held it in his hands.

CHAPTER SEVENTEEN
MALAKAI

S tanding out on the balcony, I stared out at the ocean as it crashed against the shore. The clouds in the sky were dark and moody with the sun tucked behind them. There was a slight chill to the breeze that floated across the water. A low rumble of thunder sounded across the angry sky and I watched as a bolt of lightning cast its light across the horizon a few seconds later.

Storms were typical here in the afternoons of the summer months. Personally, I looked forward to them, especially since I lived right on the coast. There was something terrifying, yet alluring about the way a thunderstorm rolled across the ocean. It was mesmerizing and at the same time, it could be deadly.

I looked down at the small piece of paper in my hand with Winter's phone number written on it. I studied the way her handwriting slanted slightly and the curvature to her script-like writing. She used to leave me notes in high school, and I used to reread them over and over when I couldn't see her.

I still had them to this day, tucked away in a box in my closet.

It had been three days since Winter gave me her number. Three days of avoiding going to the library. And three days of avoiding picking up my phone to text her.

Things were already messy between us and I knew I owed her some space. She didn't ask for it, but there was a part of me that knew she needed it. I came barreling back into her life without her even having a moment to try and process it. Considering the fact that the first night she saw me in six years sent her spiraling into a full-blown panic attack, it felt like it was the least I could do.

I needed to ease back into her life instead.

Pulling my phone out of my pocket, I pulled up a new message thread and entered Winter's number. I stared down at the screen for a moment, a rush of adrenaline hitting me like a tidal wave. Thunder rumbled across the angry sky once again and instead of seeking shelter, I sat down at the small table on my balcony.

MALAKAI

Hi darling.

There was no hesitation in the message I sent to her. I wasn't one to overanalyze things, although Winter had a peculiar way of making me question everything. I'd always been sure of myself and the words I chose.

As I stared down at my phone, I couldn't help but have a moment of doubt.

WINTER

Malakai?

A smile played on my lips and her response was like inhaling a potent toxin. One that induced a high nothing else would ever come close to touching. My mind replayed her message, hearing the sound of her voice whispering my name.

MALAKAI

Is there someone else who addresses you in a similar fashion?

WINTER

Would it matter if there was?

My jaw twitched and I lifted my eyes out to the ocean. The waves had grown stronger and were crashing against the shore with more force now. The storm was inching closer and I saw streaks of rain falling from the clouds into the water. I needed to get inside before hell poured down from the sky.

MALAKAI

I suppose that depends on whether or not you want them to address you the way I do.

Droplets of rain fell onto my skin and a sigh escaped me. I made my way back inside, still with my phone in my hand as I took a seat at the island in my kitchen. Things were always so intense between us. I didn't want to bring the heaviness upon her, but my curiosity had gotten the better of me.

Winter Reign was the one person who could make me feel safe, yet insecure at the same time. She could have anyone—anything—that she ever wanted in the world. There were times when I couldn't help myself in needing her assurance that she wanted me in the past.

This was different, though. It was as if we were starting over, yet we had rubble gathered around our feet from the destruction between us in the past.

WINTER

You're the only one, Malakai.

I swallowed roughly as I read her words over and over again until they were ingrained in my mind. The guy I saw her with before was nothing. He didn't matter now. She left him in Vermont.

MALAKAI

Do you have plans tonight? I know it is short notice, but I would like to take you out.

WINTER

I don't have anything going on. What did you have in mind?

A part of me was surprised she didn't turn me down. I wasn't sure what to expect with her anymore and a part of me hated that. Winter was never predictable. I knew her better than anyone else and I tried to read her like a chess board, yet I could never figure out what her next move was going to be. She always had a way of surprising me when I least expected it.

She was predictable when it came to other people. Always proper and polite, Winter Reign never spoke out of tone or out of place. She knew how she was expected to behave as her parents taught her from a young age. I couldn't help but admire the woman Winter had grown to be after listening to the way she spoke to Mrs. Danbury at the charity event.

Winter was playing by her own rules, she wasn't here to make sure she didn't step out of line anymore. She wasn't holding anything back with anyone, and it was different from how she used to be. I personally loved the way she had evolved.

MALAKAI

> Well, I was thinking we could maybe get dinner somewhere.

I hadn't really thought past that, considering the fact that I wasn't sure she was even going to respond to me. She was a wild card.

WINTER

> That sounds perfect. Did you have a place or a time in mind?

MALAKAI

> I'll pick you up at 7, if that is enough time for you?

I glanced at the watch on my wrist to check the time. That would give her about an hour and a half to get ready. That felt like it would be a sufficient amount of time for her, but I wasn't sure. I had dated other women since high school in an effort to expunge Winter's memory from my mind, but I never paid much attention to these kinds of things.

I never fully paid attention to anyone but Winter and her needs.

Even if I had made some decisions in the past that didn't fit what she had in mind.

WINTER

That should be fine.

MALAKAI

I'll see you soon, darling.

Closing out our message thread, I went to my web browser and searched for restaurants near me. Even though I had lived in the area for most of my life, I wanted to take Winter somewhere new. Somewhere neither of us had been before. As I scrolled through the different places, I found one that looked like a quaint little Thai spot that was tucked away from the typical foot traffic in town.

It was perfect.

————

I pulled up in front of Winter's house at seven o'clock sharp. As I put the car in park and climbed out, I watched as the front door opened and she stepped out. Time was suspended and I was momentarily frozen in place as I took in her ethereal appearance.

She had on a light gray dress that looked to be made of silk. It hugged her curves, stopping just in the middle of her thighs. Her dark hair was pinned away from her face and fell in soft waves to the center of her back.

My heart was in my throat and my chest was simultaneously constricting as I took in the sight of her. She was something I would never grow tired of looking at. I forced myself out of the trance I was caught in and walked over to the passenger side to open the door for her.

"Hi," Winter said softly with a small smile as she approached me. With her black, strappy heels, she was a little taller, but she still had to tilt her head back to look up at me.

"Hi, darling."

I pulled open the door for her and she slid inside the car. Her eyes were tender, yet there was a touch of nervousness as she glanced up at me as I went to shut the door. "I hope what I'm wearing is okay? You didn't say where we were going."

A grin pulled on my lips. "You look absolutely breathtaking, Winter. You're perfect."

"But for where we're going?"

I cocked my head. "For anywhere we could possibly go."

A wave of emotion passed through her green irises and I gently closed the door without another word. My heart had settled back in my chest as I walked around the back of the car. My cock, on the other hand, was swelling in my pants. That dress she had on… I wanted to take her back inside the house and forget about dinner entirely.

Ignoring the urge I had, I got into the car behind the steering wheel and promptly put the car in reverse. If I didn't get us moving as soon as possible, we definitely wouldn't be getting anywhere tonight. The thought of giving her any type of space or taking things slow felt absurd with her in such close proximity to me. She had a way of muddling every rational thought I could possibly possess.

I would never say I was an irrational person, I just leaned more on the edge of impulsiveness when it came to some decisions.

"You surprise me," Winter said suddenly as I pulled the car out onto her road.

I glanced over at her with an eyebrow raised. "Why is that?"

"After all these years, you still remember the code to get onto my family's property."

I looked at the road and back to her. "If your parents were smart, they would have changed it many years ago."

"How did you remember it?" she questioned me with her voice soft and gentle. There was something lingering beneath the surface of her words, yet I couldn't quite figure out what it was.

"I would never forget it," I admitted with nothing but honesty. "It's the date of your birthday but backward."

Winter fell silent but her gaze lingered on the side of my face. I couldn't allow myself to look at her again, not with the energy that was buzzing in the air between us. There was a heaviness, thick with emotion, yet there was electricity and the molecules in the space were literally electric.

She had no idea just how much I would never forget.

Silence slid around us and I waited for Winter to say something. I chanced a glance in her direction and saw the vacantness in her eyes as she stared through the windshield.

Reaching out to her, I grabbed her hand with my own and gave it a small squeeze. Her skin was warm against mine and she abruptly whipped her head to the side. Her gaze collided with mine.

"Where did you go?"

She stared at me for a moment and I alternated between looking at her and the road in front of me. "It doesn't matter."

We drove into town and down the busy streets. During the summer, it got particularly busy with the tourists mixing with the locals. There were lines outside of most of the restaurants, but I turned down one of the side streets instead.

I pulled the car along the street and put it in park before killing the engine. Winter's hand was still in mine and I turned to look at her.

"It does to me."

Her lips parted slightly and a soft breath escaped her. I watched the resignation on her face as it swept across her delicate features. "I was just thinking about all the times you used the code to sneak in. I think my parents knew but they didn't want to say anything."

Her admission caught me off guard. "Why do you say that?"

She raked her teeth over her bottom lip before releasing it. "Remember that one time you skipped school and brought me my favorite soup when I was sick? You curled up in my bed and fell asleep for a little bit. My mother came home early and saw you."

I stared back at her. "She never said anything."

Winter shook her head. "She looked between the two of us and told me that you had better leave before my father got home. She never brought it up again."

"Why didn't you ever tell me?"

Her eyes were soft and warm, inviting me into her soul. "I didn't want you to stop sneaking in."

Something about the way she spoke those words splintered my heart. I rubbed my thumb over the back of her hand as I held on to her. We were going to be late for our reservation, but I didn't even care.

"Nothing would ever keep me from you."

I watched her expression transform. Ice encapsulated her irises, pushing out the warmth that once resided there. She slowly pulled her hand from mine as she opened her door. The coldness radiated from her as she gave me one last look.

"It's funny you say that, considering you kept yourself from me for six years."

CHAPTER EIGHTEEN
WINTER

Kai sat unmoving in his car for a moment as I got out and shut the door behind me. I knew I was letting my anger get the better of me but I couldn't help myself. Something about him speaking those words just hit a nerve and it was like a switch flipped. There was still a bitterness that I was harboring inside.

Forgiveness was right there, so close I could almost taste it, but I needed more from him. I had questions I needed answers to. He was delusional if he thought he would come back here and we would pick up where we left off like that night never happened between us.

As Kai got out, there was a deep sadness situated in his stormy dark blue eyes. I let out a breath as I stood on the sidewalk and watched him walk around the front of the car to meet me. He was silent and the weight of the air around him was suffocating.

He was drowning inside and he was threatening to pull me down into the depths with him.

And if I weren't careful, I would let him do it.

"Hey," I said softly as he walked past me, not even sparing a glance in my direction. "Kai, wait."

He kept walking, yet his gait slowed a fraction. "We're already late for our reservation, Winter." His tone was frigid and clipped. I watched for a moment as he walked to the front of the small brick building and pulled open the door for me.

Only then did he look at me and his gaze sent a shiver down my spine. He stood there with his hand wrapped around the handle of the door as he held it open for me. His expression was blank and void of any warmth. He waited with an expectant look on his face.

A sigh escaped me and my footsteps followed after him without my instruction. I stepped past him, the smell of his cologne enticing my senses as I walked into the restaurant. From the outside, it didn't appear to be much but as we entered, it appeared to be a much bigger building than it seemed.

"What is this place?" I asked him quietly as we stepped up to the hostess stand. It was somewhere new to me, somewhere I had never been before. "Is this a new restaurant?"

Kai looked straight ahead. "It appears so."

I stared at the side of his face as an emptiness settled inside of me. An older woman stepped up to the stand and Kai gave her his last name. I watched, feeling like I was moving in a body that wasn't my own as she grabbed two menus before leading us to our table. It was tucked in the back corner of the restaurant and I was grateful for the privacy.

Kai pulled my chair out for me to sit down and slowly eased it back toward the table once I was seated. Even though he was crass and cold, he knew how to be a gentleman. It just depended on whether or not he felt like being a gentleman in the moments that called for it.

He took his seat across from me and lifted a menu up in front of his face to look at it. He didn't speak a single word to me and I couldn't shake the mixture of emotions that were filling me. It was a wide variety that eventually settled on sadness. And regret.

There was so much regret between us for so many different reasons.

"I'm sorry for what I said in the car. That was extremely insensitive of me."

Kai lifted his gaze from the menu and set it down on the table as his gaze penetrated mine. "You don't owe me an apology, darling." There was a softness to his tone, yet his eyes were still shockingly cold. "You're allowed to be bitter and angry with me. I would be alarmed if you weren't."

My eyes refused to leave his. "I don't want to be, though."

He sighed and folded his arms on the table. "You should, Winter. I meant it when I said you should hate me." He paused for a moment as sadness began to build its own walls inside his soul. "You always should have hated me."

"That was a lie," I admitted in a rush, my voice barely above a whisper. "I never truly hated you. There were moments I wished I did. It would have made things a lot easier for me."

Kai looked at me—no, he looked through me, directly into my soul. "When will we stop lying to one another, darling?"

His words seeped into my bloodstream and I felt them everywhere. "Do you want the truth or another lie?"

"Truth."

There was no hesitation. He sat across from me, unmoving like a perfectly sculpted statue. His eyes were on mine and there was a storm brewing deep inside the depths of his blue irises.

"Probably never."

To that, he frowned. "I do not accept that, darling. The lying and the deception between us stops here. I don't want you to tell me what you think I want to hear or keep things from me that you think I don't want to hear. I want nothing but your brutal honesty, do you understand me?"

My eyes narrowed. "The same goes for you then too."

"To be clear, I did say us, not just you."

Kai was equally infuriating and alluring. I was drawn to him like a moth to a flame. I was tethered to him by this invisible thread and regardless of the destruction between us, it refused to be severed. There was a magnetic pull I could not fight against. I was no match against Malakai Barclay.

We were both raised in affluent, influential households. Kai was highly intelligent, despite his grades from high school. He spoke with such elegance and grace, like it was a true art. He was an intellect, but no one else ever got close enough to see who he was on the inside. They took one look at him when he was younger and wrote him off as entitled and a troublemaker. He could get away with murder and never have to stand trial.

"Pardon me for not hearing that part."

Kai challenged me with his gaze. "I think you heard me clearly, but you just chose to disregard that part."

My lips parted and I was about to respond, just as our server finally appeared at our table. Kai ordered water for us and looked at me when she asked if either of us were ready to order our food yet. I nodded and we both told her what we wanted before she left the two of us alone again. There was tension in the silence between us as we waited for her to return with our drinks.

She quickly reappeared. As she left the glasses of water, I looked back to Kai whose lips were slightly curved downward in a frown. "This wasn't how I imagined dinner between us going."

My eyebrows pulled together. "What do you mean?"

"Things were supposed to be light and easy." He paused for a moment and I watched his throat bob as he took a sip of his water. "I don't know how to do that."

My expression softened as his words swirled around in my brain. There was a touch of sadness and almost disappointment mixed in his voice. It sent fissures across my heart. "Kai," I said softly as he lifted his gaze back to mine. "It's okay, I promise."

Kai stared at me for a moment as if he didn't believe me. His expression was blank yet there was a wave of relief that passed through his eyes. I noted the slight sag in his shoulders as he exhaled and nodded.

There was no awkwardness between us, but the tension remained thick. A heaviness was present and it was weighing down on both of us. Things between us had always been intense, and I didn't expect anything less. Kai had always struggled to relate to people because he was so closed off. Blame it on childhood trauma. Either way, I was always the one who made things light and in that moment, I knew that was what Kai needed from me.

"Tell me what it's been like golfing professionally." I paused for a moment, a small smile pulling on my lips. There was a part of me that felt regret for not following how he has been doing, but I couldn't bring myself to do it.

Kai fell silent for a moment, almost as if he were replaying what I asked of him before choosing a response. His lips parted and he sighed. "It's been... a lot." His tongue slipped between his lips as he wet them and continued. "It's been amazing and horrible at the same time."

I scowled just as our server brought our plates to the table. I thanked her while Kai continued to watch me. My napkin was already draped over my thighs and I left my silverware on the table as I focused on him.

"What is wrong with it?"

Kai gave me a simple shrug. "It's just a lot of pressure and a lot of traveling."

"I can imagine the pressure would be a lot to take," I said softly as I nodded. Kai poked his fork at the food in front of him. It was almost as if the conversation had made him increasingly uncomfortable and I wasn't sure why. "If there is anyone who can handle it, though, it would be you. You've always been centered when it has come to golf. Are you taking a break because of those reasons?"

He cocked his head to the side, just a fraction of an inch. He was already feeling vulnerable and our conversation had barely started. Kai slowly shook his head. "I'm taking a break because I was off. I wasn't playing like I was when I first started."

"What happened?" I questioned him as I slid my own fork into my pasta and began to swirl it around on the spoon in the dish.

"You happened, Winter," he said with a tenderness, yet there was resignation in his tone, as if he had succumbed to his fate. "You always happen."

My eyes widened slightly, yet I wasn't following. "What does that mean?"

Kai took a bite of his food and watched me as he slowly chewed. It was as if time was suspended and it stopped moving. My breathing grew shallow as my mind ran rampant with all of the possible things he could say. He swallowed and took a sip of his water and I was completely unprepared for what he was going to tell me.

"We agreed on the truth, so you can't be angry with me for being honest." He paused, setting his glass of water back down in front of him. "Six months ago, I saw you at the bar you frequented with another man. I haven't been playing right since. Every time I try to focus, for some outlandish reason, the image of you both laughing together enters my mind."

The air left my lungs in a rush and I was still hanging on to the second sentence he spoke. At that moment, I didn't care about his golf game or what was wrong with it. I didn't care about the image he had in his mind.

"You were in Vermont six months ago?" I whispered the words, not fully trusting my voice. His truth was like a knife twisting in my heart. "You were there and you didn't tell me?"

The air surrounding us was suffocating. My heart was in my stomach and I glanced around for the nearest exit. My breathing was already growing erratic. I wasn't sure I wanted him to answer either of those questions.

"That wasn't the first time, darling." His jaw clenched for a fraction of a second and I watched the storm brewing deep in his irises. "But it was most certainly the last."

CHAPTER NINETEEN
MALAKAI

Winter's eyes were wide as she stared back at me like she had seen a ghost. The color had drained from her face and I couldn't quite read the emotions that danced in her irises. I wanted to take back the words the instant they escaped me, but I couldn't. I had no choice but to go with it at this point. The truth was bound to surface eventually, I just planned on giving it to her in a more eloquent manner.

"What do you mean?" she practically whispered as her eyes searched mine with such desperation, I could feel it in my chest. "What do you mean it wasn't the first time?"

"I came to Vermont on more than one occasion." I paused for a moment, collecting my thoughts as I set my silverware down. "I needed to see for myself that you were okay. I told myself if you were thriving, I would stay away. You were, so I didn't make contact."

Her mouth was agape and she quickly snapped it

shut. Her eyebrows drew together as her face contorted. I watched her with careful consideration. It felt as if she were a grenade and I pulled the pin. Instead of running for cover, I was bracing myself for her destruction. I expected her to be angry, to yell at me. Instead, she just looked broken.

And that broke me even more.

"What gave you the impression that I was thriving?"

I folded my hands on my lap. "You were at the bar with some people who appeared to be your friends. You were smiling and laughing." My eyes swept across her face. "You didn't look like this. You looked like you were happy."

She blinked. Once. Twice. The emotion had vanished but the pain lingered in her features. "Of course I was happy. I was living my life the way I wanted to, but that didn't mean I was thriving. That didn't mean I didn't go home and stare at the ceiling while thoughts of you plagued my mind."

Her words caught me off guard. They threw me off-balance and I felt the sharp intake of my own breath. My chest tightened. I had myself convinced she had moved on and forgotten about me. Not that it was something I would ever fault her for doing, considering I was the one who pushed her away.

"How many times?" she questioned me.

"Excuse me?"

Torment mixed with the pain, deep within the cracks of the mask she tried to plaster on her face. She couldn't fool me. She never could.

"How many times did you come to Vermont?"

I mulled over her question. The truth—no more lies and deception. "Four times."

Her eyes widened the slightest bit that if I weren't solely focused on her, I wouldn't have noticed. "You came there four times to see me, but never told me?"

I shook my head. "I had already done enough damage, I was trying to spare you."

"You do realize how fucked up that is, right? You went there and didn't tell me and watched me from afar?"

"That sounds worse than it was," I tell her with an exasperated sigh. "It's not like I was stalking you. I came to make sure you were okay."

Her expression was blank. "When were you there?"

"Is that really of any importance?"

Finally, there was a flicker of emotion in her eyes again. Her eyebrows pulled together a fraction of an inch. "To me, it is."

"The first time was about a month after you were there." I paused for a moment as my mind drifted. "You were at skating practice when I finally found you. You were there with another girl and I didn't want to interrupt."

"Eden," she said quietly as her expression softened. Her mask was falling away in fragments. "She helped me find my place in Vermont. We lived together until she started dating a hockey player named Hayden King and they got a place together."

There was so much about her life that I never knew. I kept tabs on her always because, regardless of what would ever happen between us, she was always my main concern. Knowing she was okay brought me a sense of peace, like I had made the right decision even though I regretted it immensely.

"When was the next time?"

"I came back every year." My throat was thick with emotion as I prepared myself for the truth I was about to unleash on her. "I wanted you to thrive, but I also didn't. I wanted to show up and see that you didn't belong there. That your life wasn't what you deserved. I needed a reason to reinsert myself in your life but every time I showed up, I couldn't bring myself to do it."

She fell silent for a moment as her eyes searched mine. "But why? All you had to do was reach out. Approach me. Anything would have been better than nothing." She stopped as she chewed on the inside of her cheek. "You don't know how many times I wished you would just show up but you never came. You never came for me, Malakai."

Her words broke my heart into jagged fragments.

"I did come for you," I assure her, my voice barely audible. "I just knew I was never what you needed."

Winter's eyes narrowed on mine and she shook her head. "I hate when you do that."

"Do what?"

She gave me an incredulous look. "When you act like you aren't deserving of anything. We agreed on no lies, correct?"

"Indeed."

"How is this for the truth—I've always needed you, Malakai. You have always been exactly what I need." A wave of sadness and sympathy passed through her eyes. "You deserve to experience the good in the world."

I stared at her for a moment, tilting my head to the side in confusion. "How can you say these things with such conviction after what I did?"

"Because my heart has always known you. It has always known that you were it for me."

It never made sense in my mind how someone like her could possibly feel so deeply for someone like me. I was nothing; she was everything. She was the sun in the sky, the moon and the stars. She was the entire universe and I was simply just existing in her atmosphere. I would put my entire life on the line for Winter Reign.

"Why me?"

A smile pulled on her lips as she challenged me with a fire burning in the depths of her green eyes. "Because it's you. I never had a choice or a say in the matter. My soul knew you from the moment we first met. It's always been you."

Her words seeped into my bones. My heart beat erratically in my chest. The intensity between us was exhausting. We went from zero to one hundred in a matter of seconds, only to come to a full stop and switch in the opposite direction. It was maddening, yet it was like a rush to my system that no drug would ever come close to touching.

"I have one question for you."

"Ask me," she said with no hesitation.

"You told me there was no one else." I spoke the

words slowly and fought to keep the jealousy from my tone. "I saw you with another man in Vermont."

Winter frowned and shook her head. "Travis. I won't lie to you about him. We did date, but I could never bring myself to sleep with him. I tried. I tried to get over you, but it never felt right."

A weight that I hadn't noticed was instantly lifted from my chest. It felt like I could breathe easier, like there was a sense of relief. There was something more. A touch of anger that bubbled just beneath the surface. I couldn't get the image and thought of her and this guy from my mind, and it wasn't what I thought it was.

My golf career was hanging in the balance because of the way I let it affect my mental strength. All of this could have been prevented had I seen past my stubbornness and reached out to her.

I had a lot of things I would have to make up for.

"I don't like the thought of you with anyone else in any other way."

She stared at me for a moment. "I won't apologize for how I handled the pain I was feeling. I didn't have many choices. I was tired of being haunted by your ghost."

"I'm not a ghost anymore, darling. I'm here now and I have every intention of correcting the mistakes I've made in the past."

"I changed my mind about letting you fix the things you've broken." A ghost of a smile played on her lips and she shook her head once more. "There's nothing we can do about the past. What is done is already done."

Defeat rushed through my system. "So, I'm too late."

"I didn't say that." Her brow furrowed before they softened again. "There's still time, but not to fix what has already been broken. To start again, to start over."

My eyes were cemented to hers. "You want to start over?"

Winter nodded. "We can't forget our history and I would never want to." She paused for a breath as she smiled at me. "I want to start from the beginning. Our new beginning."

"I don't deserve your forgiveness, Winter."

She continued to smile. "How unfortunate that you don't get a say in that."

"Why would you forgive me so easily?"

"What does holding the hate in my heart do for either of us?" Her voice was soft as she questioned me. "I choose to forgive you because I want to give you the chance to make things right. I can't do that if I continue to hold on to the past between us."

I did not deserve her. It didn't matter what she said, I would never accept it as the truth. After what had happened between us in the past, I could not fathom why she would be so forgiving. Why would she still even want me? I was grateful that she did because I had every intention of making her mine, but I didn't expect her to be like this, especially after the rocky start we had after that charity event.

"Regardless of starting from the beginning, I have a lot of things to make up for."

Winter nodded. "We will see where things go from

here. I can't promise any of it will be easy. We both have a lot we need to heal from."

"When does our new beginning start?"

She smiled. "Whenever you're ready."

For the first time in a long time, I couldn't fight the smile that pulled on my lips.

"I've always been ready for you, darling."

CHAPTER TWENTY
WINTER

Kai was quiet as he held my hand in the car. We had finished with dinner and there was a difference in the air between us. It was no longer as heavy as it once was. There was still so much that was unknown about where the future would take us, but I was ready to find out. After everything Kai and I had been through, I really wanted to give this one last chance.

There was a part of me that was giving myself a suspicious look. Did I give in too quickly to him? It was highly probable. If there was anyone who deserved a bit of grace, it would always be him for me. The demons he struggled to fight were enough for him to be dealing with. If I could offer him some sense of peace and freedom in life, I was going to do that.

He had my heart in his hands and I didn't want to have to ask for it back. I wanted him to prove me wrong, to challenge my thoughts. I wanted him to make me believe there really was hope for us. That there could actually be an us. Punishing him and making him continue to jump through hoops wasn't conducive to a healthy relationship. It would only push us back further instead of moving forward in life.

The moment there was a shift between us tonight, I knew I had a choice to make. I had chosen to forgive him, but I would never forget the heartbreak I experienced at his hand. I just hoped it could be a part of our story instead of the way it ended.

The sun was already hidden beneath the horizon and the moon shone brightly in the sky above. I looked out the window, up at the night sky as the stars danced around the moon. Kai's hand was warm against mine and his touch was soft as he lightly stroked the back of my hand with his thumb.

"You're quiet, darling," Kai said softly as I noticed we were now on my road. He said after dinner that he would take me home since it was getting late, but I couldn't help but feel a mixture of excitement and anxiety in the pit of my stomach.

I turned my head to look over at him. The soft glow from the lights on the dashboard illuminated his features and I studied the side of his face. There was a small tattoo, tucked just behind his ear that I hadn't noticed before. It must have been hidden by his hair before. I tilted my head to the side, attempting to get a better look.

I reached out to touch him, my fingers trailing along his skin. "What is this?"

"A tattoo."

I inched closer, my eyes tracing over three small

snowflakes. Emotion welled in my throat and I swallowed over the lump lodged inside. My fingers were still against his skin, my eyes glued to the small, intricate design.

"I got it for you, Winter."

My breath caught in my throat as my heart felt like a vice grip was tightening around it. "When?"

He was silent for a moment. "Right after you left."

"But why?"

He was such a contradiction, pulling my heart in every possible direction.

"My father always said if I got a tattoo, I'd regret it, so I decided to get a tattoo of my biggest regret."

His words felt like a blow to my chest. I abruptly pulled my hand away from his neck as the pain struck my heart like a bolt of lightning.

My voice was barely audible. "I was your biggest regret?"

He pulled the car off the road onto a small pull-off spot that sat between two rows of trees. "No." Kai's gaze met mine as he put the car in park and turned to face me. "Pushing you away was my biggest regret." He paused for two heartbeats before speaking again. "This was where I used to leave my car when I would sneak into your house at night."

I stared at him for a moment, a touch of sadness filling me as my eyes searched his.

He let out a soft sigh and I watched his chest as it deflated. "I don't know how to do this right."

"What do you mean? Do what right?"

"This." He lifted our hands that were still clasped

together. "Am I supposed to take you somewhere else? Am I supposed to take you home? You're giving me a chance to start over and I refuse to mess things up."

A smile pulled on my lips as his words soothed my soul. Here, I had been thinking he wanted to take me home because he wanted to get rid of me for the night, but I was completely wrong. He'd been sitting here with anxious thoughts of not knowing what his next move should be. Kai was a strategic player. He was a master of chess and knew his opponent's next move. When it came to this thing between us, he had no idea what his next move was supposed to be because he couldn't predict anything.

"Kai… There's no right or wrong way to do things. Let your heart lead you."

His eyes were glued to mine and there was a touch of confusion and hesitation in his features. This was all foreign for him and a part of me felt honored that I was the one he had chosen to figure out this undiscovered territory with. I knew he never experienced love from his parents and I instantly felt guilty for questioning his love for me in the past.

I didn't lie when I said I felt like he did it in his own way that may not have been conventional. Nonetheless, he still loved me then.

"Your heart won't lead you astray," I assured him as I reached up with my free hand and cupped the side of his face. "Just feel and go with it."

"I don't want to hurt you," he said with so much emotion in his voice, although it was barely above a whisper. "I can't bear the thought of doing it again."

His eyelids fluttered shut as I ran my fingers along the curvature of his jaw.

His admission splintered my heart. "I trust you not to, Kai."

"What if you were right?" He was hesitant with his words and when he opened his eyes, the air left my lungs in a rush. Deep within the stormy depths of his irises, there was a mixture of fear and regret, laced with hope and adoration. "What if I don't know how to love you properly?"

Regret pierced my heart and I frowned slightly as my eyes desperately searched his. His internal critic was usually the voice of his father, but I was the one who planted these thoughts in his mind.

"Kai," I whispered as I slid my hand around the back of his neck. I closed the distance between us as I made the move I knew I needed to. It was something he needed from me and I would give him whatever reassurance he needed. "I apologize for the things I said out of anger. I was hurting and I wanted you to hurt as well."

"I deserve any and all of your anger, darling," he said softly, his lips brushing against mine. "Please don't ever feel as though you owe me an apology for expressing your feelings."

He may have been abrasive and standoffish with everyone else, but the fact that he had a soft spot reserved only for me melted my heart.

"I know you can love me properly. I just need you to believe it yourself."

He stared at me for a moment. "If you believe in me, that's all I need."

His lips crashed into mine and I expected his kiss to be bruising, but it was a stark contrast. His mouth was soft and gentle as he began his slow, torturous assault on my soul. They moved against my own lips with such a tenderness, it threatened to shatter me into a million pieces right then and there. A mixture of emotions and memories flooded me as he kissed me like he had once before.

"You're everything, Winter," he breathed as he thrust into me once more. "Fucking everything."

My lips parted as his tongue slid along the seam of my mouth. I sighed and he swallowed the sound as his tongue moved with mine. He was drawing my soul from my body, draining the oxygen from my lungs. He was devouring me in the softest, most tender manner possible.

Abruptly, he pulled away, his hand cupping the side of my face as he rested his forehead against mine. "Winter, Winter, Winter..." His breath was warm as it skated across my face. "The things you do to me."

A ragged breath escaped me as I struggled to regain composure. He had crawled back inside my heart, where he once resided. Malakai Barclay was finally home.

"I'm going to take you home now." He whispered the words softly as he lifted his lips to my forehead. They were soft against my skin and my eyes closed as I breathed him in. "I want to be a gentleman tonight but I make no promises for behaving that way in the future."

"What if I don't want you to be a gentleman?" I challenged him as he released me and moved back into his seat.

One corner of his lips lifted and he shook his head. "My sincerest apologies, darling. You may be the one who possesses me. You may be the one who has the ability to blur the thoughts in my brain. I'm asking you to please let me have some self-control and take you home."

His tone was light but as he continued, he grew tense. I cocked my head to the side as he put his car in reverse without another word and backed out onto the road. He shifted back into drive and we began the short drive back to my house.

"What are you so afraid of?"

Kai was silent as he punched in the code and we watched the gates open. Silence enveloped us and I was internally conflicted. I didn't want to push him. I wanted to respect his wishes, yet I felt like I was at a loss. It was as if we took a leap forward, only to be suspended in air by some unspoken fear.

He put his car in park as he pulled up in front of my house and left the engine running as he climbed out. I sat with my hands in my lap as he walked over and opened the door for me. His hand was warm and soft as he held it out for me and I slid mine into his while he helped me out of the car. Kai didn't let go and his fingers were laced within mine as we got to the porch.

I paused, suddenly feeling anxious under his gaze. It was unreadable and my eyes bounced back and forth between his as I tried to pinpoint the emotion he was feeling.

"I'm afraid of doing this wrong, Winter. I'm afraid of messing this up."

Minutes had passed from when I asked him what he was afraid of to him finally formulating a response. It caught me off guard and I closed the distance between us as I stepped closer to him. Instinctively, I pressed my free hand against his chest, resting it just over his heart.

"None of this will be easy, but I believe in you. I believe in us."

He released my hand and brought them both up to cup the sides of my face. "I will prove to you that I am worthy of your love, even if I don't truly believe I am." He paused for a moment, his lips gently pressing against mine before he pulled away slightly. "I will spend the rest of my life earning your forgiveness."

I tilted my head to the side ever so slightly. "You don't have to earn that, Kai. I chose to forgive you because we have both suffered enough from our choices in the past. I'm choosing for things to be different."

Kai's eyes slid back and forth between mine once before his mouth was back on mine. There was nothing gentle about the way he kissed me now. There was urgency, need, and desperation behind his movements. It felt as though he was going to burrow himself deep inside my skin. I would have gladly given him every single piece of me. Whatever he wanted, I was his for the taking.

I was so lost in him, in the moment between us. His hands were in my hair, mine were clutching his shoulders. He was kissing me senseless, devouring me with his lips. His tongue slid against mine, tangling together in their own dance. Kai was consuming me and I was quite certain I would drown in him without a moment's hesitation.

Abruptly, he pulled away, leaving both of us breathless as we came up for air. "I need to go, Winter." His voice was hoarse and rough.

"Come inside with me," I said breathlessly.

He let out a sharp breath. "Let me do this right, please?"

I pulled back, just enough to look into his eyes. There was a mixture of torment and lust burning brightly inside his irises. His jaw was set and his fingers dug into my skin. He wanted me—that much was clear—but I had to let him do this his way.

"Good night, Kai," I said as I lifted myself on my tiptoes and pressed my lips to his in a soft kiss. As I moved away, it looked like he was at war with himself internally. He didn't say another word as he watched me disappear into the house.

Shutting the door behind me, I pressed my back against it and brought my fingers to my lips as I slowly slid down onto the floor. I couldn't fight the smile as I replayed the night in my mind. I didn't want to get my hopes up because if you had hope, you had something to lose.

And I had something to lose now…

CHAPTER TWENTY-ONE
MALAKAI

As I waited outside the clubhouse, I saw Nico pull into the parking lot. I was loading my bag and arranging my clubs as he came walking over to the cart. He texted me yesterday evening after my date with Winter and asked if I wanted to golf today. I was trying to be a little more of a people person, even though I didn't particularly care to be around anyone but Winter.

I knew I needed to put some type of distance between the two of us. There was an intensity between us that was completely unmatched. It was consuming and threatened to suck us into its dark depths. It wasn't something I wanted to fight against, but I also didn't want it to be too much, too soon for her.

I would gladly be sucked into its depths with no way of ever seeing the light again, as long as it meant I had her by my side.

Winter was the one who needed time. I needed her

to know I had good intentions behind what I was doing and I wasn't going to be pushing her away again.

Nico brought one of his friends that he played hockey with along with him today. Weston Cole. I was only familiar with who he was from hearing about him or seeing different hockey highlights on TV. I had never met him in person before, so I wasn't too sure about him, but Nico had insisted he was cool and we would get along.

Nico was obviously lying to himself. He knew I didn't really get along with anyone.

"You're here early," Nico said as they both walked over to me. They were both wearing khaki golf shorts. Nico had a black polo shirt on and Wes was wearing a white one. "This is Wes. Wes, this is Kai."

"Nice to meet you, man," he said as he held his hand out for me to shake. I fought the urge to flare my nostrils and instead shook his hand.

"Nice to meet you too." I spoke the words with a pleasant tone, although I wasn't sure I really meant them. I didn't need any more people in my life. I wasn't in the market for new friends, but this was Nico's friend. And I supposed that was part of being a good friend. I would never tell him he couldn't bring someone along unless I absolutely loathed them.

Nico excused himself as he went to pay their fees and grab a cart. Wes tucked his hands into his front pockets as he stared at me for a moment. "It's a beautiful day today," he said as he tilted his head back and looked up at the sky. "Have you been golfing a lot lately? Nico mentioned you were taking a break from your tour."

I lifted my gaze to his and narrowed my eyes in warning. He couldn't see it past my sunglasses and he was too busy looking up at the bright white clouds in the sky above us instead. "I haven't been out as much as I should be."

Wes looked back at me and shifted his head to the side. "Hey," he shrugged, "sometimes we need time off to find our passion for it again."

His words struck a chord of curiosity inside of me. I wasn't usually one to add to a conversation unless it was needed, but I felt compelled to ask him. "Are you speaking from experience?"

Wes nodded. "I had a bit of a dry spell while I was in college. I was still adjusting to the competitiveness of it and I really got in my head about it." He stopped for a second and adjusted his hat on his head. "I ended up taking a little bit of time off to work on my shot and figure out why the hell I even wanted to play hockey anymore."

"Did it work?"

His lips parted as he smiled and nodded. "It did."

"Hmm."

Nico whipped the golf cart out of the spot it was in and stopped in front of us for a moment. "This is interesting. It's not often you see Kai actually engaging in conversations."

I glared at him and Wes laughed. "Leave him alone, bro," he said as he hopped onto the golf cart with Nico. "We'll meet you at the first tee."

I nodded and the two of them drove over to Nico's car so they could grab their bags and other things for our round. Turning my attention back to my bag, I finished what I was doing and drove my own golf cart over to the first tee to wait for them. The sun was hot already, even though it was still early in the morning. The Florida summers were brutal, but after traveling like I did, I welcomed the familiarity of the suffocating air.

Nico and Wes weren't far behind me and they grabbed their drivers and tees before walking over to where I was standing. We each took our turn and made it through the first few holes before Nico decided it was time to start interrogating me.

"So, did you get Winter's number so you could stop showing up at the library like her own personal stalker?"

I cut my eyes to him as I took a sip of my Gatorade and set it back down. "Yes. I went to the library to see her and she gave it to me then."

"No shit," he said with a smile and a look of surprise. "When did you do that? Have you seen her since?"

I nodded. "I went that day after we were done golfing. We had dinner last night."

Wes looked between me and Nico with curiosity. "Who's Winter?"

"The love of Kai's life that he's trying to get back," Nico explained to Wes before turning his attention back to me. "How did last night go?"

"It went well," I told him with a shrug. It wasn't

entirely a lie. There was a bit of a rocky start and I did walk away from her when she wanted me to come inside with her. Other than that, I wasn't lying. "We just went and had dinner and then I dropped her back off at her place."

Nico widened his eyes. "You didn't even go inside?"

"No," I muttered as I raised an eyebrow. "Some of us are able to exercise self-control."

"I mean, I'm just saying I'm a little surprised," he admitted with a smirk playing on his lips. "With the history the two of you have, I thought for sure you wouldn't leave her for the night."

"We did things a little backward," I explained and instantly regretted it when I saw the curious look on his face and Wes's. Wes didn't even fully know what we were talking about but he was invested.

I was the last one who needed to shoot and I did it quickly, watching my ball land on the green. Nico wasn't going to let that comment go, but I could avoid him and buy myself approximately sixty seconds before he would be fishing for an answer.

My strides were long as I made my way back to my golf cart and drove over to the green. I hopped off and grabbed my putter. There was a nervousness that settled in my hands as I gripped it between them. I wasn't playing my best in terms of putting today, but it was definitely better than it had been, which gave me a small ounce of confidence. Maybe I wasn't destined for failure.

Perhaps there was hope in my life in more aspects than one.

It felt surreal and almost as if it were a dream. Even though I had made it to a professional level with golf, that didn't mean anything came easy to me in life. I lived with a glass-half-empty mentality. It was only a matter of time before things went to shit and before the other shoe dropped. It didn't take much for things to blow up in your face and then you were left to sift through the rubble.

Wes and Nico walked over to the green and Wes stepped over to lift the pin from the hole for me to make my putt. No one spoke a word as I focused on where I needed the ball to go and made my shot. I read the green appropriately and I watched as the ball sank into the hole.

My eyes widened and I quickly washed away the look of shock. It was a seamless move and it was the first of the day. The first in such a long time. I don't know how it happened, but it was something I needed to continue to replicate. I needed to get back into a consistent groove to prove to myself I could do this. I could play professionally and handle the pressure that came along with it.

"Nice shot, Kai," Nico said from where he was standing behind me. "Are you going to elaborate on what you meant by you guys doing things backward?"

I walked over to the hole and bent down to get my ball before taking the pin from Wes. I turned to look at Nico as he was lining up his own shot. Typically, we wouldn't talk when someone was trying to focus, but I wasn't particularly amused with him.

"Exactly what I said. We ran into each other, we

ended up sleeping together, and now she's actually giving me a chance."

Wes nodded in understanding. "You're playing the long game, so you're pulling back now."

"Not necessarily pulling back. Just slowing things down a bit."

Nico lifted his gaze to look at me. "I get why you're doing it," he said with the same understanding Wes had. "You fucked up before and you don't want to fuck it up again."

"Precisely."

My phone vibrated in my pocket, drawing my attention from the guys. Nico took two putts to get his ball in the hole and he took the pin from me as I pulled my phone out and stepped away from them. A sigh escaped me as I saw my mother's name on the screen.

"Hello, Mother."

"Malakai," she spoke softly and clearly. It was early in the morning still, so she either hadn't started drinking yet or she was only on her first mimosa of the day. "I was wondering if you would like to get lunch today."

I was thankful she remembered that I told her I did not care to come back to see her at her home. "Would you be available for a late lunch—perhaps around two? I'm in the middle of a round right now."

"Yes, yes, of course," she said with more enthusiasm than I expected. "There's a small coffee shop in town called Tourmaline. Would you be interested in meeting me there?"

"That would be fine."

"Perfect. I will see you then," she responded before ending the call.

My shoulders sagged slightly as a defeated sigh escaped me. I didn't have a clue as to why she would want to see me, but I would find out in a few short hours. The guys were waiting for me as I walked back over and I could tell Nico wanted to ask.

"Shall we continue then?" he asked instead which took me by surprise.

I nodded as I climbed back onto my cart. "Absolutely."

———

"It's so good to see you again, Malakai," my mother said quietly as she sat across from me. "How have you been since I last saw you?"

I stared back at her as I took a sip of my drink. "I've been well. How have you been?"

"Oh, we're not here to talk about me," she replied with a wave of her hand. "I feel like I don't even know what is going on in my son's life and it makes me feel like a terrible mother."

My expression was blank, yet I could feel her words hit my chest. I had put enough distance between myself and my family, so I was partially to blame for her not knowing what was going on. At the same time, if she really cared, she could ask me. She could find out.

There were times in your life where you had to make the choice to cut the toxicity out of your life. I didn't cut them out, but I reduced it by avoiding my parents.

"What do you want to know?"

She didn't order any food even though she asked me here for lunch. As I studied her face, I noticed the tiredness that had settled in her eyes. She was growing older and I could see past the Botox and filler. The years of being Winston Barclay's wife was taking its toll on her.

"Well, considering the fact that you're taking a break from golf, I presume that isn't going well."

My throat bobbed. "Just a bit of a rough spot I'm working through."

She nodded as her eyes trained on mine. Even as she watched me, I noticed the vacancy in them. The way she looked at me, but it wasn't like she was actually seeing me. She was lost—somewhere far from here.

"Are you seeing anyone?"

My jaw ticked and I pushed my plate before carefully folding my hands on the table. I had ordered a sandwich, but I had yet to eat any of it. I couldn't be honest with her without fearing she would tell my father. He hated the Reigns. The last thing I needed to do was to add fuel to his raging fire. If he knew about Winter and I, he wouldn't be happy.

But then again, I never cared much about his happiness.

"I am."

Her eyes widened. "You are?"

"Yes," I nodded with my tone clipped.

"Who is it? Do I know her?" There was a touch of

hopefulness in her voice and I couldn't help but feel a stinging sensation in my heart.

I fell silent for a moment as I chose my words carefully. "I would rather not say. Things are new between us and until it's a sure thing, I would rather keep it private."

My mother winced as if I had struck her. There was nothing vicious in her expression, instead it was pained and there was a touch of disappointment crinkling the skin around her eyes. "Where did I go wrong with you, Malakai?"

"Pardon?"

She frowned. "You were never an affectionate kid, but you had a kind, gentle soul. As you got older, you grew colder and distant. Sometimes I can't help but feel like you're a stranger."

I stared at her for a moment as I tried to conceal the disbelief that flooded me. She was always the one who shielded herself from the happenings around her. I didn't believe her to be that delusional, however. I thought she knew what was going on and just chose to ignore it. The way she spoke, it was as if she was really that detached from reality, from the horrors her husband put me through.

I was at a loss for words. Even though I wanted to lay it all out for her, I knew her mind was doing it to protect her. What kind of person did it make her to stay with a man who took advantage of her and was a monster to her child for that many years? Bringing any of it up wouldn't help matters.

"I'm sorry you feel that way," I told her with my voice low.

She dropped her gaze down to the coffee in front of her. "As am I."

There was a heaviness that settled between us and it felt awkward and unnatural. I felt uncomfortable sitting across from her. I watched her for a moment as she pulled her phone out of her purse and looked at it.

It didn't take long before she began to ramble about the next charity event she was working. I watched her intently as she began to explain the logistics of it, but I wasn't fully listening to her. I had tuned her out.

She was right. We were merely strangers in this life now.

And this wasn't where I belonged.

My mother's phone rang and she excused herself, claiming she needed to take the call. I assured her it was fine as I pulled out my own and went directly to my messages. I tapped on Winter's name without any hesitation.

MALAKAI

May I see you tonight?

There was no way that giving her any space was going to work.

Not when she was where I belonged.

CHAPTER TWENTY-TWO
WINTER

As I sat at my desk at the library, I glanced around and surveyed the area. It was a quiet day and not many people had been there. There were a few college students sitting at different tables, but other than that, the place was relatively empty. I had already put the returned books away and there wasn't much left for me to do.

My mind played back over the previous night with Kai as I pulled my laptop from my bag that was tucked under my desk. I sat it down in front of me and felt as if I was metaphorically brushing a layer of dust from the top of it.

It had been many months since I opened the document that held the manuscript I was too afraid to touch. I never gave it a title and I never bothered to try and plot a story. It was more so just a series of different scenes that was me bleeding my feelings out onto the keyboard.

It was a tragic love story, but it was one I planned on

giving a happy ending to. When I first started writing it, I was in a bad place mentally. My thoughts kept circling back to Kai and I couldn't help but make the story parallel to our own. At the time, I didn't see how there could possibly be an ending that was happy, so I had closed my laptop and tucked the manuscript away.

But now, I felt a different source of inspiration. It was one that didn't come from a place of longing and heartbreak. Instead, it was as if I were seeing things from a different light, a new perspective. Perhaps even the most tragic of stories could have a happy ending.

My stomach rolled with anxiety as I opened up the document and my eyes began to scan over the words. There was so much heartbreak and pain woven within every sentence I had crafted. A part of me wanted to deconstruct it all and make it a little lighter, but I knew I couldn't. Not when that was what I was feeling from my heart at the time.

With my history of working in publishing and reading and editing hundreds of raw manuscripts, I knew what I was sitting on wasn't garbage. This story was something I could work with. It was a masterpiece in its roughest stages.

It was the story of us.

Suddenly, the screen of my laptop began to move toward the keyboard as it was closing on its own. My eyes flew up and my breath caught in my throat as I saw someone was on the other side of the desk pushing it closed. Giana Cirone. A friend I had shut out many years ago when I left Orchid City. Someone I had left behind because of her connection to Malakai.

She looked down at me with a soft smile on her face and I moved back as she closed the laptop completely. I lifted my hand to wave at her as I felt a bit shocked to see her.

"*Hey, stranger,*" she signed to me with a mischievous smile.

I smiled back at her, feeling a twinge of guilt in my chest. "*Giana,*" I signed back, even though I knew she would be able to read my lips. I learned sign language when we were kids so I would be able to talk to her then. "*How are you?*"

"*I'm good. Really good, actually. I just moved back here last month and I heard from my brother and Malakai that you were back in town too.*"

My eyebrows pulled together. "*Did Kai tell your brother?*"

She nodded and rolled her eyes. "*Even after all these years and Malakai being the way he is, my brother still has a soft spot in his heart for him.*"

I laughed softly and shook my head. "*Nico always did.*" I stopped signing for a moment as the laughter vanished and my eyes softened. "*I'm sorry I didn't really keep in contact with you or let you know I was home.*"

Giana held her hand out to stop me. "*Nope. I'm not here for apologies or anything like that. I was hoping we could just pick up where we left off, like none of that ever happened.*"

Her words caught me by surprise and I careened my head to the side. "*Why? I essentially ghosted you after I moved away. Why would you still want to be friends after that?*"

"Because I know what you were going through, Winter. You don't owe me any explanations. Do I wish we wouldn't have lost contact that whole time? Absolutely. But I'm also not going to hold that against you. I'm not going to let that stop us from having a friendship now."

Perhaps this was how Kai felt with me. I didn't feel as though I deserved her forgiveness or for her to even want to try and have a friendship with me now. She was the one who reached out to me over the years and tried to maintain our friendship; I was the one who gave her short answers and avoided seeing her.

Her brother was Kai's best friend. My mind couldn't help but group the three of them together. Anything that had to do with Nico or Giana sent my mind spiraling back to Malakai Barclay. They were a part of my life because we grew up in the same area, but it was Nico and Kai being friends that brought Giana into my life.

"If you don't want to be friends anymore, I completely understand," she signed to me as a look of understanding washed over her eyes. *"I didn't mean to come on strong. I just wanted you to know that I don't care about what has happened in the past."*

Giana had dealt with a lot in life. Being deaf proved to be a challenge with some people who just weren't understanding of it. She was used to people leaving and the rejection. And that broke my damn heart.

I shook my head at her before signing my response. *"Of course I want to be friends with you. I know I wasn't a good friend in the past and I really do apologize for that. I should have handled things differently—better."*

"We're not apologizing, Winter." She smiled at me. *"We're going to let bygones be bygones and move on. Does that sound good to you?"*

My smile matched hers. *"That sounds perfect to me."*

"Great," she signed back to me. *"So, I don't want to bother you while you're working. Did you want to get dinner and we can catch up on all the things?"*

My phone vibrated from beside me on the desk and I saw Malakai's name on the screen. I stared at it for a moment before looking back to Giana. *"Yes, of course. Let's meet at Donovan's Kitchen at five-thirty?"*

"I'll see you then," Giana signed back to me before she turned around to leave me to my work. I watched her as she disappeared through the front door, feeling a sense of peace wrapping its arms around me.

I was beginning to think that maybe coming back here wasn't as bad as I thought it was going to be.

Picking up my phone, I opened up the message from Kai, a smile pulling on my lips as my eyes scanned his message.

MALAKAI

May I see you tonight?

WINTER

I'm meeting Giana for dinner at 5:30. Did you want me to let you know when I'm leaving and you can meet me back at my house?

Three bubbles popped up instantly as he wasted no time in responding.

MALAKAI

Yes, please. Let me know when you're
ready for me and I will be there.

A smile was still situated on my lips and I read over
his message again. It was hard to pick up on a tone
when you read a text message from anyone, but Kai
was even harder. He was hard to read in person and his
text messages always came across even more
emotionless.

There was something behind his random text that
had me wondering if something happened to spark
this. It wasn't urgent that he needed to see me immediately, but we just went out for dinner last night. He said
he wanted to take things slow, so it seemed a little
contradictory that he wanted to see me again tonight.

However, I was not going to question it.

We had a lot of time we needed to make up.

WINTER

I will let you know.

MALAKAI

I look forward to hearing from you.

Part of me wanted to roll my eyes at how formal he
was, but I knew to expect that with Kai. He was just
wired a little differently than most people. It was hard
for him to show weakness and vulnerability, and he
most definitely wasn't going to do that through text
messages.

Locking the screen of my phone, I set it back down

and opened my laptop again. I wasn't sure where I was going with this story. I wasn't sure where my own story was even going, but it was time I figured it all out.

———

Donovan's Kitchen was a small yet popular restaurant in town. It was a farm-to-table one and they always had the best dishes. They changed their menus with the season and since it was summer, they were known for having some of the best fish. Giana was able to get us a reservation online and she was already seated at the table waiting for me with a glass of wine.

She smiled at me in greeting as I took a seat across from her. There was a glass of white wine sitting by my spot and I lifted the glass and took a sip as Giana raised hers and did the same.

"How was the rest of your day?" she signed to me after sitting her glass back down. *"You don't have to sign if you don't want to. I do appreciate it, but I can read your lips too."*

"It was good," I told her, keeping my voice quiet. That was one thing I had noticed a lot of people did when they tried to talk to her. As soon as they found out she was deaf, they would raise their voices like it made a difference. And they would talk slowly like she was stupid. It was insulting and I would never ever do that to my friend.

I enjoyed signing because that was the way she communicated. I was also thankful she told me just to talk because that was always easier for me too.

"It wasn't very busy, so the day kind of dragged on but then it was suddenly over. It was weird."

Giana nodded. *"My day was about the same. I was on my lunch break when I stopped by and when I got back to the rehabilitation center, there wasn't much to do out of the ordinary."*

"What rescue are you working at?" I asked her. "What are you doing there?"

"I work at Orchid City Marine Research and Rehabilitation Center. We work with various different marine animals and work on rehabilitation. I got a degree in marine biology and after interning at a rehabilitation clinic in Tampa, I knew that was what I wanted to do."

Giana had a smile on her face the entire time she signed back to me. It was clear this was her passion, but I always knew that about her. She volunteered all the time when we were in high school. She used to go out when they organized events to help turtle hatchlings get to the ocean. And she always had one of the kindest souls I'd ever encountered.

"That sounds amazing and like such a rewarding job," I told her as my smile matched hers. "It's perfect for you and something you've always wanted to do."

She nodded. We paused our conversation as we gave our server our order, then Giana directed her attention back to me. *"What about you? I know you're working as a librarian and books have always been your life."*

I laughed softly and nodded. "I got a degree in English literature and I was working at a publishing house as a junior editor before moving here. I wasn't sure what I was going to do but the library was in need of a new librarian and it fit what I was looking for, for now."

"Have you ever considered trying to write yourself? I remember you used to talk about how you wanted to be an author, but I wasn't sure if you ever did anything with that."

"I tried and kind of gave up. The stuff with Kai had messed with my head and everything I wrote hurt." I stopped for a second and shrugged. "I've been considering trying again."

Mischief danced in Giana's eyes and she lifted an eyebrow at me. *"That wouldn't have anything to do with the two of you being around each other again, would it?"*

I narrowed my eyes on her. "What makes you think we're around each other at all?"

"I have my ways," she signed and winked. *"What's going on with you both?"*

"We're taking things slow and going to see where it goes."

She stared at me for a moment. *"So, you've forgiven him then?"*

I nodded. "Holding on to it wasn't good for anyone. I lived long enough with that hate and bitterness. You know how Kai is. There's a lot more to him than everyone sees. He's been fighting his own demons for years and I think he pushed me away because he thought he was saving me from himself."

"Just promise me you'll be careful with him this time." Giana stared back at me with such intensity and concern. *"I don't want to see him hurt you again."*

"I know," I whispered as a sigh escaped me. "I'm not sure I would survive another heartbreak from him."

"He's got a lot of baggage, Winter. He's not exactly the most pleasant person either." She took a sip of her wine before continuing to sign. "I can't help but worry about you getting involved with him. What if he's no different than he was before? Malakai always had a lot of issues."

"I'll be okay, Giana," I told her with a forced smile. "I know what I'm doing with him."

She gave me a reluctant look but nodded. "I hope so."

There it was again. Hope. The one thing I knew I shouldn't have when it came to Malakai Barclay.

Yet it was the one thing I was desperately clinging to.

CHAPTER TWENTY-THREE
MALAKAI

Past

Crouching down, I looked across the green from my ball to the hole. All I had to do was make this last putt and the championship was mine. I was already leading by at least six points, but I couldn't mess up this last shot. It would just look bad and poorly executed on my part.

I stood back up, lined up my putter at the exact angle I felt would be appropriate, and pulled back on the club. It lightly met the ball with a firm, yet soft tap and I watched as it rolled across the green before sinking into the hole. A sense of satisfaction filled me, yet it was mundane.

I loved golf, I loved the sport and everything that came with it, but as I glanced out at the crowd, it all fell short. My mother was standing and talking with a few of her friends and I saw the back of my father's broad shoulders as he stalked away. The one person I wanted to see wasn't here.

Her parents forbid her from seeing me, so it was no surprise she wasn't here. That didn't mean there wasn't a part of me that wished to have her constantly by my side. Winter Reign was the only person who had ever mattered to me on this godforsaken planet.

The tournament had officially come to an end and after everyone had finished their final round, we met back at the clubhouse for the awards ceremony. I was completely detached as I was handed my trophy and forced out a rehearsed thank-you to the organizers as I received it from them.

My mother watched from afar, but there was a glossed, distant look in her eyes. It was one I had grown accustomed to. As I approached her, I looked over her shoulder for my father. He was nowhere to be found. His disinterest used to bother me. When I was growing up, I watched the other kids at tournaments as their families surrounded them and showered them with congratulatory celebrations and love. I used to wonder why I never received the same.

Now, I no longer cared.

My father congratulated me with his fists. I could do without any form of celebration or recognition. I would have rather had the bunker turn to quicksand and to have it pull me beneath the surface.

"You did exceptionally well, Malakai," my mother beamed at me as I walked over to her. She tipped back her glass of wine, draining it in one sip. "Your father had to leave early, but he is requesting our presence at DeLuca for dinner this evening."

I shook my head at her. There would be no dinner tonight. I was done subjecting myself to the ridicule of a man who played beneath me. My father golfed solely for business reasons. He prided himself in having a son with my talent, but when his friends weren't around, he rained down on me like hellfire.

I could get a hole in one on every single hole and it still wouldn't be enough for him. He would still find something to criticize or bring to my attention that I wasn't doing well. And even though I played a higher level of golf than him, I still let him plague my mind with the vile things he spoke.

"I won't be attending dinner tonight."

My mother narrowed her eyes slightly. She was challenging me and her lips parted as she was about to scold me for my disobedience. Instead, a sigh of defeat escaped her and her facial expression softened.

"Why must you do this, Malakai?" There was a mixture of disappointment and resignation in her tone. "Life would be much easier for you if you would just comply. You cause him great displeasure with your defiance."

I stared at her in disbelief. "What would complying look like? I've always caused him displeasure, even as a child."

I would never admit it to her, but I always wanted to know why he hated me the way he did. There was nothing that stood out in the forefront of my mind that I did to deserve the anger he directed at me.

A few years ago, I had caught him in a vulnerable moment. It wasn't often that he indulged in enough alcohol to get drunk, but for whatever reason he was wasted that night. He didn't lay a hand on me that night, but instead, he stood in the kitchen across from me with utter disdain in his eyes.

"You were never supposed to exist. And most certainly not in the capacity that you are."

I never knew what he really meant by that and I never dared to ask.

One thing was certain—I had carried those words with me since that night.

My mother sighed again, pulling me from my memory. "I don't know, Malakai. Your father had expectations for you to be like him. For you to follow in his footsteps so he could pass on his legacy." She frowned with a touch of sadness. "You've always been the furthest thing from him, forging your own path instead of the one he laid out for you."

I raised an eyebrow at her. "You say that like it's a bad thing."

She shook her head. "Not bad, just problematic."

I watched her as she glanced around the room, almost as if she were expecting him to appear out of thin air. Or perhaps she was looking for a way to end the conversation between us. Either way, she appeared to be uneasy with growing discomfort. She was never one to fully talk down upon me the way he had, but hearing the truth from her was a harder blow than I anticipated.

At this point in my life, I had grown so immune but

every so often there was a crack in my armor. Just a sliver—big enough to allow words to penetrate and the emotion to seep out. I quickly pushed her words from my mind, choosing to pretend they were never spoken out loud.

"Where shall I tell your father you went?"

I shrugged with indifference. "I'm sure you can formulate some believable lies. It's what we've all been programmed to do, isn't it?"

Her eyes widened and she stared at me before she recovered from the momentary shock. "We do what we must to survive, Malakai. We fall in line and assume our role. Try not to think of them as lies, but more so a necessary tactic."

"I applaud you for being the master of charades," I told her with cruelty in my tone and venom on my tongue. It wasn't often that I spoke to my mother in such a manner, but I was only able to maintain composure for so long before the volcano of anger erupted. "I, however, refuse to be his puppet. This game isn't one I care to partake in."

My mother frowned. "It would be a lot easier if you would, Malakai."

I was growing tired of this conversation and the way we were going in circles. There would never be any middle ground. My mother and I would never see eye to eye on the matter, not as long as she was under his finger. I was wasting my breath and precious time with her.

"Enjoy the rest of your evening, Mother," I said to her as I nodded before departing. She didn't offer me any words as I turned my back to her and strode away. The trophy in my hand felt heavy, as if it were weighing me down. I wanted to throw it into the waste can. I didn't feel deserving of anything good in that moment.

I didn't feel deserving in most moments.

———

I had to wait until after nightfall before I could climb up to Winter's window. She had left it cracked open for me and I lingered just outside for a moment as I watched her through the glass. She was curled up on her bed with the blankets pulled up to her chest. Her dark hair was pulled up on the top of her head in a messy bun and I watched as her eyes scanned the pages of the novel in her hands.

A pained smile pulled on my lips. I would never deserve her.

If I weren't selfish, I would have climbed down from the roof and gone back to my car parked down the street. I would have left Winter Reign alone for good. I would have slipped out of her life without a second thought or glance.

Unfortunately, I never claimed to be selfless.

Winter lifted her gaze to mine as I slid the window open and climbed inside. There was a softness in her green irises and peace settled in her expression as she slid her bookmark between the pages.

I pushed the window shut and stepped deeper into the room. "Don't stop on my account."

"Nonsense," she replied in a hushed voice as she

sat up in bed. "I was only reading to pass the time. I was beginning to wonder if you weren't going to come."

I didn't bother answering her as I kicked off my shoes and stripped down to my boxers. Winter shifted on the mattress as she pulled the blankets back for me. Climbing onto the bed, I slipped beneath the sheets and closed the distance between us. My hands instinctively reached for her and my arms wrapped around her as I pulled her flush against me.

Her skin was soft, gliding like silk across mine as she slid her hand to my chest. Her head was resting against my shoulder, fitting perfectly in the crook of my arm. It was where she belonged; she was where I belonged.

Holding her felt like coming home.

"How did today go?"

I absentmindedly traced invisible patterns across her back. "It went as expected."

"Don't be coy, Kai. How did you place in the tournament?"

I smiled to myself at the sternness in her tone. "I won."

"And that was expected?" She lifted her head to look at me and raised an eyebrow. "I don't know how you manage to be cocky and modest in the same breath."

"It's an art, darling," I said with a smirk as I rolled her onto her back and settled between her thighs. Winter laughed softly as I nipped at her bottom lip. "And for the record, I wouldn't consider myself cocky.

I'm simply confident in my ability, among other things."

Winter wiggled beneath me as I trailed my lips down the column of her throat. "What else are you confident in?"

I was deliberately slow as my lips traveled down her torso. Pushing up her cotton tank top, I kissed my way down to her stomach while moving my body toward the end of the bed. My fingers slid beneath the waistband of her panties and I dragged them down her thighs, freeing them from her feet as my knees hit the floor.

"I'm confident in knowing every inch and every curve of your body. I'm confident in knowing how to give you the pleasure you desperately need." I hooked my arms underneath her thighs before pulling her across the mattress to me. "I'm confident that no one else can ever love you the way I do."

She lifted herself up onto her elbows, her eyes wide from my words as her gaze slammed into mine. I wanted to take them back, but I couldn't. There was no sense. One day she would know the truth, but it didn't matter either way. There would never be a right time for us.

I slid my tongue against her pussy before sucking her clit between my teeth. Distracting her with my mouth was the only way I could prevent her from questioning me on my admission.

"Kai," she moaned my name as her head tipped backward before she looked back at me with a mixture of emotions swirling in her heated green eyes.

"Shh," I breathed against her flesh before pulling back far enough for my eyes to meet hers. "Be quiet for me, darling. You don't want anyone to catch us, do you?"

She shook her head, falling silent as she folded her lips between her teeth. Moving my mouth back to her, she remained quiet as she collapsed back against the bed. My tongue moved against her, licking, sucking, and tasting her pleasure until she was withering on the mattress beneath my touch.

Winter's hands were around the side of my face, pulling me upward. I rose from my knees after discarding my boxers, climbing onto the bed above her before sinking deep inside her. Her legs were wrapped around my waist and her arms around my shoulders as I shifted my hips, slowly thrusting in and out of her.

"You know, you're not the only one who is confident," she murmured against my mouth as we moved against one another, caught in a tragic melody of our own.

I pulled back, just enough to meet her gaze. Her green eyes pierced my blue ones, spearing directly through me, straight into my heart.

"No one will ever love you the way I do either."

CHAPTER TWENTY-FOUR
WINTER

Present

It's late in the evening as I sit out on my front porch, waiting for Kai to show up. I let him know when I had finished dinner with Giana and he had responded, telling me he would be over soon. I couldn't help the nervousness that was encapsulating me as I stared out at the driveway.

With the shift in the dynamic between us, I wasn't sure what was appropriate. How was I supposed to act around him? Did I seem too eager if I was sitting outside waiting for him to show up? We were supposed to be taking things slowly, but this didn't feel slow… not that I was complaining.

Off in the distance, I heard the creaking of the wrought-iron gates opening. I needed to have someone inspect that and eradicate the dreadful sound. My spine straightened as I sat up in my seat with my hands folded carefully on my lap. I saw the headlights on

Malakai's car before I could actually see the vehicle in the darkness of the night.

His sports car was painted a matte black and the entire thing was blacked out. He blended in with the darkness, just as he always had.

The engine purred as he slowly pulled up in front of my house and put his car in park before turning it off. My breath was caught in my throat as my heart pounded erratically in my chest. I needed my body to calm down, yet it wouldn't. I hated him for having such a profound effect on me like this.

As he slipped out of his seat, the door closed softly behind him and he rounded the car with his jaw set. He looked so perfect and so beautiful it hurt. His stormy eyes shined under the soft light of the moon above while it illuminated his chiseled features. He was wearing a pair of black sweatpants, paired with a matching black sweatshirt and white sneakers.

He climbed the steps and stopped on the porch in front of me. "Hello, darling," he said softly. He leaned against the pillar along the railing and his gaze collided with mine. "How was dinner with Giana?"

"It went well," I told him with honesty as I relaxed in my seat. "How was your day?"

The conversation seemed so trivial, so mundane, yet it was what I craved to have with him. Some sense of normalcy rather than the whiplash I was used to.

"I golfed in the morning with Nico and then met my mother for lunch and a healthy dose of family drama."

He said it with such indifference, as if it were something everyone dealt with. Like it was just another day in the life of Malakai Barclay. My heart constricted at the thought. His childhood trauma was still so present in his life because he had yet to escape the demons he fought daily. Associating with his parents only made it worse.

He had mentioned before about being in therapy and seeing a therapist, but he never elaborated on that. There was a difference to Kai now, even though the struggle was still visibly apparent. He was more mature and a little more levelheaded, but if he was backed into a corner he would strike like a venomous serpent.

"What happened?" I questioned him, motioning for him to sit down on the bench next to me.

A sigh escaped him as he took a seat and lazily draped his arm across the back of the bench. I could feel the warmth of his body with how close he was, but we both stared out into the dark sky.

"Nothing new. She was just being nosy about my life, playing her part as the good mother." He paused for a moment. "Her loyalty has and will always lie with my father. It's as if she thinks I am the way I am because she went wrong somewhere in life, but she isn't fully open to admitting that she went wrong when she chose to stay with my father."

I turned my head to stare at the side of his face. "You know none of that is your fault, right? Your father is an evil man, but you never deserved the treatment you received from him."

Kai looked over at me with sadness warping his expression and a pained smile on his lips. "I know. I've been in therapy for years since I was able to get out from under my father's thumb. It's easier to discuss than it is to fully accept. I have a lot of years of damage I've been trying to reverse. It's quite a difficult task to retrain your brain."

"I know," I said softly as I reached out and placed my hand on his thigh. "I know your demons are relentless, but I know you can break through it all. You're not your father, Malakai."

He stared at me for a moment, the color slowly draining from his face. "What if you're wrong? What if I do end up exactly like him?"

I shook my head, lifting my hand to cup the side of his face. "You won't. You have a heart of gold, even if you appear to be made of cruelty and ice. It's all a facade. A defense mechanism you hide behind because you're afraid to let in the good and end up hurt."

"That's my biggest fear," he admitted, his voice barely audible as his eyelids slammed shut. "I'm terrified I'll be a replica of him."

"I promise you, you won't," I assured him, turning to face him completely as I held his head in my hands. "I know you, Kai. You are not him, and you never will be."

His eyelids lifted and there was nothing but pain and desperation in his stormy irises. "I don't know how to be softer and kind. Therapy has helped provide an explanation and a guide for how to deal with my trauma, but I don't know how to let myself feel properly."

A small smile pulled on my lips. "Let me show you how, my love." I rose from the bench and straddled

Malakai's lap before settling on his thighs. "Let me be your beacon of light in the darkness of your world."

He slid one hand around my lower back, pulling me flush against his body as his other hand snaked around the back of my neck, pulling my face down to his.

"That's all you've ever been."

He claimed my mouth with his own with desperation and urgency, fierce and hungry. I was the escape he needed. He wanted to lose himself in me and I clung to him with a severity that shook my soul. In a sense, we were equally as lost, but together, we were found.

Malakai lifted me off his lap as we momentarily broke apart. In one swift movement, he lifted me into his arms, my legs instinctively wrapping around his waist. He carried me inside the house without another word as I buried my face in the crook of his neck. His feet took us deep inside, up the winding staircase and down the hallway to my bedroom.

"That was impressive," I murmured. I lifted my head to look at him as he began to lower me down onto my bed. "You remembered which room was mine."

"Where you are concerned, darling, I will never forget," Kai murmured as he released his hold on me and rose from the bed. He watched me with hungry, tormented eyes. "I shouldn't be in your room right now."

He kissed me again, but I abruptly pulled back and pushed him away from me. I moved off the mattress, so I was standing directly in front of him as I began to strip until I was completely naked. His gaze was greedy as he drank me in. I watched him as his throat bobbed while he swallowed roughly.

"Winter," he growled, his voice hoarse and thick with need as he closed the distance between us. "This isn't us taking things slowly."

I stepped closer, sliding my hands beneath the bottom of his sweatshirt and the t-shirt underneath. "There is no slow for us, Malakai," I breathed as I began to push his shirt up his torso. He took over, removing his clothing before tossing them onto the floor. "It's always been all or nothing with us. We have too much history, too much fire."

"The fire between us smolders with an intensity greater than the sun," he said softly as he stripped down until he was bare in front of me. "If we go any slower, the flames will only flourish perversely. Burn with me, darling. Burn until we're nothing but ash."

I wrapped my arms around the back of his neck and spun us around until he was standing in my place. I began to guide him until he was laying back on the bed. My knees sank into the plush mattress as I followed him, climbing on top of him. Kai lifted me up with one hand as he grabbed his cock with the other, positioning it against me.

"Always, Kai," I said breathlessly as I sank down onto him, taking his full length in one movement. "If the sea of flames engulf you, I'll be right beside you incinerating."

His hands gripped my hips, lifting me up and down as I began to move on top of him. He stared back at me, his gaze penetrating my soul. There was nothing but three words hanging between us. Three words that would shatter the world around us if either of us dared to speak them.

But his eyes—his eyes said it all.

I love you. I love you. I love you.

CHAPTER TWENTY-FIVE
MALAKAI

Winter sat on the edge of her bed wearing my t-shirt as she stared out the window. Droplets of rain pelted against the glass and she was lost in her own thoughts. She didn't notice me as I watched her intently. She was the last thing I saw when I closed my eyes last night and the first thing I saw when I opened them this morning.

I wanted the rest of my days to follow in similar fashion.

There was a softness in her expression. My eyes trailed over her high cheekbones, down the straight slope of her nose, across her plump lips. She was absolute and utter perfection. She was so beautiful, it hurt. My chest constricted, tightening like a vise around my heart as I studied her. There was no one else like Winter Reign and I knew she was it for me.

I loved her from the first time she kissed the scars on my back and wiped the blood from my lip.

The rain slowed before coming to a stop and the

clouds in the sky parted as the sun came through. The light shined through Winter's bedroom window, illuminating her face. A soft smile played on her lips and her eyelids fell shut as she let the warmth seep into her skin.

What I would have given to read her thoughts, just this once. I wanted inside her mind and her heart and soul. I wanted all of her for myself.

Her phone vibrated on the nightstand and she reached for it, glancing at me at the same time. There was a sharp intake of breath and her eyes widened slightly as they slid to mine.

"You're awake," she breathed as she ignored her phone ringing.

I shifted on the mattress, rolling onto my back. "Good morning, darling."

Her phone started vibrating again and she let out an exasperated sigh. "It's my mother," she told me as she looked up from the screen. "I'm going to see what she wants and make some coffee."

I nodded, watching her as she rose from the bed. The hem of my t-shirt brushed against the tops of her thighs. "Take your time." Winter was just about to answer the call. "Wait. Do you have an extra charger anywhere?"

Winter pointed over to the desk on the opposite side of her room. "Check in my desk. There should be a spare in there." She smiled at me and answered the call on the last ring. I watched her as she disappeared from the room. Her voice carried through the hallway and I couldn't help but smile when I heard her mention my name. It wasn't my place to eavesdrop, but hearing her tell her mother that she was getting ready to make us coffee was a pivotal moment.

Her family had made their distaste for me clear when we were younger. I couldn't say I blamed them, considering my behavior and how they protected their image and their daughter. What they didn't know was how deep our connection ran. They didn't know how much I loved their daughter and how I had desperately tried to protect her from myself even though it only ended up hurting her in the end.

I was here to make things right with her, and it was only a matter of time before our families would find out. Personally, I didn't care about any of their opinions, but I imagined Winter did. Her family had stronger ties than my own. I had no problem writing mine off if they disagreed. They had already disagreed with my existence, so what was one more disappointment?

Winter and I hadn't had the chance to discuss any of this with one another. We hadn't truly defined anything, but it seemed like she had made her mind up. She was letting me back into her life and she wasn't going to be quiet about it this time.

Sitting up in her bed, I moved until my feet were on the floor and I rose from the mattress. She had stopped talking and the smell of fresh coffee was drifting through the house. I grabbed my pants from the floor and slipped them on before making my way over to Winter's desk. I pulled open the drawer on the left and didn't find a charging cord, so I moved to the one in the middle.

My eyes scanned the space for a cord, but they froze as they landed upon my name written in messy cursive writing. The entire page was filled with words and my stomach sank. My movements were hesitant as I picked up the piece of notebook paper and held it in front of my face. I slowly scanned it, noting the darkness of the ink, the way it stained the paper. Each stroke of every letter was laced with pain.

And I began to read it.

Malakai,

I don't know why I'm even writing this to you. You made it clear that you don't want me and if I'm being honest, I can't believe you. I don't want to believe you, but I'm afraid that I have to. I can't help but wonder what I did that was so wrong. Why would you leave me? After everything between us, everything we've gone through, you were supposed to always be by my side. I promised you that I would never leave and I broke that promise to you tonight. I should have stayed, I should have fought against you... but you were like a stranger. Someone that I didn't recognize—someone I didn't even know. The coldness that you kept hidden from me was all that was left of you tonight. Which is why I have no choice but to believe that you meant every single word you said to me. Why else would you say them? My brain hurts, my heart aches. Why, Kai? Why? I wish that you would have just told me that you didn't apply to Wyncote University. That doesn't even matter to me. There's always a way to make things work, but you didn't even give me the option. You made the choice for me. I told you that I hated you tonight, but I don't think I really meant it. I don't hate you. I hate this. I hate what you did to us. I've always loved you and I know that I always will, even if that makes me the most pathetic person to ever walk the planet.

I don't imagine you'll ever read this. I'm sure it will get tossed to the side, just like you did to me.

That was mean, but I'm not crossing it out. You broke me, Kai.

I don't know how I'm going to get over you. I don't know if I ever will.

This hurts.

So bad.

But even through the pain, I still love you.

I always will.

-Winter

My heart was in my throat as I returned the letter to where I found it. My search for a charger didn't even matter anymore. Her pain had become my pain and I needed to see her. I needed her to know how fucking sorry I was. There was nothing I could do to erase the past, but I would do everything in my power to make the future better.

As I entered the kitchen, she damn near took my breath away.

Her bright green eyes found mine and her lips parted slightly. Her dark hair hung in tousled waves with pieces framing her face. Thoughts flooded my mind of sliding my fingers through her silky locks as I was buried deep inside her. My cock twitched in my pants and Winter broke eye contact as she filled a mug with coffee for me.

"Do you want any cream and sugar?" she asked as I took it from her.

I shook my head and took a seat at the island while she poured her own cup. "No, thank you."

She turned back around to face me with an eyebrow raised. She didn't comment on the way I took my coffee, but I couldn't help but smile as she dumped a gracious amount of French vanilla-flavored creamer into her own. I studied the curiosity in her expression as she plunged a spoon into the warm liquid and began to stir.

"You told your mother I was here."

Winter stopped stirring. She lifted her eyes back to mine. "Was I not supposed to?"

"You're free to tell her or whomever what you wish." I lifted my mug to my lips, feeling the coffee scorch my esophagus as I took a sip. "I was simply surprised, is all."

"Why were you surprised?" she questioned me before taking a sip of her own drink.

I shrugged. "Your parents were pretty adamant on us not being together before. They weren't particularly quiet about their contempt for me."

She tipped her head to the side as she watched me for a moment. Her ceramic coffee mug clinked against the quartz counter as she set it down and walked around the side of the island. I turned my head and body, following her movements until she was standing at my knees.

"We're both consenting adults who can make our own decisions." She placed her hands on my thighs. "I don't care what they think, Malakai. You were never a choice for me, you were always my destiny." She lifted her hands to my face. "This was always inevitable."

My heart crawled into my throat. "Does this mean you are mine, Winter Reign?"

"I've always been yours, Kai."

My hands found her waist and I pulled her against me. "You have, haven't you?"

She smiled back at me and nodded. "You were just stubborn and tried to fight it."

"Well, it's a good thing I lost the battle." I stared into the swirling green hues of her eyes. Curiosity struck me and I couldn't help but feel a surge of anxiety. "What did your mother say?"

Winter's smile didn't falter. "She called to see how I had settled into the house. She had heard from her lawyer that the paperwork had been squared away and it had been a few weeks since we last talked on the phone since they were busy traveling." She paused for a moment. "We've talked through text but she wanted to check in on me and see how things actually were."

I pulled my lips between my teeth before releasing them with a soft pop. "As much as I appreciate the sentiment and you explaining what she called for, that's not what I'm asking about, darling."

"Oh, I know." Mischief danced in her eyes as she laughed quietly. "It's kind of fun to watch you be the one to squirm and sweat."

A soft chuckle rumbled in my chest as I abruptly rose to my feet and lifted Winter into the air. She let out a yelp as I turned us around and set her down on the counter. "I'm glad my distress is amusing you."

"Sorry." She laughed and shook her head as she slid her hands around the back of my neck. "She didn't seem fazed. She asked about you, about us, and said she was surprised this hadn't happened sooner."

Her words left me momentarily speechless. I was

frozen in place and my fingertips were digging into her hips. My eyes desperately search hers for clarity. "She was surprised?"

"I told you how she walked in on you sleeping in my bed that one day." She let out a soft breath as she slid her fingers through my hair. "She knew there was no way to keep us apart and it was only a matter of time before the universe would be pulling us back together. This force between us, it's not something you can fight forever."

I swallowed roughly over the ball of emotion lodged in my throat. "I stopped fighting long ago, darling."

"Do you promise you won't push me away again?" There was hesitancy in her tone and a touch of panic. Her eyes were solely focused on mine. "I won't survive another heartbreak from you."

"I promise," I told her with nothing but conviction and truth. "I swear to you that I will never break your heart again, Winter. I wish I wouldn't have in the past, but I can't take that back now."

There was a touch of sadness in her eyes as her lips lifted again. "It's okay, Kai. We found each other again and that's all that matters. The past is what got us to where we are now."

I hated her words, but I craved her forgiveness. I would never be worthy of her, but I wanted to be.

"I found a letter in your desk."

I watched as shock settled within her features and her eyes widened slightly. Winter stared back at me, her lips parting as a nervous breath escaped her. "Did you read it?"

The sadness pulled me deep into its depths as I nodded. "I did."

"I was never going to send it to you." She paused for a moment, her voice dropping to a whisper. "I was so hurt, Kai. It was more to help me process what had happened that night."

I tilted my head to the side. "Why weren't you going to send it? I wish you would have. I would have given anything to read those words six years ago."

Confusion washed through her bright irises. "Because it wouldn't have made a difference."

My breath caught in my throat as her words sank in. She was right. It probably wouldn't have made a difference. I was set in my ways and convinced that pushing her away was what was best for her. Would a letter have changed that? Most likely not.

"Be honest with me," she said, breaking through my thoughts. "If I would have sent it, would you have read it?"

A muscle in my jaw flexed. "Probably not. Forcing you away was the hardest thing I ever did. I'm not sure I would have been able to look at it. I didn't need anything to sway the decision I made."

She stared at me. "The decision you made for both of us."

"The worst decision I've ever made." My nostrils flared and my chest expanded as I inhaled deeply. I slowly released the breath, staring down at the one who my heart truly belonged to. "I fucked up, Winter. I did take the choice away from you. I pushed you away, thinking it was the right thing, but all I did was cause so much pain between us. So many years apart that we can't get back now."

Winter's expression softened. Her eyes shifted between mine before settling on my gaze. I was lost in her eyes, lost in her essence. She slowly pulled my face down to hers and her lips brushed mine as she whispered against my skin.

"We just have a lot of lost time to make up for then."

CHAPTER TWENTY-SIX
WINTER

K ai was sitting up in the stands like he used to do when we were kids as I skated around the ice rink. There was something freeing about the way my ice skates slid across the surface. I was in my element, completely lost in the moment, yet in the back of my mind I couldn't help but remember that he was there watching my every move.

And every time I glanced over in his direction, I couldn't help but notice the smile on his lips. It was the one he had reserved for me and me only. Kai was never a warm and welcoming person to others, but he was different with me.

He always was.

When we were in high school, he would drive me to my practices and sit in the freezing building while he watched me the entire time. I knew he didn't care about figure skating and would have rather been on a golf course instead, yet still, he stayed.

As the freestyle time was coming to an end, I made

my way over to the boards and I saw Kai as he was descending from the loft area where spectators could sit. He met me at the door with his smile illuminating his face. It reached his eyes, revealing the dimples in his cheeks.

"You looked devastatingly beautiful out there," he said as his arms encircled my waist. "I always loved watching you skate."

I laced my hands behind his neck, pulling his face down to mine. "You came and watched me, so now it's my time to repay the favor."

Kai lifted an eyebrow. "There's no repayment needed. Watching you has always been my pleasure, darling."

Lifting on my toes, I pressed my lips to his before breaking apart. "You said you were having trouble putting and I want to help."

A look of confusion washed over his expression. "Winter... you hate golfing."

"I know, but I have an idea," I said as I stepped out of his reach. His hand quickly found mine as we walked over to a bench and I sat down to untie my skates. Kai pushed my hands away as he reached for my ankle and lifted my foot to untie them himself. "I was thinking, if I came with you out on the course, maybe it would help to distract the thoughts that keep interrupting your mental space."

"I can't unsee you with another guy."

I rolled my eyes at him as he set my foot down, handed me my skate, and grabbed my other ankle. "So, see me instead. See me with you and not him."

His blue eyes met mine in a rush and he was silent for a moment. "Okay. At this point, nothing else has worked and I have nothing to lose. Let's try it."

Malakai set down my other foot and I dried off my skates before putting them back into my bag. I slid my feet back into my shoes and watched him as he was pulling out his phone.

"I'm going to call the country club and see if they have any tee times available today."

I nodded as I rose to my feet. "I just need to speak to the director of skating and then I'll be ready to go."

Kai reached out and grabbed my bag from me as he lifted his phone to his ear. "I'll meet you out front."

He turned and began to walk toward the exit as I made my way over to the front desk. Linda was out of her office so I left a message for her with an inquiry for more information on coaching. It wasn't something I was sure I would be able to dedicate a lot of time to, but if I could help give back to the rink that sculpted me into the skater I was, I wanted to do that.

―――――

Sitting in my seat on the golf cart, I watched Kai swing his golf club with such force, it made a cracking sound as it connected with the dimpled white ball. My lips parted and I stared down the fairway as his ball went soaring through the air. His talent always amazed me. He was designed to master this sport and with the way his muscles flexed and rippled with his movements, I had no problem watching him play.

He strode back to the cart with a ghost of a smile playing on his lips. "Did you want to hit one?"

A soft laugh escaped me and I shook my head. "I'm just here to watch."

"Enjoying the view?"

I smiled at him as he dropped into his seat. "Immensely."

"Excellent."

His hand was on my thigh, lightly tracing patterns as he drove through the grass to where his ball was. I watched again as he took another shot, landing it directly on the green a few yards from the hole. His jaw was tense as he climbed back onto the golf cart.

I followed him onto the green and walked over to the hole as I pulled the pin out and held it. I watched him carefully as he assessed the slope and angle with his jaw still clenched. He took a practice swing and lined up his shot. The muscles in his arms were tightened and the veins running up his forearms were on display.

He pulled back and then froze just before the ball. He squeezed his eyes shut, giving his head a vicious shake. I watched the turmoil and torment across his expression as he looked from his ball to the hole. This was the struggle he had been experiencing and I felt nothing but guilt for the way it was affecting him.

"Relax, Kai," I said softly. It was proper etiquette to remain silent as someone took a shot, but I couldn't stand here and watch him internally suffering. "Control your breathing and loosen your muscles."

His chest rose as his lungs expanded with the deep

breath he inhaled. He remained unmoving, still staring at the hole. His body had relaxed slightly, but his jaw was still clenched with determination.

"Malakai," I spoke a little louder, but my voice remained soft. "Look at me."

His gaze met mine in a rush and it felt like the oxygen was being ripped from my lungs. "Every time I go to hit it, I see your face and you laughing at something that imbecile said."

"I'm here with you, Kai. Not him. He doesn't exist in my life." I paused for a moment, swallowing back the emotion that welled in my throat. "You do. My world is caught in your orbit, circling around you. Forever consumed." I let out a breath.

He stared back at me with such intensity, it shook me to my core. I never felt more exposed in front of him in my life. I was bare, bones and flesh as he ripped open my rib cage and made his way back to the home he had made for himself in my heart.

"You *are* my life, Winter." Emotion brewed in the abysmal depths of his stormy eyes. "My existence is eternally obsolete without you."

I was forever lost to him. "You will never have to live in a world without me."

His eyes lingered on mine for a moment longer before he directed his attention back to his putter. He lined up his shot and took it. I held my breath, watching as anticipation fluttered in my stomach as the ball rolled across the green, coming directly toward me. It was a flawless shot and the ball sank into the hole with absolute precision and skill.

Kai's eyes widened and his feet were cemented to the ground as he stared at the hole in front of me. I exhaled, a smile lifting my lips. He tore his gaze away and it flashed to mine as he looked at me with pure shock.

"I can't remember the last time that happened," he said, his voice barely audible. He smiled at me. A full smile that reached his eyes that were filled with adoration. His dimples were out again. "It was because of you, Winter. God—it's always been you."

I leaned down and picked up his ball before putting the pin back in place. As I stood back up, I walked toward him and tossed the ball to him. "Come on," I smiled when I reached him and shifted onto my toes to kiss his soft lips. "Let's go do it again."

———

Kai finished the rest of the course, scoring better than he had in months. Every shot he made, his gaze met mine first and it was as if it helped him get out of his head. He focused on me, on the game in front of him. And he played flawlessly. He truly made it seem like it was easy with how effortless he looked.

We decided on dinner at the restaurant at the country club. My footsteps felt lighter as I stepped inside, feeling like I had just helped Kai conquer the world. He asked me to come in and get a table for us while he took his bag back to the car and he returned the golf cart. The restaurant was relatively busy, but I was able to get a table for us.

My back was facing the door and I was preoccupied with looking at the menu when he arrived. The seat across from me was pulled out and I lifted my gaze. My lips parted as I was about to ramble about something insignificant when it felt like the floor was falling out from beneath my feet. A much older version of Kai was staring at me as he took a seat across from me.

Winston Barclay.

His hair was the same shade of sand like Kai's, although it was peppered with gray from his age. His angular face was hardened and he watched me with a cruel look in his blue eyes.

"Hello, Winter." His voice was low, his tone as cold as ice. "I was hoping to run into you soon."

My stomach was in my throat and I stared back at him like a deer in headlights. My fight or flight instincts were kicking in. The adrenaline was coursing through my system and I wasn't sure I could handle it. My heart was threatening to beat out of my chest.

Not only did Kai's father hate me because of my interest in Kai, he hated my family even more. Winston Barclay was a dirty businessman and everyone knew it. He wasn't afraid of insider trading and breaking laws to capitalize and grow his empire. My parents didn't agree with his methods and when they turned down a business deal with him, they were immediately moved on to his shit list.

"Hello, Mr. Barclay," I forced the words out, although I couldn't quite force a smile onto my face. My stomach was sour and my heart pounded harder and harder as the seconds stretched between us. I glanced around, looking for Kai.

He was assessing me with his frigid stare. "From my understanding, you and my son have been spending a decent amount of time together."

I was struggling to maintain my composure. My surroundings were growing closer, yet louder and brighter. I was in sensory overload, thanks to my anxiety, and I was bordering on the edge of a panic attack. I counted my breaths in my head, trying to slow my heart rate.

"People talk, Miss Reign. It was only a matter of time until I found out." He paused for a moment as he folded his hands on the table. "You need to walk away from him. You are not helping his golf career and quite frankly, he belongs with someone of higher status than a Reign."

His words were like a blow to the chest. My lungs constricted and I struggled to inhale. The room was thick with tension and it was only increasingly becoming more suffocating with every passing second. My mouth was dry, yet I was frozen. My glass of water was right in front of me, but I couldn't move. I was paralyzed with fear as he caught me off guard and my mind was spiraling.

This man hated his son, he rooted against him and wanted him to fail, but he didn't want him to fail that badly. He still expected Kai to meet his expectations, even if it would never be enough for him. And in Winston's eyes, I would never be enough for Kai. I was inferior because of him hating my parents.

"I won't walk away from him again," I said quietly, finally forcing the words from my mouth. I was shaking in my seat, standing up to the one person I feared the most. I hated him for what he did to Kai; I was also equally terrified of what he could still do to Kai.

Winston clicked his tongue and shook his head as he lifted the glass of water that was meant for Kai to his lips. He took a long sip. "I'm not asking you, Winter. I am telling you." He set the glass down and his eyes hardened. "You will walk away from my son and you will not look back. If you do not go of your own accord, I will have it arranged."

There was a chill from his threat that rippled down my spine.

"What are you doing here?" Kai's voice sounded from behind me.

His father gave me one last cold glare before lifting his gaze to Kai. "Malakai." He motioned to the seat beside me. "Take a seat. The three of us will dine together."

"Absolutely not." Kai's hands were on the back of my seat, pulling it away from the table. I finally turned my head to the side to meet his gaze. Everything was moving too fast and the motion made me feel dizzy. I couldn't breathe. My heart was beating so hard it was going to burst. My tongue felt like it was going to lodge in the back of my throat. Nothing felt right and I needed to get out of there.

Kai's eyebrows were drawn together as he scanned my face with concern. I stared back at him as realization dawned on him. He held his hand out for me and I slid my palm against his. "Come on, Winter."

"Sit down, Malakai."

His father's voice was stern, yet he wouldn't raise his voice here and cause a scene. It sounded so distant as I rose to my feet. My knees felt weak, but Kai was there. He was here. He was leading me away, without a second glance or word to his father.

One hand was on the small of my back, guiding me, as the other held on to my arm. "I got you, darling. It's okay." His voice was soft. So soft and so gentle as he led me outside to his car. Everything was distorted and I was floating. It was almost as if I were in a dream-like state. None of this was real.

Kai's voice was soft against my ear as he helped me into the car. "I'm here, Winter. You're safe with me."

He was real.

He was always real.

CHAPTER TWENTY-SEVEN

MALAKAI

The moment I saw her face and saw the glossed-over look in her frightened eyes, I knew what was happening. Winter was spiraling in her mind, deep into a panic attack. She had them when we were younger. Sometimes they were triggered by nothing, but most times there was some event that sent her anxiety into overdrive.

I hated when this happened to her because there was no immediate fix. I knew it had to run its course and all I could do was be there for her. Winter needed to get as far away from my father and crowds, so I was taking her back to my condo. She would have been better with somewhere familiar, but it was closer than her house.

And she had me.

I was all the familiarity she needed.

Winter was perfectly still with her eyes shut and her head leaning against the window of my car. I pulled into the garage underneath my building and put the car in park. She still didn't move even after I killed the engine. I stared at her chest until I saw it rise and fall a few times.

I never felt as helpless as I did in moments like this.

My movements were rushed as I climbed out of the car and walked to the passenger's side. I slowly opened the door, careful to not disrupt her too much. Winter moved her head and sat up straighter. She cracked her eyelids, undoubtedly trying to block out some of the harsh lights from inside the parking garage.

"Where are we?" Winter questioned me, her voice barely audible.

"I brought you back to my place, darling." I reached out, brushing the hair from her face. "Let's get you inside, okay?"

"Okay," she murmured as she unbuckled her seat belt. I held my hands out to her and she took one and placed her other hand on the door to help herself out. After shutting the door and locking it, I held on to her hand while giving her some space to get her bearings as we walked into the building.

She didn't utter a single word as we stepped inside my condo.

"Quiet and dark, right?" I asked her quietly as I pushed the door shut behind us and pulled her deeper inside.

Winter nodded, letting me lead her to my bedroom. I pulled her inside the dark room and moved the blankets out of the way as I made a spot for her to lay.

Winter lowered herself onto the bed and I followed along with her. Her back was pressed against my chest and I pulled the blankets over us as I wrapped my arm around her waist and held her tightly.

"Just breathe," I murmured as I lifted my hand from her waist and began to stroke her hair. In the past, it was what she liked. It helped to distract her. "One, two, three, four, five, through your nose. Hold for one, two, three, four, five. Now exhale for one, two, three, four, five, six, seven."

Winter followed my instructions, breathing in, holding her breath, and then exhaling. The silence settled around us. I continued to stroke her hair as she kept following the breathing exercise.

"Kai?" My name was but a whisper on her lips.

"Yes, darling?"

"Please, don't stop talking to me." She let out a soft breath. "Your voice... it helps."

"Just breathe with me. I'll count and you focus on controlling your breathing." I murmured the words, keeping my tone soft and gentle, just like her soul. "I'm right here. I'll always be right here. You are my existence."

I began to count, the numbers becoming a chant or a mantra as I kept repeating them. Winter continued to breathe, focusing on my words, on the sound of my voice. A few minutes passed before she began to relax in my arms, before her breathing was slowing itself.

She abruptly rolled to face me. The soft glow from the moon outside my window cast its light across her face. Her green eyes met mine. "Thank you for helping me."

"How are you feeling?" I asked her as I slid my hand along the side of her face. "Has it subsided at all?"

She nodded. "It's lingering a bit, but it's much more tolerable than it was." Her gaze dropped to my mouth before lifting back to my eyes. "Distract me, Kai. Make it all go away."

I stared at her for a few heartbeats. "Are you sure? I don't want it to be too much for you."

"I need you, Kai," she breathed as she pressed her body flush against mine. "You're the only thing that can make me feel better. You make me feel safe, like nothing could ever hurt me."

"Nothing ever will, darling," I assured her as I slid my hands down her body. My face inched closer to hers. "I will always protect you with my life. In this life and the next. Your safety will always be of the utmost importance to me."

I gently pushed her onto her back, rolling with her until my arms were caging her in. I settled between her thighs, my mouth a breath away from hers. Her eyelids fluttered shut as I brought my lips down to hers.

"Promise me, Malakai," Winter murmured against them. There was desperation and need in her tone as she pushed her hands beneath my shirt. Her nails raked over my skin. "Promise me you'll never leave."

I wanted to know what my father had said to her before I arrived at the restaurant tonight. He said something that left her rattled like this. I pushed back the anger, knowing I couldn't ask her, not like this. Emotion lodged itself in my throat. "I promise."

Her lips were soft against mine and I moved with tenderness. I wanted to be gentle with her, but Winter had other plans. Her hands were urgent, pushing my clothes away. Her mouth was bruising against mine as we breathed each other in. She was consuming me and I was ready to let her. She could have whatever she needed from me without a second thought.

Layer by layer, we removed our clothing until they were scattered across my bedroom floor. Winter was beneath me, open and accepting as I slid inside her with one fluid motion. Instinctively, her legs wrapped around my waist, her ankles hooking together behind my back. My hands were in her hair, exposing her neck as I dropped my mouth down to her throat.

Winter clawed at my back as I thrust into her, harder and harder as I tasted her flesh beneath me. I trailed my lips across the column of her throat, nipping at her skin before making my way to her jawline. A moan escaped her and I swallowed her sounds as my mouth crushed against hers once again.

She was greedy, taking everything she wanted, and I wanted to give her every piece of me. Whatever she wanted, it was hers. She could have the last breath from my lungs and I would die a happy man.

Sliding my hands down her thighs, I parted them and pinned her against the mattress as I positioned myself on my knees. Lifting her legs, I flattened them against my body and she hooked her ankles behind my neck. She stared up at me, lust and need swirling in her green irises. From this angle, I had the perfect view of every inch of her skin. Her chest rose and fell in rapid succession with every shallow breath she took.

"You're fucking breathtaking, Winter," I breathed, my voice barely audible. It wasn't often that I swore, but in moments like this, I couldn't help myself.

Her lips parted and she moaned again as I lifted her hips and slid deep inside her. Wrapping my arms around her thighs, I held her legs against my body and began to thrust in and out of her. Her hands were fisting the sheets, her breasts bouncing with every movement.

"Please don't stop," she moaned, twisting the sheets in her hands.

Holding her legs with one arm, I reached for her hand and pulled it away from the sheet. I moved it down her torso until her fingers were pressed between us.

"Touch yourself, darling," I murmured as I shifted my hips again. "I want to watch you play with that pretty pussy while I'm deep inside you."

Her gaze was trained on mine as she began to move her fingers across her clit. I watched her as I slowly began to move inside her. My heart pounded inside my chest. Her breaths were growing more ragged as she rolled her fingers over her clit, over and over. Her pussy was clenching me tighter as I kept thrusting into her.

"That's it, darling," I growled as my fingers dug into the flesh of her thighs. My hips began to piston faster and the entire bed was groaning from the force of our movements. I pounded harder into her. "Make yourself come all over my cock."

"Harder," she moaned as her eyes began to roll back into her head. She was so tight around me, pushing me closer to the edge. "Don't stop."

The warmth was rapidly building in the pit of my stomach, spilling into my veins. It spread through my body like wildfire. My balls constricted against my body. I drove into her harder and harder, deeper and deeper with each thrust until she was a mess of moans. She cried out as her fingers brushed across her clit once more, sending her free falling into the abyss of ecstasy.

She shattered around me, and that was all it took to send me falling with her. I thrust into her once more, my fingers bruising her thighs. My face contorted, my eyes slamming shut as my orgasm tore through my body with such force, it was literally mind-blowing. Stars consumed my vision as I spilled my cum inside her.

We rode the waves of euphoria together and I slowly pulled out of her in a daze. Winter was breathless as she watched me disappear from the room for a brief moment before returning with a washcloth. I carefully cleaned her up, my body still on fire from the inferno that constantly burned between us.

I discarded the washcloth on the floor and climbed back onto the bed with her, pulling her flush against my body as I held her tightly. Burying my face in her hair, I breathed her scent in deeply. Winter yawned as she relaxed against me, our skin melting together.

"Sleep, darling," I murmured as my own eyelids fell shut. "I'll be here when you wake."

The sound of her steady breathing settled my soul.

Feeling her in my arms was all I ever needed. I held her tighter as sleep began to pull me under, deep into the depths where she still lingered in my dreams. Winter Reign consumed my every thought. Awake or asleep, she was all I ever saw.

And now that I had her, I would never let her go.

CHAPTER TWENTY-EIGHT
WINTER

Kai's breathing was slow and even and it warmed my skin as it fanned across my neck. His arm was heavy, wrapped tightly around my waist. I slowly turned within his grasp to face him. He stirred slightly, but he didn't wake up. His expression was so soft, so relaxed. It made him appear younger and innocent. Like the years and the life he'd experienced had never hardened him. There wasn't a single line of torment written across his face.

A soft smile pulled on my lips, but it instantly vanished as I replayed the evening in my head. The words his father had spoken to me... I couldn't escape them no matter how hard I tried to force them from my memory.

"You need to walk away from him. You are not helping his golf career and quite frankly, he belongs with someone of higher status than a Reign."

"I'm not asking you, Winter. I am telling you."

"You will walk away from my son and you will not look

back. If you do not go on your own accord, I will have it arranged."

A shiver ran down my spine and I felt uncomfortable in my own skin. I didn't know what he meant by his threat, but I had no intentions of ever finding out. Winston Barclay had power and money, along with unlimited resources. It was a deadly combination and it wasn't one I wanted to explore.

I didn't want to walk away from Kai, but I couldn't help but wonder if I should. I had no idea whether or not his father would follow through with his threat. He said he would have it arranged if I did not go on my own. What could that possibly mean? And what could it mean for either of us if I didn't listen to him?

I was afraid of what he would do to me, but more importantly, I was petrified of what he would do to Kai. I knew Kai was older and bigger now. He could hold his own against his father, but in reality, that didn't mean anything. His father could easily pay someone to do whatever he wanted them to do.

Tears pricked my eyes as I stared at how devastatingly beautiful Malakai Barclay was. My heart constricted as I trailed over the perfectly sculpted planes of his face. He was truly a work of art. One I could stare at for hours upon hours, I'd never grow old of how he looked.

There was no real option for me. I could stay and jeopardize both of our lives, or I could leave. Leaving was the sure solution. It was the safest one. And I was more concerned with preserving Kai's life than preserving my heart.

He had broken it once before and I was going to be the one to break it this time.

Kai stirred slightly as I lifted his arm and rolled away from him. It took everything in me to force my body to move. Tears stained my cheeks as I stood along the edge of the bed and watched him for a moment. If I woke him, he'd never let me leave. He would promise me we would figure it out, and I couldn't do that.

I couldn't take any more promises that would never be guaranteed.

As I collected my things, I put my clothes back on and grabbed one of Kai's sweatshirts from the floor. I had to leave with a piece of him if I couldn't have all of him. My phone was in my purse and I pulled it out to check the time. It was a quarter till midnight. We must have fallen asleep early after our dinner had prematurely ended.

I looked at Kai one last time and allowed myself a few heartbreaking seconds to study and memorize his face. I wanted him imprinted in my memory. My heart cracked in two and I wiped the tears away from my cheeks. This was the way it had to be if I wanted to keep him safe from the devil himself.

Stepping out of his bedroom, I opened up my text messages and sent one to Giana. She was a perpetual night owl, so I was hoping she would still be awake at this time. I could have taken an Uber home, but I didn't want to be alone. Not when my heart was falling into pieces on the floor. And I couldn't call my sister. Sutton wouldn't understand or she would blame it all on Kai.

WINTER

Hey. Are you awake?

Giana texted me back almost immediately. I walked through Kai's condo until I was reaching the door that would let me out into the building. I couldn't help the tears as they began to fall again.

GIANA

I am. What's going on? Is everything okay?

I swallowed back the emotion as I quietly exited his condo and closed the door behind me. I waited until I was successfully out of the building before responding to her. My hands hastily wiped the tears away from my eyes. I needed to hold myself together. I made this decision for us, so I needed to accept it and move forward. My feet hit the pavement and I put distance between myself and Kai as I walked down the sidewalk through the dark.

WINTER

Can you give me a ride home?

GIANA

Absolutely. Where are you?

There was a coffee shop about two blocks away from Kai's place. I sent Giana the address and sat down on the stoop as I waited for her to come get me. I should have just taken an Uber. It would have been more practical and I wouldn't have been burdening anyone else.

It only took her about ten minutes to get there before an unfamiliar car pulled up. Giana hopped out of the passenger's side and I noticed there was another girl sitting behind the steering wheel.

"That's Harper, Nico's girlfriend," she signed to me as she motioned to the car. *"She's cool and harmless. Get in."*

I stared at her for a moment before my shoulders sagged in defeat. I climbed into the back seat and the pretty blonde up front turned to look at me. She flashed her bright white teeth at me as she smiled.

"Hi, Winter," she said with a tenderness to her voice. "Giana told me about you. I hope you don't mind that I'm the one driving and not her. She's had a little bit to drink this evening."

I forced a small smile in return. "It's nice to meet you, and of course, it's fine."

Instead of getting back into the passenger's seat, Giana forced her way into the back seat with me. I raised an eyebrow at her and she flicked the overhead light on while she rolled her eyes in response. She reached up to the front of the car, handing Harper her phone with my address already in it. Harper was news to me and I couldn't help the curiosity of hearing that Nico had a girlfriend.

She wasn't familiar with the area since she needed directions to drive fifteen minutes from here. Giana settled back in her seat and Harper began to drive as G turned to face me.

"Why did we just pick you up on the corner of the street? I know Kai lives around here." The expression on her face

matched the exact tone I got from the way she signed her words to me. *"Were you at his place?"*

I nodded. "He was asleep when I left."

Her eyebrows drew together. *"I'm so confused. So, he didn't do anything wrong?"*

I shook my head at her. "I ran into his father earlier today and he made it clear that I needed to walk away from Kai forever." I paused for a moment as I took a deep breath. "He made it clear that if I didn't listen to him, he would make it happen himself."

She stared at me for a moment as she processed my words. I could have signed back to her, but the words just came tumbling from my mouth. Harper remained silent in the front seat, but I knew she was listening to everything I was saying. A part of me didn't even care at this point.

"Does Kai know what he said to you?" she signed with a suspicious look on her face. One that was also mixed with a touch of anger.

"No. I didn't tell him."

Giana tipped her head back and closed her eyes for a moment before she turned to look out the window. Silence settled around us and we rode in it for a few minutes. I wasn't sure what else to say but with the way Giana was looking at me now, I couldn't help but feel like maybe I had made a mistake by leaving.

Harper let out a breath as she pulled her car into my driveway. "I need the code to get in."

I told her it and she punched the numbers in as Giana began to sign to me again.

"You have to tell him, Winter." She shook her head in

disapproval and gave me a knowing look. *"Would you want him to do the same to you?"*

"Well, no," I told her in a rush as Harper put her car in park in front of my house. "I did it to keep him safe. You know how cruel his father is. The last thing I need him to do is come after Kai."

"That's not your choice to make, babe. Malakai is a grown man. You need to tell him what happened and let him make his own decisions."

Her words took me by surprise. I didn't expect her to be like Sutton would have been, but I also didn't anticipate her fully being on his side. Not that there were sides to take. I just expected her to agree with me on the decision I had made.

"You know he's not going to let this go, right? As soon as he realizes you left, he's going to come looking for you. That man would burn down the entire world looking for you." She raised her eyebrows at me. *"You're going to have to tell him because he's not going to give you a choice."*

A sigh escaped me and I nodded. "I know. I was afraid he would come looking for me and I'm not sure what to do about that."

Harper turned to look at us, the side of her face illuminated from an unknown source of light. "Were you expecting someone else?"

My eyebrows lifted as I looked out the window and saw another car racing down the driveway. My heart all but stopped in my chest and I glanced at Giana.

"That didn't take him long," she signed to me with a ghost of a smile playing on her lips. *"I told you he'd come looking for you."*

The headlights were bright and blinding as they shined directly on me like a spotlight. I was momentarily frozen in place as time felt suspended. I looked between Giana and Harper. "Thanks for the ride."

"Good luck," Harper said with a touch of encouragement.

Giana smiled. *"Don't fight it, Winter. Let him in."*

I nodded at her and slowly got out of the car. Harper put it in drive and slowly drove away. Kai killed the engine of his car, his movements slow and calculated as he climbed out. His strides were long and he didn't stop until he was standing directly in front of me.

"Hello, darling." There was a hardness in his gaze, but his voice was smooth like honey.

I inhaled sharply as he looked down at his sweatshirt in my hand and back to my eyes. The air had left my lungs and I couldn't formulate any words. He cocked an eyebrow at me, but didn't comment on the stolen shirt.

"I appreciate the effort, but you can't run away from me that easily."

CHAPTER TWENTY-NINE
MALAKAI

W inter stared back at me as if she were completely in shock. Almost as if she wasn't expecting me to show up. *Foolish girl...*

When I woke up and found my bed empty, I had thought Winter slipped out to go to the bathroom. When I heard the front door to my condo closing, I knew she was leaving me instead of coming back to me. I gave her enough time to change her mind and come back, but she never returned.

I knew she was running and home was the only place she would go at this hour. After her panic attack, I thought things were okay. Apparently I was gravely mistaken. Something else was going on and I wasn't leaving until I had an answer from her I was satisfied with.

"Why are you running from me, Winter?"

Her slender throat moved as she swallowed hard. I watched the shock and reservation vanish from her expression. My eyebrows scrunched together in confusion as a wave of fear washed over her eyes.

"Come inside with me," she said quietly as she slipped her hand in mine and led me toward the house. She was silent as she pulled me inside and locked the door behind us. She didn't speak another word as we ended up in the living room and she curled up in the corner of the sectional couch.

I had never been more confused and conflicted than I was in that moment. I knew there was something she hadn't told me, but her fear left me feeling unsettled.

"What's going on?" My tone was soft and gentle as I sat on the couch beside her. "Tell me what's wrong."

Her eyes searched mine for a moment as she pulled a blanket over her body, almost as a defense mechanism. "Your father. He doesn't want us together."

My stomach sank and dread filled the pit of it as I watched her nervously shift on the couch. I knew he had been the reason behind her panic attack, I just didn't know what he had said that set her off. She was slowly giving me the pieces I needed to put the entire picture together.

"What did he say to you?"

Her tongue darted out as she wet her lips. "He knew we were seeing each other. He thinks I'm only hurting your golf career and that you deserve someone of higher status." She paused for a moment and my blood was already beginning to boil. "Our families have never really gotten along, so this is all to be expected."

"You know he's wrong, right? You know what, I don't bother myself with his thoughts or opinions," I reminded her as I placed my hand on her knee. Everything she was telling me was something I would have expected from my father, but I knew it wasn't what had set her off. There was more she wasn't telling me.

Tears fell from her eyes, solidifying my thoughts. I scooted closer, closing the distance between us as I lifted my hands up to cup the sides of her face. I caught her tears with the pads of my thumbs and brushed them away from her silky skin.

"Did he hurt you?" I questioned her, struggling to keep my tone even. It was taking everything in me to not go burn my parents' house to the ground with him inside it.

Winter shook her head. "No, he didn't. I only saw him at the restaurant when he sat across from me."

"What really happened? What aren't you telling me?"

"He told me I needed to leave you. I need to walk away and if I don't, he will make sure I do." Her words came out in a rush and her voice was splintering around them. "I didn't leave because I wanted to, Malakai. I left because he made it clear that I didn't have a choice."

My heart stopped in my chest as my eyes desperately searched hers. Emotions I couldn't dissect instantly flooded me. They were seeping into my system and running rampant through my veins. I wanted to gut him.

"No one ever gets to make that choice for you, Winter." I was struggling to keep my tone even and I was failing. There was a chill in my tone that I couldn't eradicate. "I am going to kill him."

"Stop," she said, shaking her head. Her hands were reaching for me as I pushed off the couch in a rush. I was on my feet and she was following after me. "Kai, please. Don't do something irrational or something that is driven by your emotions right now."

I turned around to look at her, my hands finding the sides of her face once again. "When have you ever known me to make a rash decision, darling? Everything I do is calculated. I don't move without a plan."

"What is your plan?"

Killing my father wasn't exactly an option. I did have enough money and resources that I could potentially get away with it, but it was too risky. He was someone who if he went missing, people would start looking. People I didn't want to be looking.

"Don't worry. Everything will be okay." I pulled her to me, pressing my lips against her forehead. "You don't have to be afraid of him. He will never hurt you. I promised you I would always keep you safe."

"It's not me I'm worried about," she said in a rush, breathing against my chest as I held her close. "I'm afraid of what he will do to you."

I leaned her head back so she was looking up at me. "I promise you he won't be doing anything to me. I'm just going to go over and have a conversation with him. He doesn't get to threaten you and think he can get away with it."

"It's the middle of the night, Kai," she protested,

fisting her hands in my shirt. "Just stay, please. We can worry about it tomorrow."

I shook my head at her as I pressed my lips to hers in a haste before pulling away. "I'm sorry, this is something that can't wait. The more it festers inside me, the worse it will be. I need to deal with it now."

There was a troubled look lingering in her features, but there was also resignation. Winter knew better than to try and stand between me and something I had already decided upon. What he did was unacceptable. It was unforgivable. And I needed to be the one to make sure he knew that.

It was time for me to take back the power he had stripped me of many years ago.

"Everything else in this world is insignificant in comparison to you. I will always protect you, no matter the cost or sacrifice."

Winter bit down on her bottom lip and nodded. "Promise me you'll be safe. Promise me you'll come back to me."

She said it as if I were walking into a burning building and in a way, I was. My father was unpredictable. I wasn't exactly sure what I was going up against, but none of that mattered. I would never allow another person to make Winter feel frightened and unsafe. No one would ever make her feel as though she had to walk away from me to keep us both safe.

He put her in a position I would never allow him to do again.

"You are my home," I whispered against her lips as I

kissed her once more and released her. "I'll always come back to you."

———

As I stepped inside my parents' home, I couldn't fight the anger as it rippled through my body. I slammed the door behind me with such force, it knocked a picture onto the floor. Glass scattered around it as it landed with a crash, but I paid it no mind. I was already moving, striding through the vast rooms, flipping on every light switch I passed. There was a soft light glowing from under the door to my father's office and I heard the TV from their bedroom upstairs.

The rage was boiling inside and it was taking everything in me to not destroy everything in my path. My footsteps were loud and heavy and I was making my presence known as I stomped in the direction of my father's office. My hands reached the knobs and I twisted them, before shoving the doors open. There was enough force behind my movements that had them slamming into the walls.

"What the hell?" my father said loudly as he jumped up from the plush seat behind his massive mahogany desk. He narrowed his eyes as he realized it was me. "What are you doing, Malakai? What is wrong with you?"

My heart pounded erratically in my chest as I paused just inside his office and stared him down. "My tolerance for you has officially dissolved."

He let out an exasperated sigh as he rounded his

desk and stood in front of it. "It is the middle of the night. What do you want?"

"I want nothing from you," I seethed. I stepped farther into the room, closing the distance between us. "All I ever wanted was a real father and you proved that wasn't an option. I accepted it many years ago that I would never be what you wanted me to be, but you crossed a line tonight. You will not speak to Winter, you will not look at Winter, you will forget her existence."

He rolled his eyes and pursed his lips. "You're really here about *that* girl? Jesus, this is pathetic. She's nothing, Malakai, and you need to realize that."

It took me two and a half strides to reach him. My hand was fisting the collar of his shirt and I pressed it against his throat as I lifted him onto his toes. My fist was beneath his chin and his hands were wrapping around my wrists. "That's where you are wrong, Father. She is everything. If you even breathe in her direction again, I will kill you myself."

"Malakai," my mother gasped from behind me, her voice an octave higher than normal. "Let go of your father."

I stared at him as he didn't even attempt to fight me off. "Do not fucking try me, *Dad*. I will not hesitate, even if it lands me in prison for the rest of my life."

"They still have the death penalty in our state, you idiot."

"Even better," I smiled viciously at him. "Then I can track you down in hell and do it over and over again."

"Malakai!" My mother's voice was louder and her hands were frantically pulling at my arms. "Stop it!"

I let go of him, abruptly dropping him to his feet as I took a rushed step backward. My breathing was erratic and my heart threatened to pound out of my chest. I came here to tell him off, not put my hands on him like he would have to me. The thought alone shook me to my core. Was I really any different than him?

"You are dead to me," I told my father as I stared him down. "I put up with your abuse for so many years. I'm done. You won't do it to me and you sure as hell won't do it to Winter. This will be the last time you see me or speak to me."

His gaze hardened as he glared back at me. "Very well. I will have your name removed from the will. You will never get anything from us again."

"I never needed you." I shook my head at him as a harsh laugh escaped me. "Burn in hell, Father."

I spun on my heel, leaving him standing where he was as I strode out of his office. The rage had simmered and was replaced with an unfamiliar pain. I knew my father never truly cared about me, but there was no hesitation with him completely removing me from the Barclay family. It was almost as if he was waiting for this moment, he just needed me to be the one to pull the trigger first.

My mother was hot on my heels as I continued to make my way to the front door. "Malakai, wait!"

I stopped short and she almost ran into my back. Turning around to face her, I didn't miss the look of confusion and torment on her face. "Please don't try and change my mind, Mother."

"I won't do that," she said softly as she shook her head. "I'm sorry for him. You know how he can be."

I lifted my hand to stop her. "No more excuses, Mom. I am done. Nothing will change that and honestly, I wish to never speak to him again." I paused for a moment. "That doesn't have to change our relationship, but I will ask that you respect my boundaries and do not try to fix this. It is over."

She swallowed and nodded. "As you wish. I would still like to stay in contact with you." Her voice cracked slightly. "You're my only child. I'm sorry I was never a good mother to you."

"You did your best."

There were tears in her eyes. It was strange. There was no glossiness from the alcohol. She must have passed out earlier and I had woken her when I rushed into the house. For the first time in a long time, she was more sober than I had ever seen her.

Turning my back to her, I reached for the front door and pulled it open. My mother's hand gripped my shoulder and I glanced back at her, watching as she retreated.

"I love you, Malakai," she practically whispered from where she stood.

A muscle in my jaw twitched and I gave her a curt nod before exiting the house.

I couldn't remember the last time she spoke those words to me.

And I couldn't repeat them—not to someone who didn't understand the meaning of love…

CHAPTER THIRTY
WINTER

I was pacing around the house when I saw a set of headlights coming down the driveway once again. It was already well past one o'clock in the morning and my anxiety was running rampant through my body. It was invading every crevice of my mind, but seeing the lights brought a sense of relief. It had to be Kai. It wouldn't have been anyone else.

And if he was here, then that meant he was safe.

My feet carried me to the front door and I pulled it open just as he parked his car. My shoulders sagged as relief chased the panic away. It felt like I could finally breathe and I could breathe easily. Kai got out of the car and began to walk toward me with his eyes on mine. I couldn't stop myself as I rushed over to him.

My hands found his face and my eyes frantically scanned him. In a sense, it was almost a bad habit from when we were younger. I was used to Kai coming to me after he had been abused. It was a habit, looking for blood or bruises. "Are you okay?"

He wrapped his hands around my wrists and looked down at me. "I'm fine, darling."

"He didn't do anything to you?"

Kai shook his head. "I told you he wouldn't. I simply went there to speak with him." The corners of his lips lifted, but there was a look of torment in his eyes. "You never have to worry about him again, okay?"

My eyes desperately searched his as my heart pounded erratically in my chest. I couldn't help but wonder what really happened. "What did you do?" I didn't expect Kai to do anything bad, yet I couldn't help but feel the weight of his words. I didn't doubt the fact that he would burn down the entire world for me.

He shook his head again. "We talked and that was it. I told you I wouldn't do anything stupid, and I didn't."

"I believe you," I assured him, my voice quiet and tender. "It's late. Let's go inside."

Kai dropped his hands away from my wrists and I watched his expression transform as a shadow passed through his face. He took a step back and dropped his gaze to the ground. Confusion swept through me and I stared at him for a moment before I slid my hand into his. He didn't say anything. His eyes met mine with a pained look, but he let me lead him inside.

Something happened, something shifted, and I wasn't sure what it was. Despite the coldness that radiated from him and the way he always had his guard up around people, Kai wasn't as closed off as he made people believe. Inside he was riddled with trauma and when it plagued his mind, he was delicate. Like a piece of glass resting on the edge of turmoil.

He hated to be vulnerable; he never wanted anyone to see him break.

Kai remained silent as I led him through the house and up to my bedroom. I released his hand as I pulled the blankets back on the bed and climbed inside. He followed behind me, his body tense as he pulled me flush against him. My head was resting on his chest as I wrapped my arm around his torso. It was like there was something inside of him that was preventing him from relaxing. His demons had resurfaced from whatever words were exchanged between him and his father.

"Talk to me, Malakai," I whispered as I lifted my head to look at him. "You promised you would always come back to me, but you're not here right now."

His stormy blue eyes barreled into mine, effectively stealing the air from my lungs with the torment hanging heavily inside them. "I'm right here."

I shook my head. "Physically, perhaps. You're lost in your mind."

A muscle in his jaw twitched and his nostrils flared. He didn't push me away, but the coldness was rolling off of him in waves. "You really want to know what happened? Fine. I confronted my father. I told him that what he did was unacceptable and he's not to look at you, speak to you, think of you again. I meant what I said, Winter. I would burn down the entire fucking world for you. I would destroy anyone who stepped in my way." He paused as a ragged breath escaped him. "I love you, Winter. So fucking much that it hurts, but you're the sweetest pain I've ever experienced."

It had felt like I had waited an eternity to hear him finally speak the words aloud.

"I love you," I whispered back to him, the emotion welling inside my chest. My heart felt like it was going to explode. Like a ticking time bomb waiting to detonate. "I've always loved you."

"I always knew I loved you, but it wasn't until tonight that I realized the truth behind it. I never felt like I was capable of loving because I never truly felt love... not until I met you." The words tumbled from his perfect lips and his body was relaxing beneath mine. "You are my heart, Winter Reign."

Kai's hands were in my hair and his lips were crashing into my own. What oxygen was left in my lungs, he swiftly stole. His mouth was tender and gentle, yet needy and urgent as it moved against mine. My lips parted as his tongue slid along the seam of my mouth and he slid inside. I was completely consumed by him. We were lost in one another as our tongues tangled and our souls melted.

He was in my veins and there was nothing that could ever eradicate him.

We broke apart, breathless, as we came up for air. He pulled me back against him and we fell into the silence of the night as he wrapped me in his arms and held me close. His fingers were light against my arms as he trailed them over my skin.

"I'm afraid that I will end up like him."

His voice cracked, splintering into fragments around

the words as he finally admitted what was haunting him. I wrapped my arms tighter around him.

"You're not your father, Kai. You will never be like him."

He sighed. "I grabbed him by the collar of his shirt and pressed my fist against his throat. Tonight wasn't the first time things between us got physical."

I pulled away from him and rolled onto him as I stared down into his troubled blues. "Listen to me. You are *nothing* like him, Malakai. You are tender and compassionate. Just because you don't want others to see your vulnerable side doesn't mean you are cold and cruel like him. I know *you*. Your heart is too pure, your soul is too pure."

He fell silent again. I counted three heartbeats and it felt like an eternity before he spoke again. "You truly believe that? Even after everything, you sincerely believe my heart is pure for me to ever be like him? The devil raised me, darling. Isn't it only proper that I end up following in his footsteps?"

I shook my head at him as I flattened my palms against his cheeks. Kai's eyelids fluttered shut and I pressed my lips to his forehead. "Hell was never where you belonged, my love. It's always been right here with me. You're forging your own path. One that is fueled by the way he raised you, but you're not following it. You're breaking the wheel. Your fear of wanting to not be like him is what will prevent you from being a replica of your father."

"He showed me what I never want to be."

I pulled back once again to look into his soul. "I

know you. I know your heart. It's made of gold, unlike his, which is black and rotten."

Kai's eyelids opened and he stared directly into my soul as he pulled my face down to his. "I hope you're right," he whispered against my lips. "You make me want to be the best version of myself. I want to give you the world, Winter. I want to see myself as the person you see when you look at me. I want to be everything you deserve."

"You're more than I ever deserved."

He shook his head as his lips swept across mine. His movements were fluid and smooth as he rolled me onto my back before hovering above me.

"Let me love you." His lips touched mine again. "Let me love you the way you should be loved."

Tears pricked my eyes as his words seeped into my soul. "You already do."

He slowly stripped me bare, kissing and touching every inch of my skin until I was naked beneath him. I watched him as he undressed and settled between my legs. His eyes were on mine, filled with so many conflicting emotions as he slid inside me, filling me to the brim.

A shallow breath escaped me and his mouth was on my neck. His lips were soft and gentle as he trailed them across my jawline.

"In this life—the next life—wherever our souls go… you will always be mine," he whispered against my skin as he reached inside my heart. "I've loved you for an eternity and I'll love you for an eternity more."

EPILOGUE
MALAKAI

Six Months Later

I trailed behind Winter, watching her with an amused look as she slowly walked down the cobblestone streets, staring up at the buildings around us in amazement. There was a chill in the air and she paused while wrapping her coat tighter around her body. She glanced over her shoulder, a smile reaching her eyes.

"This place is seriously so magical," she said softly as I stepped up beside her. "I feel like I'm in a *Harry Potter* movie or something."

I reached for her waist, pulling her flush against my body. "Honestly," I said with a smile as I looked down into her eyes. "That's exactly why I wanted to bring you to Edinburgh. You've always been so obsessed with *Harry Potter*, I figured this was as real as we could get without going to an amusement park or something."

Pure joy glimmered in her green irises as she

wrapped her arms around the back of my neck. "I thought you wanted to go to Scotland to play golf at St. Andrews?"

A soft chuckle rumbled in my chest and I shook my head. "Darling, I've already played there before. I wanted to bring you here because I want you to experience the world."

"I've been abroad with my parents before, but never like this."

I smiled at her. "Exactly my point."

She stood on her tiptoes and pressed her lips to mine. "I literally do not deserve you."

"You let me be the judge of that," I murmured against her mouth before claiming her lips with my own. She tasted like candy and I wanted to revel in this moment with her—I wanted to revel in every single moment with her. She was the constant in my life and I would never let her go.

We stood in the middle of the street, wrapped up in one another as our tongues danced together. A car blew its horn and Winter jumped in my arms. A nervous laugh slipped from her lips as we pulled back from one another. Grabbing her hand, I broke out into a jog as I pulled her to safety on the sidewalk and threw up an apologetic hand to the driver.

We were both laughing and I stopped as I caught Winter staring at me. There was a mixture of emotions swirling in her bright green eyes.

"I love you like this," she said softly, still smiling at me. "Happiness looks good on you."

I shook my head at her as I pulled her along with me

to continue down the street. "You look good on me, darling."

The past six months had changed me in ways I never thought were possible. Completely cutting ties with my father was entirely liberating. I finally felt free from the hold he had always had over me. I still struggled with the dark thoughts that plagued my mind from time to time, but it had gotten easier over the past few months. I found a new therapist, one who dealt specifically with the types of trauma I had, and it helped immensely.

I had missed my chance at the Masters Tournament this year, but I was back on my golf game, thanks to Winter. She was nothing but encouraging. I convinced her to quit her job as a librarian and travel with me. I didn't want to be without her and she had her own dreams of becoming a published author. I urged her to chase her dreams and she was doing it.

She managed to write a full book and find an agent, and her manuscript was currently being reviewed by a major publisher. We were both living our dream life together and I wouldn't have changed a single thing about it.

None of it really mattered, though—as long as I had her.

I was still healing, but Winter was right. I was happier than I had ever been in my life before, and I owed it to her. My therapist insisted it wasn't healthy to base my happiness off another person, but that rule didn't apply to me. Winter was my safe place, she always had been. And with my own healing process, I found that I was deserving of her. I deserved to be happy and to live this life I was living.

I may have made changes, but at the end of the day, Winter was the only thing that truly mattered. I couldn't care less about anyone else on this planet but her.

My relationship with my mother wasn't anything special, but we were both trying to navigate having a healthier one than what we had before. She kept her word and never once brought up my father.

Winter's family was more accepting of us being together than I imagined they would be and I was eternally grateful. Her family was important to her and having them supporting our relationship meant more to me than I could ever put into words.

Since we were traveling, she wasn't able to commit to coaching figure skating back home, but whenever we were back in town, that was the first place she visited. She made it a point to volunteer any spare time she had when we were in Orchid City to helping little kids learn how to skate, how to perfect the art she had mastered.

We found a quaint little restaurant tucked in a hole-in-the-wall-looking place. We dined by candlelight and it was absolutely glorious. Winter lit up the entire room with her presence alone. I was captivated by her, caught in her web. I couldn't stop staring at her, watching her every chance I got. The way she spoke, the way she breathed. She was the most alluring, ethereal being under the sun.

After dinner, we stepped back out onto the street and began our walk back to the hotel. It was already late and dark and the streets were practically vacant. Her hand fit perfectly in mine and I pulled her to a stop as I spun her around to face me.

"What's wrong?" she questioned me with her bright green eyes searching mine.

A smile pulled on my lips. "Absolutely nothing. I just wanted to do this."

Her lips parted and her eyebrows pinched together in confusion but I was already pulling her flush against my body. My hand slid around the back of her head, my fingers plunging into her hair as I angled her face up to mine. My lips crashed into hers in an instant.

Winter didn't miss a beat, her movements matching mine as she clung onto me. I walked her backward, just into the small alley beside us before pushing her up against the stone wall. Her hands were fisting my shirt, her head tipping back even farther as she let me into her mouth. My tongue slid across hers, tasting the wine from our dinner.

She kissed me back with such an intensity, it felt like we were going to combust. I wanted to strip her bare and lift her up to fuck her against the wall.

"Jesus," I breathed as I broke away from her. My heart clenched in my chest and I pressed my forehead against hers. "I'm so hopelessly in love with you, Winter Reign. You are my absolute weakness."

"Why did you stop?" She pouted, her voice just as breathless as mine.

"Because if I didn't stop, I would have ended up taking you right here up against this wall."

Winter was quiet for a beat. "What if I told you I wanted to?"

I pulled back enough to look into her eyes. "Is that what you want, darling? You want me to fuck you right here where anyone could easily see us?"

"Yes," she murmured. "That's exactly what I want."

Good God. My cock was already hard in my pants and all I needed was her to speak those words for me to throw any rational thought out the window. "As you wish, darling." She had a dress on, which made this an absolutely perfect opportunity. "Lose the panties."

She obeyed as I stepped back, just enough to give her room to slip them off. I took them from her and tucked the lace into my pocket. A mischievous grin played on her lips and her gaze dropped down to my hands as I undid the button and zipper to my dress pants.

I pulled my cock out and slid my hands under her thighs as I lifted her up. She was positioned just above me and I slowly lowered her onto my length. A moan escaped her as she took me completely.

"Jesus. You're always so wet and ready for me."

"Only for you," she assured me as she wrapped her hands around the nape of my neck and brought her lips down to mine. "Only ever for you, Malakai."

"Mine."

She moaned into my mouth as I gripped her ass and began to pound into her. The stone wall had to have been digging into her back, but neither of us cared. The only thing that mattered was me being inside of her right now. I was lifting her up and down, her insides stroking my cock as she clenched around me.

Her fingers were digging into my shoulders as she clung to me. Our mouths melted into one another and I swallowed her moans as I kept thrusting in and out of her. Our surroundings had completely vanished. We were the only things that mattered in this world, in this universe.

A warmth built rapidly in my stomach, it spread through my body as my balls constricted. I was getting closer and closer and I could feel that she was too. She panted against my mouth and I slammed into her again with such force. Winter was a mess of moans, not caring if anyone could hear or see us as she lost herself around me.

Her pussy clenched me in a vise grip as her orgasm tore through her body. She shook and quivered under my touch and I thrust into her one last time before my own orgasm erupted. I spilled myself inside her, slowly thrusting in and out until she was filled to the hilt with my cum.

I held her in place, still pressed up against the wall with my cock inside her. My cum was leaking out of her, but I didn't care. She lifted her head to look down at me as she let out a ragged breath.

"Mine," I growled as I nipped at her bottom lip.

"Yours."

EXTENDED EPILOGUE

MALAKAI

two years later

As I stood in front of the mirror, I fiddled with my tie, untying it and retying it again for the fourth time in a row. There was nothing wrong with it. It was me. My brain. The thoughts that plagued my mind were literally driving me insane.

Nico was rambling about something from where he was sitting with Wes, but I wasn't hearing a single word he was saying. The only thing I was listening to was that horrid little voice in my head that was telling me lies. Or maybe they were truths.

"Kai."

What if Winter didn't want this with me? We had been together long enough—loved each other long enough—it only seemed fitting that we do this. But what if she was just agreeing to make me happy?

That stupid little voice. It was making me question whether or not she was questioning all of this.

"Kai."

I whipped my head in Nico's direction. "What?" I all but snapped at him as the anxiety and endless pessimistic thoughts continued to plague me.

He was staring at me with a touch of concern in his expression. He wasn't helping. Maybe he knew she didn't want this and that was what the look was for. He cocked an eyebrow. "Are you good, man?"

My jaw was clamped together. No, I was most certainly not good. My palms were sweating. My stomach was rolling with nausea. There wasn't a single piece of me that wasn't second-guessing any of this. But I had to know if she was. I had to know if this was really what she wanted, if *I* was really what she wanted.

"I'll be back," I said in a rush as I spun on my heel and headed toward the door.

"Ah, shit," I heard Wes's voice as he spoke to Nico. "His nerves are getting to him. He's definitely going to get sick."

Ignoring his words, I pushed through the French doors that led out onto the patio. It was a short walk— only fourteen steps, to be exact—until I was reaching a different set of doors that led to the room Winter was in. My hands found the handles and I was pushing them down while simultaneously pulling them open. I should have walked away, but I couldn't. I needed to see her immediately.

The first set of eyes that met mine were Giana's. They instantly widened in shock before shifting into pure anger. *"What are you doing here?"* she signed furiously as she began to march toward me. I glanced around the room, yet Winter wasn't there. *"Get out! You're not supposed to be in here right now. You're not supposed to see her yet."*

"Where is she?" I questioned Giana while simultaneously signing to her. My voice was hoarse, filled with emotion, yet full of panic. "I need to see her. It's an emergency."

Giana shook her head. *"No way. If you're not dying, get out of here."*

Jesus, it felt like I was dying inside.

"Malakai?" I heard Winter's soft voice. A wave of relief instantly flooded me, but it didn't drown out the panic. "What are you doing in here? Is everything okay?"

I looked past Giana and the oxygen instantly left my lungs in a rush. The white lace strapless gown hugged her curves before slowly fanning out around her feet. My eyes traveled over the material and up to her face. Her dark hair was in soft waves, pulled back from her face with two small braids on either side of her head.

She was absolutely breathtaking.

Giana glanced over her shoulder and looked back at me. She let out an exasperated sigh and threw her hands up in defeat before signing, *"Oh, hell."* She turned her attention back to Winter.

"It's fine, Giana. He can be in here." Winter offered her a small smile as she signed in response to Giana. *"Give us a few minutes, okay?"*

Giana nodded, but when she turned back around to face me, she gave me a murderous glare. I waited for her to hurl an insult at me or scold me, but she didn't.

Instead, she left the room, softly closing the doors behind her as she left Winter and I alone.

"You know it's bad luck seeing me before the wedding?"

I swallowed roughly over the emotion in my throat. "I needed to see you."

Winter closed the distance between us. She appeared ethereal as she practically floated across the room to me. She was naturally beautiful and her makeup illuminated her features. It was like she had drifted to Earth from the clouds above.

I did not deserve her.

"What's wrong?" Her voice was soft and tender as she reached out to me. "Are you second-guessing this?"

My eyelids fluttered shut as I felt her palm against my cheek. "I would never." I slowly opened my eyes again to search hers. "I needed to know that you weren't."

Her eyebrows were drawn together. "I have been waiting for this day since I fell in love with you, Malakai."

"Are you sure that you want this? Are you sure that I am what you want and who you want?"

She stepped closer until her body was flush against mine. Her arms linked behind my neck and I tilted my head down to look into her bright eyes. "I've never been more sure of anything in my life. You are all I have ever and will ever want. You are the love of my life. In this life, and the next life. It will always be you, Malakai." She paused for a moment as a smile touched her lips. "It's always been you."

"I just—I don't know." I was stumbling over my words. My voice dropped to a whisper. "There are times that this doesn't feel real. Sometimes I imagine that I'm going to wake up from this dream and you won't be here with me. I just needed to make sure this was what you wanted, not just something you felt you had to do."

The lilt of her laughter warmed my soul. "Oh, my love," she said softly as she pulled my face down to hers. Her lips brushed against mine. "This isn't a dream. I want this life with you and no one else."

"What happens if you change your mind one day?"

I watched the hues of green swirl in her irises. "That would never happen. I told you before that you were always my destiny."

My hands encircled her waist, feeling the lace of her dress beneath my fingertips. "We were written in the stars," I whispered against her lips as I breathed her in.

"And the stars never lie."

CHECK OUT THE ORCHID CITY SERIES

If you loved The Lie of Us and want more of the Orchid City world, check out Meet Me in the Penalty Box which is the first book from the Orchid City series!

Continue reading for a look inside!

PROLOGUE
NICO

As I walked off the ice and headed back to the locker room, my hair was soaked and stuck to the back of my neck. There was nothing like hitting the ice for practice and having your coach tell you that you're not practicing with pucks. After the loss that we had on Sunday, I wasn't surprised. We got spanked and it wasn't the pleasurable kind of spanking.

"Damn, that man is ruthless," Lincoln mumbled as we both dropped down onto the bench beside each other. He was in his rookie year too, so we were both working our asses off to prove that we belonged playing on this level.

Ice hockey was competitive as hell and if you weren't keeping up with the best, you'd easily get left behind. Dropping back to the AHL wouldn't be a death sentence, but it wasn't what I wanted. I wanted it all, or nothing.

And luckily, I was right where I needed to be in

terms of impressing our coach and being an asset to the team.

Coach Anderson didn't fuck around and I wasn't about to be the one who got on his bad side. We had one issue this entire season and it was about me getting into some unnecessary fights. I dialed it back a bit since we had a talk about it and everything had been good between us ever since.

"Cirone," Miles, one of our new equipment guys, said as he walked over to me. "Let me get your practice socks so I can get you new ones."

I pulled the clear tape from the material and balled it up and set it on the bench beside me before I continued undressing. Miles looked at the ball of tape and held out his hand for it as I handed him my socks.

"Do you want me to throw the tape out for you?"

My eyes widened and I shook my head. "Absolutely not."

Wes chuckled from a few guys down. "You never touch Nico's tape," he warned Miles. Wes and I played on the same team together in the AHL before we were moved up to the NHL. He knew my weird quirks and superstitions.

"What's the deal with the tape?" Miles questioned the two of us, genuinely interested.

I shrugged off the rest of my equipment and put it all back in its respective place. "My mom started this thing when I was a kid. I used to piss her off with leaving balls of tape everywhere, so every season she would collect them. It kind of started this weird thing that I do now."

Wes laughed again and Lincoln shook his head. "Go on, tell him more," Lincoln urged. "It gets even more interesting."

I looked between my two teammates. "Like neither of you have your own weird things you do." I paused and directed my attention at Wes. "You sleep in your damn suit every night before a game."

Wes simply shrugged. "It's good luck, bro."

"And so is my ball of tape."

Miles looked between the three of us. "You know what, I don't need to know the specifics. I know now to leave your tape untouched, so we're good."

He quickly moved away from all of us and everyone went back to their routine. Some of the guys headed into the shower to wash away the sweat before leaving. Wes walked over to me as I grabbed my keys, phone, and wallet.

"What are you doing tonight, Nico? Some of us are going to meet up at that new club Mirage. You game?"

I shrugged, even though my body was telling me I needed to go home and go to bed. "Sure, why not. I'm going to run home and shower and I'll meet you guys there?"

"Sounds good," Wes said with a smile before he left the locker room. I wasn't far behind him and some of the other guys came out in a larger group. I was still getting to know a lot of the guys and they had been pretty accepting so far.

After hopping into my black Mercedes, I headed out through the ramp that led down to where all the players parked. The man sitting at the booth lifted the gate and waved as I drove through. My apartment was only a five-minute drive from the arena and there wasn't much traffic so I got home without any issues.

From one parking garage to another, I slid my car into its spot and took the elevator up to my floor. It was a building of condos and each floor was its own separate unit. I didn't make enough of a salary for a place like this, but my mother had an insane trust built for me and she left me a fortune when she passed away.

The thought weighed heavily on my heart and as I stepped into the shower, I couldn't help but tilt my head back and wonder where she was in the universe. I hoped wherever she was, I was making her proud. She was diagnosed with cancer when I was finishing up college. Her prognosis wasn't good and she didn't last very long with us after she found out.

She was alive when I was drafted into the NHL and I'd never forget the look on her face. It was a memory I had cemented inside my brain. She never got to see my NHL debut, but I knew she was with me that day. I missed her, but there was nothing I could do about it now except hope that I was continuing to make her proud.

After showering, I got dressed and added my ball of tape to the massive one I'd been collecting during the season. I had been keeping it in my guest room and thankfully, no one ever asked to see inside the room. To the guys, it wasn't anything to be ashamed of. Someone who didn't understand it might not find it as amusing.

By the time I left my apartment, it was already well into the night and I was pulling into the parking lot at the club by ten-thirty. Wes had already texted me to let me know they were here and to head to the VIP section.

"Took you long enough," Lincoln said as I took a seat next to him in the booth. There was a bottle of champagne in a bucket in the center of the table, but everyone had mixed drinks and was taking shots.

I shrugged as I grabbed one of the shots and swallowed it back. The liquor burned as it slid down my esophagus, but I welcomed the feeling. "Let's be real— you guys were probably here for five minutes before I showed up."

Wes clapped his hand on my shoulder and gave me a swift shake. "Hey, buddy," he said with a smile in his voice. "Linc was just missing you, is all."

Lincoln laughed loudly. "I'm here for one thing and one thing only tonight," he said with a smirk. "And you are not it, Cirone."

"Bummer," I chuckled as I grabbed one of the mixed drinks that Wes had. Otto, Mac, and Cole were sitting in the booth talking to some girls who had wandered over. A few of the other guys were here somewhere, but who knew where they wandered off to.

Lincoln stood up from where he was sitting. "I'm heading out to scope out the scene. Either of you want to come with me?"

Wes shook his head as he leaned back in his spot and slowly sipped his bourbon and ginger ale while pulling out his phone. "Nah. I'm just going to lay low for a little."

Lincoln glanced over at me. "Cirone?"

I shrugged as I picked up my drink and stood up. It

was the same thing Wes was drinking. "Fuck it. I don't have anything else going on, so I'm down."

Lincoln smiled and he began to wander through the VIP section. I followed after him as the sound of the bass pounded through the speakers and directly into my bones. It was loud as hell but the DJ had a nasty mix going, so I was feeling it as we walked down the stairs and into the main area of the club.

I waded through the sea of dancing bodies and lost Lincoln somewhere along the way. I didn't need him as my wingman. I was highly capable of finding someone without him. Plus, Wes was a better wingman than he was anyway.

As I pushed my way through the throng of people, eventually the crowd broke open to where the bar was. My eyes scanned the area and I took a seat as I finished my drink. Setting it down, I ordered another when the bartender came over to me. Just as I placed my order, someone ran into my back, pushing me forward slightly in my seat.

"Oh my god, I am so sorry."

The sound of her voice slid across my eardrums like silk and I slowly turned around to face her. She was still standing close and I caught a whiff of her floral perfume. The corners of my lips lifted as her blue eyes met mine. Under the flashing colored lights from above, her blonde hair changed hues with each flash.

She was petite and looked like I could probably bench-press her entire body. A tight black dress hugged her curves and I allowed myself the opportunity to quickly check her out as she moved to the seat next to me.

"There are so many damn people in here. Someone pushed me into your back." She paused for a moment, pulling a credit card from her clutch. "Let me buy you an apology drink?"

Reaching out, I placed my hand over hers and pushed the card back into her small bag as I shook my head. "You don't owe me anything." I smiled at her as she turned to face me. "I have a better idea. How about I buy you a drink instead?"

My eyes were drawn to her plump lips. They were stained a dark red from her lipstick and I wanted the matching stains on my own lips. "I like that idea."

"What are you drinking?"

Just as I asked her, the bartender walked back over with my drink and I listened as she ordered a vodka soda. I assessed her as she was talking to the bartender. My eyes traveled over her high cheekbones and down her straight nose. She reached up and tucked her straight hair behind her ear.

She turned to face me. "Do they make their drinks strong here?"

I glanced at the bartender and took a sip of my own drink. "Usually. Judging by this drink, I think it's safe to say they do. Is this your first time here?"

She nodded. "I just moved here a week ago for a new job. One of the girls I met through work invited me out here, but she brought her boyfriend and I'm not in the mood to be a third wheel."

Luckily for her, I was only looking for a second wheel.

"What do you do for work?" I inquired as she got her drink and took a sip of it.

She set her glass down just as the DJ switched the song to a different one. "I'm a photographer." Her face lit up and she began to move in her seat to the beat of the music. "Why is that always a question people ask when you first meet someone?"

"I feel like it's an easy icebreaker," I said with a shrug. "Plus, you did say that you just moved here because of your new job, so I figured I'd be polite and ask about it."

This earned a smirk from her. "Ah. Trying to make it seem like your intentions are pure and wholesome, right?"

I laughed and shook my head at her. "My intentions are only the purest and most wholesome." I leaned closer to her, my lips brushing against her ear. "I'm actually an angel and as innocent as they come."

She snorted and pushed me back before hopping out of her seat. "I highly doubt that," she winked as she grabbed her drink with one hand and grabbed my bicep with the other. "Dance with me?"

I grabbed my drink and slowly rose to my feet. "I thought you'd never ask."

Her palm was warm against mine as I threaded my fingers through hers and followed her into the crowd. She abruptly stopped and I dropped her hand, grabbing her waist to hold her upright as I crashed into her back.

She lifted her arm up, snaking it around the back of my neck as she began to move in front of me.

Her back was pressed flush against my torso. We had about a foot difference in height so her ass was just below my pelvis as she began to roll her hips. I moved along with her, grinding against her as I slid my hand across the front of her dress, stopping with my fingers splayed across the bottom of her stomach.

Holding her drink in one hand, she spun around in my grip and I was holding the small of her back as she faced me. Her other arm was back around my neck and her velvet skin slid against mine. I wanted to toss my glass onto the floor so I could hold her with both hands. I wanted to explore her body and get lost in the valleys and planes of her torso.

We were pressed flush against each other, two strangers in the darkness of the club as we moved together to the music. She leaned her head back, her ocean blue eyes colliding with mine as she gazed up at me. Her lips parted slightly and my gaze dropped down to her mouth before finding her eyes again.

"Kiss me," she murmured. I could barely hear her over the music, but her body spoke louder. "Make me forget it all."

My face dipped down to hers. "What are you trying to forget, love?"

"The asshole who broke my heart."

I pulled back slightly, a ghost of a smile playing on my lips as I searched her eyes. "So, you're looking for someone to replace the memory of him tonight?"

She flashed me her bright white teeth and her eyes danced under the flashing lights. "Exactly."

Everyone around us continued to dance along to the music, but we weren't moving with them anymore. Instead, my face was dipping down to hers and I was claiming her mouth with my own. She tasted like the vodka she was drinking and her nails dug into the back of my neck as I traced the seam of her lips with my tongue.

Gripping onto her waist, I slid my tongue against hers, breathing her in as she moved against me. This wasn't usually my style with a girl that I had just met. I mean, by the end of the night, I was usually on my way back to their place with them, but I usually tried to play it cool at first.

She made it clear what her intentions were and I wasn't going to deny her a fucking thing.

Our tongues were tangled together and there was an urgency behind our kiss. My lips bruised hers and I wanted more. Fuck playing it cool, fuck waiting till later. Abruptly breaking apart, I left her breathless and she stared up at me with wide eyes.

I pulled at the material of her dress as I spun on my heel. Her hand slid into mine and I headed through the crowd. I needed to get her alone. Somewhere I could do whatever she wanted me to do.

She followed along after me as we moved toward the back of the building and discarded our drinks along the way. We climbed the stairs and I led her through the VIP area. I caught Wes's eye as I strode past the booth the guys were in. He raised an eyebrow and nodded in approval. There was a back room tucked off to the side. I had no idea what was in it, but we were about to find out.

Grabbing the handle, I turned it to the side and it opened with ease. I pushed it open and pulled the girl in with me before shutting it behind us. Her hands were on my back and heat rolled off her in waves.

"I can't see a thing. Is there a light in here?"

I turned around to face her, my fingers trailing up her neck and across her jaw. "I don't want anyone to interrupt us."

I could hear the smile in her voice in the darkness. "Good idea."

She leaned up on her toes and our mouths collided in a rush. Her arms were around the back of my neck and she ran her fingers through my hair as she held on to me. I grabbed her hips and slowly backed her up until she was flush against something.

"Wait," she broke away, breathless. "I don't even know your name…"

I pulled away for a moment, sliding my hand into my pocket as I pulled out my phone to check our surroundings. It was just a storage closet and there was a worktable behind her. Turning off the screen, I slid it back into my pocket before I grabbed her thighs and lifted her up.

The sharp intake of her breath filled the room and her hands clutched at my shoulders as I had her sitting on the table with me standing between her legs. My cock throbbed in my pants and she hooked her legs around my waist, pulling me flush against her.

"Nico," I told her as I dropped my mouth to her neck. "But you can call me whatever the fuck you want."

"Mmm, Nico," she hummed as she reached for the bottom of my dress shirt and pulled it out of my pants. Her nails were sharp against the skin on my back. "Different. I like it."

"I like the way my name sounds rolling off your tongue, but you know what I really want to hear, love?"

She looked up at me as I pulled the straps of her dress down her arms. "What's that?"

"I want to hear you screaming it instead."

I slid the straps of her dress down to her elbows before trailing my hands across her collarbones. My lips found hers again as my fingers traced the dips and curves of her body. Sliding the material under her breasts, the feel of her skin was soft against my palms and I rolled her nipples between my fingers.

She moaned into my mouth and I swallowed the sound. Her hands found the waistband of my pants and she worked them open. Shifting my hips back, I gave her access to my cock as she slid her hands under my boxers.

A pounding sounded on the other side of the door and she stilled against me with my cock throbbing in her hand. "Someone knows we're in here," she breathed against my lips.

"Fuck," I mumbled as I released her breasts and pulled back. Whoever was on the other side knocked on it again and I heard my name. "Goddammit." I grabbed the straps of her dress and pulled them back up to cover her up. "Hold on."

Her heels hit the floor as she dropped down off the table and I pulled up my zipper and buttoned my pants as I walked over to the door. The hinges groaned as I pulled on it with force, feeling the frustration building inside. My balls ached and I needed to be inside her.

Wes was standing on the other side with a look of regret on his face. "Sorry to interrupt, bro, but I need your help with Linc."

"What about him? I'm not his babysitter."

He frowned and swayed a bit. "He left with these two girls. I don't know what the hell happened, but they kicked him out of his car." He paused for a moment and lifted his backward baseball hat from his head before putting it back in place. "I shouldn't drive and I didn't know if you could."

Goddammit. I only had one drink and barely drank the second one I ordered. If there was anyone sober enough to drive here, it was me. I glanced back at the girl with ocean eyes who was staring at me from across the small room.

As much as I wanted to finish what we started, she was just a stranger at the end of the day. These guys were my family and we had to have each other's backs on and off the ice.

I turned back to Wes. "Give me a minute and we'll go get his dumb ass."

"Thanks, Nico."

Leaving the door cracked open, light shined into the

small room as I closed the distance between the girl and me. "I hate to leave like this, but I gotta go."

She smiled up at me. "I get it. You go do whatever you have to do and maybe one day our paths will cross again."

"Let me see your phone," I said to her as I held out my hand.

She raised an eyebrow and pulled it from her clutch. After unlocking the screen, she handed it to me. I took it from her and called my phone from hers.

"There, now you have my number," I told her as I handed it back and slid my hand up to cup the side of her face. "I'm not done with you. Call me if you decide you want to finish this sometime."

I claimed her lips once more with a teasing kiss and grabbed her hand before pulling her out of the room with me. Wes was waiting by the booth and I stopped next to him as I watched her disappear back into the crowd.

"Who was that?"

Shit. I pulled out my phone and saw that I had her number, but I never got her name. A slow smile pulled on my lips.

"I have no idea," I paused as I slid my phone back into my pocket, "but I have every intention of finding out."

ACKNOWLEDGMENTS

To my husband: You are the best thing that has ever happened to me. I will always be forever grateful for your nonstop support and love. And for answering all of my stupid questions. And for also picking up the slack when I'm in my head. Dade County.

To my beta readers from throughout the series (Alex, Lauren, Caroline, Emma, Erica): Your help and encouragement has literally been priceless. I love you and appreciate you all!

Rumi: You know how to make shit shine. I love you forever.

Cat: 637. That is all.

Cassie: Never hugs and always drugs.

Alex: You are the absolute best! I appreciate the fuck out of you.

Christina: THANK YOU ALWAYS

My street team and ARC team: You guys are seriously so amazing. I appreciate you all and your support never goes unnoticed!

My author friends (I'm not going to list everyone, but you know who you are): We all know that sometimes this industry is toxic as hell. We all know that sometimes the people here want nothing but the worst for you. I cannot say that about all of you, though. The support, the way we all stand by each other. It's something special that I will treasure forever.

My bookish friends (again, I'm not going to list because I'm bound to forget a name lol): All I have to say is I am so glad that books brought us together. You are an integral part of my life now and that means so much to me.

And last but not least, my readers. You are all what keeps me writing. If you didn't show your love for these stories I create, there would literally be no point in me creating them. I will always be so grateful for each and every one of you. Seriously, I think I have the best readers out there.

ABOUT THE AUTHOR

Cali Melle is a contemporary romance author who loves writing stories that will pull at your heartstrings. You can always expect her stories to come fully equipped with heartthrobs and a happy ending, along with some steamy scenes and some sports action. In her free time, Cali can usually be found spending time with her family or with her nose in a book.

ALSO BY CALI MELLE

WYNCOTE WOLVES SERIES

Cross Checked Hearts

Deflected Hearts

Playing Offsides

The Faceoff

The Goalie Who Stole Christmas

Splintered Ice

Coast to Coast

Off-Ice Collision

ORCHID CITY SERIES

Meet Me in the Penalty Box

The Lie of Us

The Tides Between Us

Written in Ice

Printed in the USA
CPSIA information can be obtained
at www.ICGtesting.com
LVHW041532170923
758448LV00008B/236